To

Pat Angell

Thanks for your
friendship and support.
Those were good years
at Oak Park.

Hayes

Moonbeams from a Jar

Moonbeams from a Jar

Hayes F. Fletcher

VANTAGE PRESS
New York

Jacket design and illustrations by C. Winston Fletcher
Copyright research by Katherine Fletcher

FIRST EDITION

Copyright © 2006 by Hayes F. Fletcher

Published by Vantage Press, Inc.
419 Park Ave. South, New York, NY 10016

Manufactured in the United States of America
ISBN: 0-533-15371-9

Library of Congress Catalog Card No.: 2005909073

0 9 8 7 6 5 4 3 2 1

Acknowledgments

In the early stages of writing this novel, I entertained doubts about the purpose and relevance of these narratives. While vacationing in New Mexico, my wife and I spent a day at the Museum of Indian Arts and Culture in Santa Fe.

After reading the inscriptions on the wall and viewing the historical displays, I understood why it was important to share these stories. One engraving, written by Anthony Dorame, provided part of the inspiration to continue the book. He wrote, "Cycles are circles that travel in straight lines. Stories come from the land whispered by sand and echoed in rock and told again in the moist breath of water and in low conversations of cottonwood trees. Others are told in stories made of paint, clay, fiber, bone and hide."

My stories are based partly on a fertile imagination and partly on actual experiences from my years growing up in a Methodist parsonage in small rural towns.

I dedicate this book to my parents, the late Harold and Ivie Fletcher, whose dignity and love were the foundations of a home and family that made it easy to move into the world of fiction with integrity, objectivity, and veracity.

I am also deeply indebted to my seven siblings—six brothers and one sister—Sue, Coy, Jim, Winston, Hollis, George, and Thomas, all of whom are living except Hollis, who died in infancy, and Sue, who died in 2003. Although only three children are featured in the novel, all of my siblings, through their support and the gift of memory, provided important threads for the experiential fabric needed to complete the tapestry of our lives. Many of the incidents they shared were personal and distinct, but contributed to the whole.

v

Special recognition must be given to Winston, on whom the character Wes is based. From the depths of his remarkable memory, he provided stories, anecdotes, and data that embellished and verified my own recollections and perceptions. Being an accomplished artist, he pictorialized the written word with his vivid sketches of people and events.

To Anita, my wife of forty-eight years, who had faith in me and encouraged, prodded, stimulated, and prevailed upon me to submit to my intense desire to write this novel. She is a grammarian without peer, a thoughtful inquisitor, a sharp-penciled editor, and the love of my life. Without her inspiration and certitude, this novel would still be a conceptualized construction buried in the deep recesses of my mind.

This is also written for my four children—Marc, Suzanne, Katherine, Grant—and their children. The inscription on the wall of the Santa Fe museum reminds us that "We must not forget what we now remember."

I am imploring my progenies to store in their memory the history of their forebears and pass it on so that it will not be forgotten.

Moonbeams from a Jar

Prologue

Tragedy paid an unwelcome visit to the small West Tennessee town of Adairsville. An ominous cloud had settled over the village, leaving the townsfolk bewildered and distraught. There had been many funerals in Adairsville, but none quite like this.

Junior Macgregor, age fourteen, the son of one of the town's prominent citizens, was laid out in an expensive casket placed near the chancel of the Methodist Church. The bright sun couldn't dispel the foreboding gloom that consumed those who were in attendance on that hot and humid day in late June, 1942.

Walking toward the church with my father, Brother Milton Turnage, the minister of the church, I asked why Junior had to die. Daddy was a thoughtful person and chose his words carefully. He paused briefly as he pondered my question.

"Vance," he said, "I'm not sure I can answer that, but one thing I'm certain about: God didn't want this to happen. We must hold fast to the thought that Junior did nothing to deserve this."

Daddy walked on ahead toward the church while I went to look for my older brother, Wes. He met me at the edge of the churchyard and we sat down on a bench carved out of a rough log.

In an effort to break the somber mood, Wes said, "I still can't get used to seeing those churches all bunched together like . . . well . . . like croakers on a log."

It was an unusual sight. The Methodist Church sat in the middle, and on each side, like bookends, were two other churches—Baptist and Presbyterian. I smiled as I remembered

1

Daddy telling us how Mr. Alfred Adair had given the land with the understanding that the town's four churches had to build there.

Daddy said, "The Church of Christ refused Mr. Adair's generosity, believing that being too close to the other denominations might contaminate their biblical purity." Mr. Adair relented and gave the land anyway.

For more than forty years, the three churches stood side by side as bulwarks of "faith, hope, and charity." However, as Daddy pointed out, their proximity to one another was physical only. In doctrine and theology, they were very different. Methodists traced their lineage to John Wesley and the Church of England. Presbyterians were proud of their founder, John Knox of Scotland, who developed the doctrine of predestination. Baptists, however, believed they were direct descendants of John the Baptist, anointed to "prepare the way for the Lord."

Sunday nights when the air hung heavy and the wind was lazy, the churches opened their windows to invite in a breeze. Congregations could hear each other as they raised their voices in song and prayer. The story has been told many times that one evening the Methodists were singing a favorite hymn and when they came to the verse that asked, *"Will there be any stars in my crown?"* the Baptist responded with a line from an old hymn that said, *"No, Not One."* Old timers would say, "That story sorta grew with time and retelling."

There was one other church near Adairsville. People of color worshipped in a converted schoolhouse on New Shiloh Road, the New Salem Missionary Baptist Church. New Salem's preacher, The Reverend Hezekiah Lacy, was a beloved member of the community, known for exhorting his parishioners to lofty aspirations. When he wasn't exhorting, he worked at the local sawmill.

My father was highly regarded by most members of the community and felt honored to be counted among the other professionals with college degrees in this town of approximately 5,000. The exact number wasn't known because the census takers didn't count the Negroes (my father taught us never to use the word "nigra" or the other word that some whites used), and many of the white sharecroppers who lived in small shacks far off dusty rural roads.

2

Many of these people were very poor, living without hope. For most of the year, the townspeople ignored their plight. Whether it was an act of Christian charity or an effort to satisfy their consciences, the churches always put on a food drive the week before Thanksgiving. People brought canned goods and vegetables to the church and Mr. Taylor, owner of the grocery store, provided the turkeys paid for by special offerings taken at the churches.

Every poor family received a basket a few days before Thanksgiving. Regardless of the motive, the food kept families from going hungry on a day when other people were enjoying the blessings of abundance. As Daddy observed in a sermon, "The fact that this charity is not extended to the other months of the year is a flaw in the community's character."

My history teacher told about how families in Adairsville had survived the Depression by working on projects initiated in 1935 by President Roosevelt's Works Progress Administration. Since more than a fourth of the American work force was unemployed in the early thirties, the W.P.A. put over eight million people to work preparing highways, building bridges, restoring state and federal parks, digging irrigation ditches, and dredging river beds. The building of the Pickwick Dam by the Tennessee Valley Authority not only created many jobs for workers in five states, it provided electrical power to thousands of families in the surrounding areas.

In Macon County, where Adairsville was located, you didn't hear any unkind words about President Roosevelt. The only registered voters were Democrats and Mayor Shipley often stated that "If you run into a Republican in this county, give him a map because he's lost." There were other things people said about Republicans, but Daddy wouldn't allow us to repeat them.

The courthouse, occupying a prominent place at the end of Main Street, was built of Arkansas limestone and painted a dull white. Court Square was a favorite gathering place on Saturdays for farmers to whittle and share stories. After a raging fire wiped out most of the wood frame buildings located near the courthouse, new brick and mortar stores were built next to the old ones on both sides of Main Street. One of the few structures left

3

standing after the fire, the Cotton Exchange Building, became the Merchants Bank and Trust.

Just about everything we needed could be found in a six-block area. There were stores that sold groceries, dry goods, fresh meat, hardware, medicine and sundries, clothes, garden seeds, animal feed, and furniture. A printing shop published leaflets, brochures, posters, church bulletins, and *The Clarion Standard*.

At Mason's Grill, you got local gossip along with hot, black coffee in the morning and at noon the best pit barbecue in West Tennessee. There was a barbershop and a beauty parlor, also good places for hearing the latest gossip. Just off Main Street was a pool hall where men could drink beer, cuss, and lose money on billiard games. Kids were not allowed.

We washed down Moon Pies with R. C. Cola and Nehi Grape soda at Taylor's grocery. At the back of the store a pot-bellied stove kept the coffee hot in the winter. Men in overalls and straw hats leaned back in their chairs, put their brogans on the fender of the stove, and talked about the weather, politics, and war. A game of checkers and dominoes was always in progress. A round of hoop cheese sat on a butcher's block with a sharp knife sticking in it. Crackers were kept in a large barrel next to the cheese. Fresh sliced baloney, stored in a meat cooler, was put between two slices of bread and slathered with mayonnaise. If I had more than a dime to spend, I would treat myself to a long, black cord of licorice.

Trying to dispel the gloom, Wes and I talked about how much Junior loved Fesmire's Drug Store. Brightly lit with long bulbs that reflected off the tin ceiling and honeycomb tile floors, it was one of the most popular spots in town. The apothecary, where prescriptions were filled and bottled medicines dispensed, was located in the back. Stained glass oak cabinetry stood next to shelves lined with greeting cards, toys, jewelry, fashion accessories, and toiletries. In the corner, a magazine rack was stocked with periodicals, journals, and comic books.

At the front of the store was a soda fountain complete with Hamilton Beach malt mixers. Straddling a revolving chrome bar stool in front of the marble-topped counter, I watched "Happy" fill cones with double dips of homemade ice cream or prepare

4

lime rickeys, egg creams, and frothy phosphates. I thought about how Junior always wanted three dips—chocolate, strawberry, and vanilla.

The magazine rack provided a glimpse of both real and fantasy worlds. It was there that we read comic books and occasionally bought a favorite, tucking it away in our back pocket for reading later.

Outside the store was the setting for those memorable days when a smiling Filipino man came and dazzled us with the magic of the Duncan Yo-yo. He taught us how to "walk the dog," "rock the cradle," and go "around the world" with a wooden yo-yo that cost twenty-five cents. Junior never understood why the "yo-yo man" was always a Filipino. I asked Mr. Fesmire and he said he'd never given it much thought. After that, I didn't either. The drug store was also the place where we waited for the nice lady to give out free samples of a new product called Adams Dentyne Gum.

From the drugstore, we would walk to the Dixie Theater, that sacred place where we met every Saturday afternoon to re-create the innocent rite of hero-worship. For fifteen cents, we bought four hours of Charles Starrett, Red Ryder, Roy Rogers, Gene Autry, Mickey Mouse, and *Pathe News* with Lowell Thomas. Popcorn was extra.

The lumberyard was several blocks off Main Street. Just to the north was the Grange Lodge, a large frame building in need of paint and a new sign. About a half mile down New Shiloh Road was the cotton gin and gristmill owned by Curtis Shipley, who also owned the car dealership and the movie theater. His brother, Carl, was the mayor.

We were pretty much on our own in Adairsville and were never bored. If we left early in the morning and didn't return until late afternoon, no one worried or went looking for us. We played football and softball on vacant lots; swam in Jordan's Creek; fished in the river; spent hours in the local park playing box hockey; swung on swings made from boards and link chain; watched old men play dominoes and checkers. We played dodge ball and kick-the-can and hide-and-go-seek. We got cut, scratched, and broke bones and teeth, but in time everything healed. We got sick with the flu and fever. We had our tonsils taken out while sitting in a dentist's chair in Jackson, Tennessee. Children got polio and were crippled for life. Some died with pneumonia and smallpox and whooping cough.

We made up games with broomsticks and corks. We shot Red Ryder B.B. guns and never put out anyone's eye in spite of Mother's warnings. We spent hours building go-carts out of scraps of lumber and old coaster wagon wheels, and then found the highest hill to test them. After running into hedges and fences and walls, we realized we had forgotten one thing—brakes. We flew hand-made kites in March breezes and rode sleds down hills in winter snows. In the summer, we caught lightning bugs and put them in pint-size Mason fruit jars.

Junior didn't care much for school and often played hooky. I thought school was okay most of the time but not much fun in the heat of August. There were teachers I liked and others I didn't. Some students were smarter than others and when they failed a grade, they weren't promoted to the next grade. Students dropped out of school and that was okay. Truancy enforcement was for city kids. Some made it through high school and a few went to college. Most of the others remained here and became farmers or merchants; or, as Uncle John said, "worthless drunks."

Daddy would correct him and say, "Now John, no one's worthless in the sight of God."

Others returned as attorneys or bankers or politicians.

I loved this town and Wes and I were glad we moved here from the city. For most people in Adairsville, it was a good life. However, there were days when tragedy interrupted the tranquil routine. This was one of those days.

1

This was my first funeral and I hoped it would be my last. Neither one of us wanted to come, but Daddy thought the proper way to say goodbye to Junior and pay our respects was to attend his funeral.

Wes said, "Vance, you won't believe how long that car is that brought Junior's body up here."

I wasn't interested in the length of a car and I sure didn't want to hear Wes talk about something carrying the body of our friend.

"Vance," he whispered as we started into the church, "I think I saw Slowfoot over by the bushes."

"What's he doing here?" I asked.

"I don't know. It's not like him to come out . . . like . . . you know . . . for something like this. It's weird. He's hiding . . . I think . . . behind that big crepe myrtle bush and peeking out like he's afraid someone will see him."

I guess he would be, since people blamed him for anything bad that happened in Adairsville.

There were rumors that he lived alone somewhere over by the Ridges and no one seemed to know where he got money for food and clothes. Most people just ignored him and considered him harmless; others thought he was the devil himself. I was sure about one thing: I didn't want anything to do with him and had been told by Daddy to leave him be and that's exactly what I intended to do. I was still trying to figure out why Slowfoot would be hanging around the church when Wes nudged me toward a pew in the back.

The church was filling up with all kinds of folks dressed in their Sunday best. The Methodist Church was a dull brick building with a stubby tower that appeared to need a steeple. Daddy had talked about the kind of spire he wanted to put on top but never found a way to raise the money to pay for it.

Ten years ago, an annex was built across the back for Sunday school classes and a fellowship hall. A canopy over the entrance would have made the entrance more inviting and kept worshippers dry on rainy days, but there was none. Concrete steps without a railing led to two large white doors.

Inside was different. The sanctuary had an inviting, simple beauty, uncluttered by unnecessary trappings and adornments. The round stained glass window above the choir loft had pictures of Jesus holding a staff and standing next to a lamb. On a sunny day, the colors in the glass were bright and cheerful. When I got bored during one of Daddy's sermons, I would study that picture and try to figure out its meaning.

Attached to the backs of the dark oak pews were hymnal racks and communion glass holders. In the center of the chancel and in front of the communion table was a large pulpit with a banker's lamp clamped to it. There was no altar. In a deliberate attempt to distinguish themselves from Catholics, Protestant churches wanted nothing that resembled an altar. The closest Catholic Church was thirty miles away and many people thought that was too close.

Daddy had a more charitable feeling toward the Catholics and frequently remarked about their contributions to Christian education and piety in the development of the South following the Civil War. While serving a church in Memphis, he had become friends with a Catholic priest and they often talked theology and church history over coffee in a local café.

Beautiful flowers filled the front of the church and emitted a strong, sweet smell. I wondered where they came from and what they would do with them after the service. Later, I learned that they were placed at the graveside and left to wither and die.

One of the ushers gave us a printed bulletin. On one side was the order for the service; on the other was a eulogy for Junior. We were surprised when we read the heading: IN MEMORIAM: JOHN CHARLES MACGREGOR, JR. 1928–1942. Wes poked me in

8

the ribs and pointed to the name. It was then we realized that we never knew Junior's real name and hadn't given much thought to it.

"Bet he would've liked John or Johnny better than Junior," Wes whispered.

"Or Chuck," I added.

Just a few months after we met Junior, Wes had written our names on the sidewalk with a piece of chalk. Junior's name was spelled "Jr." Junior grabbed the chalk and scratched through what Wes had written, then wrote in capital letters, "JUNIOR." I guess he thought a proper name needs more than two letters, and from then on that's the way we spelled it and that's the way his teachers spelled it. It seemed strange that you could know someone for four and a half years and not even know his real name. However, Junior probably never knew our full names either.

I noticed people walking by the open casket as they moved toward their seats and I said, "I sure don't want to see a dead person, even if it is Junior."

"We might have to go and take a quick look at the end of the service," Wes said.

It'll definitely be a quick look, I thought.

Miss Simpkins, the local piano teacher and church organist, began playing a plaintive hymn and people wiped their eyes with white handkerchiefs. I was thinking about Junior and wondering again why he had to die so young. He was the same age as Wes and just two years older than me. It was said many times that he was a little slow. We weren't sure what that meant, but knew that Junior wasn't like most of our other friends. Not that we didn't like him; we did. It was just that sometimes he acted weird and did strange things.

Robert Earl Cowser, the town bully and son of the local banker, taunted Junior and made fun of him. He would say things like, "When God passed out brains, Junior thought he said rain and ran inside."

Wes and I didn't like for anyone to talk about Junior that way, but we kept quiet because we were afraid of Robert Earl. We had heard some wild stories about how he boasted of killing and torturing animals. We never saw him do any of these things, but we believed he was mean enough to do anything.

Of course, it was true that some of the things Junior did were cruel, but Wes and I thought he was just trying to fit in. For instance, when we had snowball fights, Junior would be the first to build his fort and stock it with snowballs. However, Junior didn't just make hard snowballs, he put walnuts in the middle so they would throw better and hit harder. The younger boys were always the first to run home crying and tell their parents that Junior had hit them with a snowball with a walnut in it. Wes and I finally figured it was best to be on Junior's team.

Wes leaned over and whispered, "Guess Junior won't be playing '*Apple core, Baltimore*', anymore."

One of the ushers gave Wes a stern look, so I just nodded in agreement.

Junior would scare the pants off everybody whenever he decided to join the game. Everyone else ate the apple down to the core and then said, "*Apple core, Baltimore*, who's your best friend?" You'd choose someone you didn't like and say his name. The friend got splattered upside the head with an apple core. Junior, however, would forget to eat the apple down to the core. In fact, most of the time, he didn't even take a bite out of the apple before he said, "*Apple core, Baltimore*." Everyone would run for cover. Junior always found a "best friend" to aim at with a hard, uneaten apple.

The worst prank of all was when we played kick-the-can. This was a game usually saved for after supper, just as darkness was settling in. Junior would substitute the empty can with one filled with mud. The poor fellow who got there first and kicked the mud-filled missile usually went home with a very sore foot. Junior would roll in the grass and laugh until he cried. Wes and I quit playing kick-the-can with Junior.

Tying a string to the legs of a June bug and watching it fly around in circles was one of our favorite games late in the afternoon. Junior would usually have two strings and a June bug attached to each one. He flew them at the same time and if the beetles didn't fly fast enough to suit him, he reeled them in and crushed them with his foot. Sometimes Wes would tell Daddy about Junior's strange behavior and he would say, "You

10

have to be patient with Junior. He's a little slow through no fault of his own."

The congregation stood and sang the hymn "The Old Rugged Cross." I was thinking that Junior wouldn't like that song. He would have wanted music with a little more spirit and joy.

Wes pointed to Junior's father sitting in the front pew and said, "Wonder if Mr. J. C. thought Junior was a little slow."

J. C. Macgregor was the owner of the local hardware store and considered to be prosperous. Their solid brick house on Main Street was one of the finest in Adairsville. Although Junior never worked at the store and now never would, the sign above the entrance read MACGREGOR AND SON HARDWARE STORE. It would remain that way.

Junior's mother had died nine years ago and he never seemed to understand what had happened to her or where she had gone. Sometimes his eyes would reflect a faraway look and he would say, "I think Mama's coming home tomorrow."

Wes would say, "I sure hope so, Junior, I sure hope so."

He would smile and not mention it again for several months.

Junior wore very thick glasses and when he smiled, his eyes would light up like sparkling stars and the glasses would magnify the brightness. He loved to use the glasses to set paper on fire. On a hot day, he would put a piece of paper on the ground and let his glasses create a prism. The heat from the sun would penetrate the lens and soon there would be smoke, then fire. Junior called it his special magic.

Robert Earl got angry every time Junior did this and would scream at Junior and call him "four eyes." Junior was not so slow that he didn't know he was being mocked. Junior would get even with Robert Earl by throwing firecrackers at his feet and watching him dance around trying to get away. Sometimes Junior wouldn't toss the lit firecracker fast enough and it would go off in his hand. He would just stand there looking at his burnt thumb and forefinger, smile, and say unconvincingly, "It don't hurt one bit."

Junior learned how to take mercury from a thermometer and rub it on a nickel to make it bright and shiny. He would then sell it to Robert Earl for a dime. In a few days, the mercury would wear off and return the nickel to its dull luster. Robert

Earl would threaten Junior if he didn't give him his dime back, but Junior would just smile and say, "Finders keepers," a retort that made sense only to Junior.

Daddy read some verses from the Bible and then said a prayer. The choir, made up mostly of women with untrained voices, sang, *"It is well with my soul."*

When peace, like a river, attendeth my way,
And sorrows like sea billows roll;
Whatever my lot, Thou hast taught me to say,
It is well, it is well with my soul.

I really didn't know about a soul, but I wondered if everything was well with Junior's soul.

"You think Daddy's going to say anything about how Junior died?" Wes whispered. Wes always covered his mouth when he whispered, thinking, I guess, that if people couldn't see his lips moving, they wouldn't know he was talking.

"I hope not," I replied.

The choir finished and Daddy began his sermon. Almost everyone said that he was the best preacher Adairsville ever had. Even Mattie Malone, the town busybody and a thorn in the flesh of every preacher who served that church, would admit, "Brother Turnage sure can spin a tale."

Wes and I sometimes wished that our father were anything but a preacher. Being a preacher's kid was not easy. Our mother, Grace, would say that people always expected more of us than they should. Sometimes kids at school would try to get me and Wes to say a bad word so they could tell everyone that we were no better than anyone else. "Dad boil it" or "gosh darn" were about as close to bad words as they ever got out of us. When Daddy would get upset enough to swear, he'd say, "Aw shaw" or "good grief." When she was shocked, surprised, or angry, Mother would say, "Lord have mercy." She told us that she was not taking the Lord's name in vain. "It's like a prayer," she would say. She prayed a lot.

As Daddy talked about heaven and about Junior's love of life, I thought about a Psalm I'd learned in Vacation Bible School. It said life was like "walking through the valley of the

12

shadow of death." Wes had told me it meant that as God was with us, we shouldn't be afraid to go anywhere. I had asked if that included going where Slowfoot lived.

"As long as we believe that God is walking with us," Wes had said with authority. I often wondered how Wes knew these things.

Wes and I both knew that Junior had walked through some kind of valley of death, but we didn't know why. I thought of what had happened just a few days ago when Sheriff Roy Perkins drove into our driveway.

Daddy and Sheriff Perkins were very good friends and often sat on the porch talking politics, baseball, and the latest news about the war. The sheriff walked to the front porch and asked to see Daddy. Mother said she would send him out, and then offered the sheriff some iced tea. He said, "No, but thanks." Later Daddy said he knew right away that something was wrong when he looked at his friend's face. They walked to the edge of the yard and talked in low voices.

"Something really bad has happened," Wes guessed.

Ruth Ann, our sister, came out on the porch and asked what was going on. She had just turned seventeen and for the past year had turned most of her attention to boys. When we were little, Wes and I had a hard time saying Ruth Ann, so we shortened it to Rue and that's what we called her from then on. It was okay with her, but Mother and Daddy didn't like the nickname and continued to call her Ruth Ann.

Rue was a fierce protector of her brothers. Once when Wes and I were playing in Jefferson Davis Park, some of the town bullies decided to keep us off the swings. I ran home and told Rue. In a few minutes, Rue came striding across the playground with a softball bat in her hand. When the bullies saw her coming, they ran in the opposite direction. Word got out that the bullies had decided they might take on the Turnage boys one at a time, but they would never take on Rue.

After a while, Daddy and Sheriff Perkins came back to the front porch. The Sheriff said he had a few questions to ask Wes and me.

"When was the last time you saw Junior?"

Wes spoke since he was the oldest. "We played marbles with him at the park yesterday morning," Wes said, looking at me for confirmation.

"Yeah, that's right," I said. "Junior had a new bag of marbles and some steelies he wanted to show us."

"What time was that?" the sheriff asked.

"It was late morning, I think," Wes said.

"Yeah, I'm sure it was because he said he had been with Slowfoot before he met up with us," I said.

"What time did he leave the park, and did he say where he was going?" the sheriff asked, while he jotted down something in a little notebook.

Wes and I began shuffling nervously as we pondered these unusual questions.

Daddy said, "It's okay, just answer the questions."

"It must've been about noon or so, and near lunch time, when we all left the park. I don't remember for sure, but I don't think Junior said where he was going. We just thought he was headed home," Wes said.

"Was he riding his bicycle?" Daddy asked.

"Yeah," I said.

Rue, not known for her shyness, couldn't hold back any longer. She asked, "What's wrong? Has something happened to Junior?"

The sheriff put his notebook in his shirt pocket and said, "Junior didn't come home last night and no one knows where he is. His bicycle is gone and his father's afraid he's run off."

This was not the first time Junior had not come home when he was expected, but it was the first time he had been gone overnight. Daddy explained that the Sheriff was putting together a search party and they would be leaving soon to look for him.

When Mother asked why it had taken so long to discover Junior missing, the sheriff explained that Mr. Macgregor had come in late last night and left early this morning. He thought Junior was still asleep. When he came home for lunch, he discovered that his son's bed had not been slept in.

When Wes and I asked if we could go with them, Daddy said, "You'd better stay here. It'll be your bedtime soon and we don't know how long it'll take to find him."

He turned to Mother, patted her arm, and said, "I'll be back as soon as I can."

It took the search party only about four hours to locate Junior's bicycle down by the river, but then it was too dark to continue searching. Parker, the Negro who worked for Uncle John, had led them to the landing. Parker told the sheriff that he went there often to fish because it was easy to get to from the highway. There was a dirt road going down to the landing near where the ferry docked, just below the new toll bridge that spanned the river. Most people resented paying fifty cents a car and five cents a passenger, so they continued using the ferry, which cost twenty-five cents. The bridge was built of steel dulled with black paint and some said it looked like a broken down roller coaster.

Parker said he'd seen Junior about a week ago riding his bicycle down that road. "He got off his bike and went down by the water and just sat there staring at the river. I waved at him, but he acted like he never seen me."

In the light of early morning, two deputies went out in a small boat and dropped draglines in an effort to find Junior's body. Daddy was searching by the pilings under the bridge when he spotted what looked like a body tangled in some dead branches about ten feet from shore. He and Sheriff Perkins waded into the muddy, snake-infested water to retrieve the body. Daddy wouldn't tell us what Junior looked like when they found him, but Parker told us later that Mr. Macgregor had "covered his body with a blanket as soon as they fetched him from the water, and nobody got a good look except the sheriff, Brother Turnage, and Mr. Macgregor."

Robert Earl told everyone that Junior had turned blue and had a big gash on the back of his head.

"It was just like he'd been hit with something hard and there was blood all over his head and shirt," Robert Earl explained as he patted the top of his head.

When Wes asked Daddy about that, he told him not pay any attention to gossip. Daddy frowned and gave out a long sigh as he said, "It's bad enough that Junior had a tragic accident. We don't need to make it any worse than it is."

Wes and I knew by the tone of his voice that we weren't going to be told anything else.

The choir and congregation sang, *"God be with you till we meet again."* As everyone filed past the casket, Wes and I headed for the door. Outside the Church, Robert Earl started sputtering about Junior. Wes pushed him aside and said we didn't want to talk about it.

"You're just jealous cause I know something you don't," Robert Earl said with a sneer. He was muttering something as we walked away.

"Someday, I'm gonna forget I'm a preacher's kid and knock his block off," Wes said, clinching his fist to show he meant business.

The people walked up the hill behind the church to the community cemetery. Six high school basketball players carried the bronze casket. After Daddy read some more Scripture and said the Lord's Prayer, people walked by the casket and tossed dirt on it. I thought that was strange and decided Junior didn't need any more dirt thrown at him.

As we walked back to the church, we talked about Junior. Wes said that Junior might have been a little slow mentally, but he was brave and daring. In a field behind our house, we had built a platform and trapeze. We would jump from the platform onto the trapeze and then swing like they did in the circus. We played a game of "chicken" to see how many times we would let the trapeze swing before jumping from the platform to catch it. We tried to wait until the swing had almost stopped. "The longer the count, the greater the risk," was our motto. Junior always took the longest count before he jumped. Once, he hit the trapeze when it was almost standing still, and swung violently forward, losing his grip and landing flat on his back. He was unconscious for several minutes and white foam came from his mouth. When his father came to get him, he let us know that he was not amused by our game. Neither was our father. The platform became a tree house and the trapeze became tomato stakes.

Mother was not at the funeral. She and members of the Bykota Circle were preparing food in the basement of the

church, a custom in most rural communities. People had an opportunity to visit with the family while they ate baked ham, green beans, snap peas, potato salad, fried chicken, corn pudding, and chess pie.

Most of the ladies in the church liked Mother and thought she was a good preacher's wife, even though some knew of her dislike of Adairsville when she first arrived. Mother preferred Memphis, where Daddy had been pastor for five years. According to Daddy, the Bishop believed that preachers should move often to have a variety of experiences, and the congregation would benefit from different kinds of preachers.

Mother did not agree and said, "Now Milton, you go up there and tell the Bishop that we're happy here and don't want to move."

Daddy said, "Grace, you know it doesn't work that way. We go where we're sent."

Mother cried all the way to Adairsville, and her crying turned to sobbing when she saw the old wood stove in the kitchen, the icebox on the back porch, and the outdoor privy sitting starkly in a patch of weeds. However, she got used to the small rural town and soon came to like it, especially when the church bought a new electric range to replace the wood stove and a Frigidaire to replace the icebox.

Mother had a green thumb and loved to garden. When President Roosevelt asked everyone to plant a "Victory Garden," Mother needed no encouragement. She turned a small patch of barren field behind the house into one of the finest vegetable gardens in the county. It didn't matter whether it was spring, summer, or fall; Mother could grow things. The shelves of our root cellar were lined with jars of canned vegetables, jams, jellies, tomato and kraut juice, and the floor was covered with baskets of sweet and Irish potatoes, and red onions. Dried herbs hung from the ceiling above crocks filled with cucumbers pickling in salty brine. During the tornado season, the root cellar was used as a storm cellar.

She talked Daddy into fencing in an area behind the privy for her hens and roosters. They were a nuisance, but they provided fresh eggs for breakfast and fried chicken for supper. She had a real talent for decorating—and with very little money—but lots of love and know-how, she made the three-bedroom parsonage into a comfortable home.

Mother wrote in her journal almost every day and composed poetry, but was reluctant to let anyone read it. Mother once left one of her poems on the kitchen table and Rue read it. She asked Mother how she started writing poetry.

Mother told her that when she was a little girl, she would write simple verses and hide them in her notebook. One day, the teacher was checking the students' notebooks and found Mother's poems. She was surprised to learn of Mother's talent and encouraged her to continue writing.

"When I was in the eighth grade, an English teacher came to live with us and agreed to help me with my writing in exchange for her room and board," Mother told Rue.

"Day after day, we sat on a bench under a canopy of wisteria and she taught me all the basic qualities of good poetry—the beauty of language, the use of imaginative power, rhyming, and, of course, iambic pentameter. We read the poems of Emily Dickinson, Walt Whitman, Robert Burns, and even some of the sonnets of Shakespeare. It was a wonderful experience and I have loved poetry since the first day we talked. And that's how I came to write these silly poems," Mother said with a smile.

After picking up a few pieces of chicken and some biscuits from the food tables in the basement, Wes and I decided to head for home. On our way, we went by Jordan's Creek, where all the kids swam. Wes and Junior had tied a large hemp rope to a tree limb where we could swing out over the creek and drop into the water. If there were no girls around, we swam naked. Jordan's Creek got its name from Brother Sharp, a Baptist preacher who had visited the Holy Land more than thirty years ago. He was so inspired after seeing where Jesus had been baptized, he brought back a jar of water from the river and poured it into the creek, thus christening it Jordan's Creek.

The creek became the favorite place for the Baptists to baptize their new converts. It made no difference that over the years teenage boys had relieved themselves of bodily fluids in the creek on a daily basis. To Brother Sharp and those who continued to immerse new Christians in that creek, it was still holy water.

One Sunday afternoon, Wes and I sat on a ridge above Jordan's Creek and watched a baptism service. Brother Rogers, pastor of the Baptist Church, told the folks standing on the bank to think about the River Jordan, where Jesus was baptized nineteen-hundred years ago. Before the people were led down to the water, a quartet sang a song about that river:

> Shall we gather at the river, where bright angel feet have
> trod;
> With its crystal tide forever, flowing by the throne of God?

Then all the people sang the chorus and their voices echoed through the trees and hills surrounding the creek:

> Yes, we'll gather at the river, the beautiful, the beautiful
> river,
> Gather with the saints at the river, that flows by the throne
> of God.

The preacher led a large woman into the muddy water and pushed her backward until she was completely under.

Wes said, "I sure hope she keeps her mouth closed."

After watching this strange ritual, I decided not to pee in Jordan's Creek anymore.

After dinner that evening, we sat in the swing on the porch trying to sort out what had happened that day. Daddy, looking very tired, came out, sat down on the steps, and leaned against the post.

He was more than six feet tall and was blessed with a handsome face. He shaved every day and was rarely seen without a clean white shirt with the cuffs buttoned. His hair was brownish with flecks of gray. His glasses were on his forehead as often as they were on his nose. Someone once told him he looked like Bing Crosby. Daddy feigned surprise and acted embarrassed, but we began to notice that when he was in the yard raking leaves, his hat was tilted at a certain angle and his collar turned up just the way Mr. Crosby was pictured in magazines. The comparison ended when Daddy opened his mouth to sing. Unlike Mr. Crosby, he was tone-deaf.

20

The heat mixed with the humidity was stifling. There was no wind to encourage a breeze. The leaves on the trees appeared limp, as though they shared our gloom. An eerie quietness, punctuated only by the shrill sounds of katydids humming and crickets chirping, settled on the night. The glow produced by lightning bugs cut into the thick darkness. I felt a hollowness deep within me I had never felt before.

We sat in silence for a long time and then Wes tried to tell Daddy how we felt about Junior and how sad we were that he was gone. He nodded.

"Daddy, do you think there'll be snow in heaven?" I asked.

Daddy said, "Now, why on earth would you ask a question like that?"

I said, "I don't know . . . I was just thinking that since Junior liked snowball fights, it would be kinda nice if God would have some snow for him in heaven."

"And some walnuts," Wes added.

Daddy pondered the question for a moment and then said, "If God wants Junior to have snowball fights, he'll provide the snow."

Later, as we lay in bed with the lights still on, we thought about what Daddy had said.

"Do you think God will understand about Junior's problem?" I asked.

"Well," Wes answered thoughtfully, "you know Daddy always preaches that God understands everything and loves everybody. I know one thing for sure: there won't be anyone in heaven making fun of Junior or calling him names."

We closed our eyes, but we were both afraid of what dreams might come out of the darkness.

2

It had been three weeks since we watched Junior's body lowered into the ground. We missed our weird friend and sometimes I choked back tears thinking about him. There was still gossip around town about his death. Doc Townsend came over to the house one evening and talked to Daddy for more than an hour. We heard Daddy tell Mother that Doc Townsend said an autopsy had shown that there was no water in his lungs. Wes and I didn't make anything of that at the time, but we made a note to ask Daddy later what an autopsy was.

We had hoed cotton for two days the week before and decided we weren't suited for this kind of work. Both of us were trying to earn enough money during the summer to buy a bicycle we could share, but I figured there must be a better way to do it than standing under a boiling sun and chopping weeds with a hoe.

Later in the summer, we would pluck and sort apples for Uncle John, and in the fall, when school let out for cotton-picking, we would pick cotton for Charlie Parsons. I also sold the *Grit*, a national newspaper read by most farmers and merchants in rural communities, and ran errands for Mr. Macgregor.

When I was five or six, if someone wanted me to do something I didn't want to do, I said, "I'd rather eat worms than do that." I felt that way about farming. Now I understood what Daddy was talking about when he told the story of how he came to be a preacher. Daddy went home one day and told his farmer father that he had seen a sign in the sky and believed it was a message from God.

His father, who was Papa to us, listened skeptically and said, "So what did God say to you?"

Daddy said that the clouds had formed two letters as clear as day and they were G.P.

"So what does that mean?" Papa asked impatiently.

Daddy said that God was telling him to "Go Preach."

Papa thought for a moment and then smiled. "Maybe he was telling you to go plow," he said, as he walked away.

Papa said that he always knew Daddy wasn't cut out to be a farmer so he didn't argue with him when Daddy left to go to a small Methodist college to prepare for the ministry.

Sometimes during the early evening at the end of one of those long, hot summer days, we would sit on the porch and Mother would tell us stories about her childhood while she shelled peas or snapped beans.

Once when Daddy was away on a revival, she told us about their courtship and marriage.

"Your Daddy was just about the most handsome man in the county," she began. "He had lots of admirers and most of the young girls had set their bonnet for him."

Mother, the youngest of six children, was born in Tipton County and named Mary Grace Mercer. Her parents owned a large farm in Burlison, Tennessee, about ten miles from Giltedge, where Daddy spent his childhood and youth. She grew up in a fine rambling-frame house surrounded by red barns, silos, expansive pastures filled with cows and horses, and a barnyard where pigs wallowed in mud and chickens roamed freely. The fertile soil produced ample crops of cotton, soy beans, corn, and barley. The farm was well equipped with the best implements and tools.

For some reason, we were never close to her family and did not spend much time with them. When we did visit, it was usually only for one night or for the family reunion held every July.

Daddy and Mother dated a few times before he went off to college, but she knew he had other prospects, so she didn't give their courtship much thought. Her father didn't think Daddy was good enough for her, but Grandpa didn't think any man was good enough for his daughters.

When Daddy came home from college to work in the fields during the summer, he would borrow his uncle's buggy and ride

23

over to spend Sunday afternoons with Mother, mostly sitting in a swing on the front porch of the Mercer home.

Mother smiled when she recalled a special Sunday. "When he couldn't find a buggy or wagon, he walked the ten miles in the hot sun just to spend a few hours sitting and talking. I suddenly realized that your daddy was a serious suitor, and although it didn't please my father, it made me happy."

She told us about the time they took a picnic basket, walked through the fields, spread their lunch on a blanket by a stream, and Daddy told her that he was going to be a preacher.

"As soon as word got out that your daddy was studying for the ministry, those girls gathered around him like bees to honey. Being a preacher's wife was something special even though my daddy didn't feel the same. He thought farming was a more noble profession than preaching. 'Farmers live off the land; preachers live off farmers,' he would say. My mother, your granny, was a doctor's daughter from Covington and a strong-minded woman. She let him know that she didn't agree.

" 'What we grow on this farm feeds the body; what preachers give us is food for the soul. Now you tell me, which is more important?' she would ask.

"My father would just grunt something and walk away. He was no match for her," Mother said proudly.

During Thanksgiving holidays, Mother and Daddy talked about getting married. Even though Mother wanted to wait until he finished college, Daddy convinced her that he could finish college after they married.

Two weeks later, on a Saturday afternoon, Daddy borrowed a Model T Ford sedan, picked her up, and they drove to a preacher's house in Munford. Mother was so scared and shy, she wouldn't get out, so Daddy persuaded the preacher to come out to the road and perform the marriage ceremony while they sat in the car.

Mother smiled as she looked toward the setting sun and said, "It was certainly not the kind of wedding I had dreamed of and I often wished we could have spoken our vows in church, but that's the way we did it and I was happy to be the wife of Milton Turnage."

From the pictures in a weathered photo album, she was a beautiful nineteen-year-old when she married.

Since they couldn't afford to buy or rent a house, they went to live with Daddy's parents in Giltedge and Mother admitted that it was not a good way to begin a marriage. After a few months of living in a bedroom and sharing the household duties with her mother-in-law, Mother had had enough.

Daddy, who had dropped out of college to work on the farm and earn some money, came home late one evening and found Mother lying on the bed sobbing.

Mother told him to get a place for them to live or she was moving back home. Two days later, Daddy hitched up two mules to a wagon, drove to Memphis, returning late in the evening with a load of used furniture for their first home: a two-bedroom house he had rented in Atoka. He didn't go back to college but continued his education through a special correspondence course offered by the Methodist Church. Within a year, he was ordained and assigned his first church.

She concluded her story as darkness was settling in and the June bugs were in full voice, drowning out the cricket sounds. It was a special time and we knew there would be other evenings when we would learn more about our parents.

It was Saturday and Wes had raised the window shades to let in the morning sun and remind me that it was time to get up and get dressed, but the smell of coffee was the only incentive I needed. Our grandmother had taught us to like coffee when we were no more than three or four years old. Mother, who only drank tea, was not happy with Grandmother Turnage's influence. Because of rationing, we had only a small amount of sugar for our coffee and none for our cereal. We learned to eat hot and cold cereal seasoned with salt. Mother had taught Rue how to make candy out of sorghum molasses, vinegar, and baking soda. It wasn't as good as store-bought, but it was better than nothing.

Except for gas for cars, rationing was more of an inconvenience than a sacrifice. Daddy didn't have a problem because preachers and doctors got plenty of gas coupons. Not many people complained about rationing because President Roosevelt had told us we were helping with the war effort.

25

Wes and I made plans to go to the cave over by the Ridges for some clay and to see if anyone had been living there lately. After a breakfast of pancakes and eggs, we headed for Uncle John's apple orchard. John Menloe, the postmaster and a large landowner, lived across the road from us in a fine two-story brick house with green shutters. It seemed that we had always called him Uncle John, but we couldn't remember why. Behind his house was about a hundred acres of fenced pastures, a red barn, a brick silo and one of the finest orchards in Macon County. People came from miles away to buy apples at the roadside stand located on Highway 64. He gave us bushels of apples to use for canning and drying. Mother made fried apple pies that were "fit for a king," as Sheriff Perkins would say.

Uncle John's father gave the land for the park, but he wouldn't let them name it after him.

"No," he said, "I think it's time we honored old President Jefferson Davis."

He also paid for the statue erected near the gates. Except for those in Shiloh Park, this was one of the finest bronze statues in the state. Our history teacher, Mr. Webb, would tell us lengthy stories about Jefferson Davis and suggest that we be respectful when we visited the park.

To get to the cave, we had to go through the orchard and across a wide field of clover, enclosed with a barbed wire fence. This was the pasture where we kept our cow that Uncle John had loaned us so we could have fresh milk every day. Wes and I had to take her to the pasture in the morning and fetch her for milking at night. We had to make sure that Moo Moo, a name that was understood by anyone who spent much time around her, didn't get out of that pasture and into the patches of wild onions and bitter weeds. Mother would get upset if she found those unwelcome flavors in the milk.

"Lord have mercy," she would say when she tasted the milk. "We have to throw it out. It's not fit enough even for pig slop."

After getting Moo Moo settled in her proper place, we walked briskly across the field and crawled under the barbed fence into a thicket of trees and berry bushes. We had two buckets for the clay and a sack with ham and biscuits for lunch. We stopped by Uncle John's well near the barn to fill a fruit jar with water.

We began going to the cave a year or so after moving to Adairsville. We got interested in clay because of a talk we heard during assembly at school. Once a month, grades one through eight met in the gym to hear a lecture by one of the teachers or someone outside the community. Since most of the presentations were boring, students wiggled in their seats and shot spit balls at one another.

The speaker for one of the meetings was an agriculture teacher brought in by the Grange, an educational and social organization primarily for farmers. He talked mostly about clay, and Wes and I both found ourselves listening. He described the way clay was formed and how loams were different from one area to another. We learned about the type of clay in the caves out by the Ridges. He described how much each civilization depended on clay for its existence and how the first potters learned to make jars, pots, and other things essential to cooking and storage. There was one thing he said that I never forgot:

"There is an Indian legend that tells us that clay is a form of life. A sacred relationship between the potter and the clay begins when the clay is first taken from the ground."

Wes grabbed a pencil and wrote it down in his tablet.

At first, we used the clay to make cars, soldiers, and miniature forts. Once we built a train by molding the cars in squares and sketching out windows on each side. We used coca cola tops for wheels and linked the cars with wire hooks before putting them in the sun to harden. Nowadays, we made ashtrays, crude clay pots, and saucers. We sold a few of the pieces at church rummage sales.

Wes said we needed enough clay to make some larger pots.

"That will take a lot of digging," I said, looking up at the sun as it started giving out its early morning heat.

"And you never know," Wes said, "ole Slowfoot might be there to help us."

I didn't think that was funny and let Wes know that he might be going alone if he kept talking like that. Robert Earl had said that Slowfoot was mean as a cornered rattlesnake and

27

we'd better never make him mad. Wes didn't believe Slowfoot would hurt a flea but wasn't about to find out.

"If I were Slowfoot, I'd be afraid of Robert Earl," I said laughing.

Approaching the cave, we noticed a small stream of water in front of the entrance, probably caused by rain the night before. We put down our buckets and lunch sack and took a quick look around the area before going in. The cave was no more than about twenty feet deep and seven feet high. The entrance to the cave was about ten feet across.

Uncle John had told us there used to be large mounds where the caves were now, but the erosion cut into the banks and created the caves. Some people believed they were once Indian burial grounds and there were stories about finding skeletons and pottery. Daddy told us he didn't think any of that was true and no one had ever produced one single bone or piece of pottery from the caves. He said the only Indian burial grounds in the area were over near Pinson, a small town south of Jackson. Maggie Townsend, Doc Townsend's wife, spread it all over town that Brother Turnage was the smartest man she had ever met. We thought she was right, so we believed Daddy when he told us not to worry about disturbing Indian burial grounds.

Everything looked safe, so we took our buckets into the cave, stepping over the water. As usual, empty bean and potted meat cans were scattered about the cave. There were some soda pop bottles, which were not there a few weeks ago. We figured hobos left them while passing through Adairsville. Leaning against the back wall was a stick with a fork on the end, which looked like someone had whittled it with a knife. Wes guessed that the hobos used the stick for cooking meat, maybe a rabbit or squirrel. The burnt wood in the cave indicated they had built fires for cooking and for keeping warm at night.

Wes and I started digging out handfuls of clay and filling the first bucket. When it was full, we carried it across the stream and set it outside, then went back into the cave to fill the second bucket. After that was done, we took it outside and returned to the cave to eat our lunch. When we opened the lunch sack, we found that Mother had put in two fried apple pies along with the ham and biscuits. It was a hot, humid day, but the cave was cool and the water in the fruit jar was still fresh.

As we were finishing our pies, we thought we heard something move at the mouth of the cave.

"Did you hear that?" I asked Wes.

"Sure did," he said, staring out at the opening. "I think we'd better get outta here."

We put the fruit jar in the bag and started toward the opening. Suddenly Wes took a step backward and cried out, "Wait, Vance, don't move! Look in the stream and tell me what you see."

I stopped in my tracks and it didn't take long to see what Wes was pointing at.

"It's a snake, Wes," I said quivering. "A big snake and we've been walking right over it all morning."

We moved as far back in the cave as we could.

"We're trapped," I said.

The snake raised his head to get a good look at us.

"He looks mean and angry," I volunteered.

"Looks like Robert Earl," Wes said, trying to be funny.

"What are we gonna do?" I said in a high-pitched voice. "We could be here all day and have to spend the night in the cave. Daddy would have to form a search party and come looking for us."

"Don't say stupid things like that, Vance, it only makes it worse," Wes said.

Wes thought we needed to figure out what kind of snake it was before we did anything. He said he'd read in *National Geographic* that there were over 2,700 snake species, and they all had jaws that could swallow large animals whole. Wes questioned aloud whether this was a constrictor snake that squeezes its prey or a venomous snake that kills by injecting poison into its victims.

I said, "Wes, what are you talking about? This ain't the time to be discussing the habits of snakes."

Wes often surprised and irritated me with stuff like this that just came flowing out of his mouth. However, this was just too much.

"Well, I can read and I do go to school. If you would read real magazines instead of Captain Marvel and Superman comics, you might know about these things too," Wes said sternly.

I was not amused. "I read as much as you do, but I've never taken a fancy to snakes."

Wes continued with his lecture. "They have no ears, but they can detect vibrations, and their tongues are sensitive to smell, taste, and touch."

"The point is," I said impatiently, "whatta we gonna do about that . . . that snake staring at us with his beady eyes? And whether he's got ears or not, he looks like . . . you know . . . yeah, like he's hearing everything we say."

Wes was still not sure what kind of snake it was. Mother had told us never to kill a corn snake or a garden snake because they ate pesky insects that harmed her vegetables.

Wes finally decided it was a copperhead.

"They're poisonous, aren't they?" I said, beginning to shiver from either fear or the dampness of the cave.

"Why don't you get a closer look, Vance, and tell me what you see," Wes said, laughing. "If it's got a flat head and a gold color to his body, it's a copperhead," he explained.

I said I really didn't care what kind of snake it was, I just wanted to get out.

"We either have to kill it or figure a way to get by it without getting bit," Wes said, as he stood up and moved to the corner of the cave.

I watched as Wes picked up the forked stick and started jabbing it into the soft clay, testing it to see how strong it was.

I waited to hear his plan before saying anything. Wes explained calmly that we would pack the cans with clay and use them like walnut-filled snowballs.

"We'll kill the snake by throwing the cans at his head," Wes said.

"But if we start throwing cans at him, he'll either move away or come after us," I said in a whiny voice.

"Not if we pin him down with this forked stick," Wes said in a voice that believed in his plan. I didn't argue; I just started packing the cans with clay.

When Wes motioned he was ready, he took the stick and moved toward the opening. The snake lifted its head higher and began to hiss.

"He's mad, Wes," I said.

"That's good. It means he won't run."

Wes held the stick like a spear and stepped carefully toward the snake. With all his force, he plunged the fork at the head of the snake, pinning him down in the stream.

"Throw the cans," he yelled.

I had two in my hands and moved in as close as I could. The snake was wiggling and thrashing in the water, but couldn't break away from the trap set by the stick.

"Throw the cans," Wes yelled again. "Think about Junior and throw them like snowballs filled with hicker nuts."

I hurled the first and missed by more than a foot. The second barely grazed the back of the snake.

The next one I picked up was the large bean can and it felt almost too heavy to lift above my head. I could see Wes starting to sweat and I knew he was depending on me. I stepped closer and threw with all the strength I had left. The large bean can plunged hard into the little stream, missing the snake and splashing muddy water all over us.

I was trying to fill another can when I realized that a man's shadow had fallen across the mouth of the cave. Wes saw him about the same time. We both knew it was Slowfoot. This was the closest we had ever been to him and all we could do was stare with our mouths open.

He was tall and thin as a rail. He held a walking stick with both hands, clutching it to his chest. His tanned skin stretched tightly across his long face like old leather. His eyes were narrow and, when he squinted in the sun, they looked black. He wore a shapeless dark brown felt hat with sweat rings. His face was expressionless: no smile and no frown. We couldn't speak and he chose not to.

He dropped his walking stick and pulled a knife from his pocket. With a quick flick of his hand, the knife opened and the long shiny blade sparkled in the sunlight. Unable to breathe, I moved to the back of the cave, but Wes just stood there holding on to the stick that held the angry snake.

Slowfoot stared thoughtfully at the snake for a moment, then quickly folded his knife and put it back in his pocket. He picked up a large stone, held it in both hands as if he was weighing it, then lifted it high above his head and threw it with

31

such strength that it broke the stick and caused Wes to fall backward. Slowfoot then reached down, picked up the stunned snake with his bare hand, and hurled it into the bushes. We opened our mouths but nothing came out. Slowfoot stood for a moment looking at us, then turned and walked away.

Wes finally found his voice and yelled, "Mister, thanks . . . thanks Mister Slow . . . er sir."

Slowfoot paused a moment, but did not turn around. He then continued to walk through the bushes and out of sight.

We still didn't have our wits about us, but we knew we had to get out of there. We jumped the puddle, picked up our clay and lunch bag, and ran toward the fence. Scurrying under it, my pants snagged on a barb in the wire. Wes came back, untangled me, and muttered something about this not being a good time to get clumsy. We walked as fast as we could across the pasture toward the gate where Moo Moo was waiting. We opened it and, without speaking, walked slowly toward the barn, still trying to catch our breath.

When we reached the barn, Parker and his two boys were pitching hay from the loft. Parker waved as he climbed down. He had worked for Uncle John for a long time and lived in a house at the north end of the orchard. Still dazed, we sat down on the ground and waited for his boys, Seth and Moses, to jump from the loft into the hay.

Parker had five children, four living at home and one who had enlisted in the Air Corps. When people asked about his son in the army, Parker was quick to correct them.

"Euclid's an airman and gonna be a pilot real soon."

We often played games, crated apples, and picked cotton with Seth and Moses, who were about our age. Parker's girls were named Amelia and Shelby. Alva, Parker's wife, worked mostly for Mrs. Menloe—cooking, cleaning, and washing. She practically raised Lucy Menloe and bragged about "what a fine lady she is." Lucy was now a sophomore at Southwestern College in Memphis.

We loved being around Parker and his boys. He was always joking and telling tall tales; some we believed and others we didn't. He liked to tell us how he picked the names for his two youngest boys.

"John Moses is named for Mr. John and for Moses in the Bible. You see, Moses is the man who gave us the Commandments. Now Seth Thomas here is named after the third son of Adam and the man who made all them clocks," he would say proudly.

"When Seth was born, we'd already decided on his first name, but didn't have another one in mind. Well, Mr. John came over to the house with one of those eight-day Seth Thomas clocks . . . you know . . . like you put on the mantle. He said it was a gift for our new son. So I said to Alma, that's it, our boy will be called Seth Thomas Browne."

I liked the name but sometimes I would tease him by saying, "Here comes Seth Thomas, always on time."

When Junior wanted to get back at Seth for something, he'd call him "Tick-tock." Seth and Parker didn't take too kindly to the nickname.

When we told Parker that we had seen Slowfoot over by the cave, he laughed and said, "Did he spook you?"

"No, we're not scared of him," I said.

"No need to be," Parker continued. "He's harmless. When I'm working over in the north forty, I seen him a time or two. He's got a shack over by the Ridges, built right against a dirt bank, as far as I can tell. I've only been over there once looking for a stray, but I got no reason to be fearing him," Parker said, glancing over at his boys.

For some reason, we didn't tell Parker what had happened at the cave.

Changing the subject, he said, "You boys gonna help me out at hog-killing, ain't you?"

We said we would because we were saving up for a bike and knew Uncle John would pay us.

"Now, why do you need a bike when you can ride Mr. John's horse anytime?" Parker asked.

By the look on their faces, we could tell that Seth and Moses understood about the bike, even if Parker didn't.

Seth, the oldest, said to Wes, "I bet I can pick more cotton than you this year 'cause I'm bigger now."

"No way you gonna beat me, Seth," Wes said.

I was betting on Seth.

On our way through the apple orchard, we spotted Uncle John sitting in a swing in his backyard. As we sat on the ground next to him, we told Uncle John everything that had happened that day.

He smiled and said, "You boys were lucky 'ole Slowfoot came by. You don't wanna get a copperhead's dander up. They're mean and deadly when they feel trapped."

Whittling on a stick, he said thoughtfully, "You know, people got him all wrong. He's not like what they say."

We nodded in agreement.

Uncle John continued. "He's been short on luck most of his life. He was born with a clubfoot and one leg shorter than the other and that's why he walks the way he does and that's how he got that nickname. The way he lives might not seem normal, but it's not up to us to say."

He paused and scratched his head. "Can't always judge a man by his peculiarities."

"Slowfoot's not his real name, is it?" I asked.

"Nah, but if you want to know the whole story, you need to talk to Alma Lee Stewart. Her family lived not far from where Slowfoot was born and raised."

Wes and I looked at each other and both were thinking the same thing. We'd have to figure out a way to get out to Chapel Hill Road real soon to see our adopted grandmother.

3

"Alma, don't let these boys get in your way or talk your head off," Daddy said, as he dropped us off and promised to pick us up in a couple of hours.

"Don't you worry about us, Brother Turnage. You know how I love to have these children come visit me."

Miss Alma Lee Stewart lived alone in a one-story frame house on Chapel Hill Road about five miles northwest of Main Street. The first time we met her, she called us her grandchildren and insisted that we call her Granny Lee instead of Miss Alma. Wes and I always looked forward to visiting with her and sitting on her porch that went across the front and down one side of the house, and was large enough for a swing, four rocking chairs, and a glass-top table for serving afternoon tea.

Over the massive stone fireplace, which dominated the large living room, was a wide mantel that held framed pictures, ceramic bowls, and miniature statues carved from wood. An oil lamp with a chimney darkened by smoke sat on a pine table by the radio. Huge chairs with soft cushions were placed at an angle in front of the fireplace. In the corner of the room was a roll-top writing desk with small drawers along the top. There were shelves on each side of the fireplace filled with books, some worn from handling and others that had been purchased recently. Granny Lee loved to read all kinds of books—novels, poetry, love stories, history and biography. She was especially fond of Shakespeare and always seemed to be able to work in a quote or two no matter what the conversation. Uncle John said she should have been a librarian. She loaned us books, making us promise to take care of them and discuss them with her after we finished reading them. Wes' favorites were *Treasure Island* and *Kidnapped* by Robert Louis Stevenson, a famous Scottish writer.

Kidnapped told the story of how a jury made up entirely of Campbell Clan members found Allan Breck Stewart, one of Granny Lee's ancestors, guilty of killing Colin Campbell. When we talked about the book, she explained the role of clans in most of the Scottish wars.

"Scotland is a poor country, partly because of animosity and greed. They didn't have time to farm or develop industry because they were always fighting."

The kitchen was large enough for a dining table and chairs and a sofa placed in front of a brick fireplace once used for all the cooking. She still kept a cast-iron pot attached to a metal rod which allowed the pot to hang over the fire and then swing out for ladling soup or stew or beans filled with ham hocks. Granny Lee's kitchen had wonderful smells of food being cooked, cookies just out of the oven, and her famous rhubarb pie cooling on the windowsill. She always had cold lemonade in the summer and hot cocoa in the winter to wash down oatmeal cookies or bran muffins filled with nuts and fruits.

In the back of her house was the original log cabin her mother and father had lived in when they first moved to Adairsville. She called the cabin her private studio and used it for quilting and weaving. She had two large looms, which her mother had brought from North Carolina, and shelves stacked high with cones of wool and cotton yarns in a rainbow of colors. One room held a wooden frame for making quilts. Granny Lee showed us how she took pieces of layered cloth, patchwork as she called it, and stitched them together to create colorful quilts.

She told stories of how the Hopi Indians in Arizona were taught quilting by the Mormon missionaries and had included the quilts in some of their most important rituals.

"There are also tales about how the freed slaves used quilts as message pads to guide other slaves out of the South to the North on the Underground Railroad," she said, pointing to her own personal patterns on a quilt.

Once a month, Granny Lee had quilting and weaving gatherings in her home to teach these skills to local women, just as her mother had been taught by the mountain women back in North Carolina. She had helped organize quilting bees all over the county and increased the population of looms four-fold.

We loved to watch her weave and sometimes she would let us push the pedals and run the shuttle through the warp as she explained the process, using words we didn't understand and couldn't remember. As she worked, she would tell us stories about how her grandparents came to this country from Scotland, settled in a rural area of North Carolina near Grandfather Mountain, and made a living growing tobacco and selling handmade looms to textile mills. She still had an old spinning wheel in the barn used by her mother for spinning wool and cotton into threads used on the looms.

She was proud of her heritage and could trace the Stewart name all the way back to Scottish kings and wealthy landowners.

"Now this is the Stewart plaid," she would say proudly as she displayed a shawl she had woven. "It's known as the 'Royal Tartan' and is still the official tartan of the Royal House of Scotland."

Wes and I liked looking at the colorful patterns woven into her scarves, and studying the framed Stewart coat of arms. We were always eager to hear more about this strange land so far away.

Because of the long winters and the industrialization of weaving, her parents came across the mountains to Tennessee in 1865—ten years before Granny Lee was born. They bought 150 acres of land on Chapel Hill Road and grew fine cotton and raised cattle and hogs for market. They also had one of the largest pecan groves in Tennessee. Granny Lee had intended to go to college after finishing high school, but when she was a senior, her mother died of tuberculosis. She stayed home, worked on the farm, and took care of the house and her father.

"That didn't leave much time for beaus, so I just never got around to finding someone to marry," she said, laughing.

After her father died in 1910, she sold off the entire farm except for ten acres, which included the pecan grove, the house, log cabin, and the barn.

She drove a 1936 Ford Coupe, wore well-tailored, but not fancy, clothes bought in Atlanta, and was an active Presbyterian who didn't believe in predestination. She was very generous and gave money to the Presbyterian Church for the stained glass windows and the organ, and paid for the benches installed in the flower garden next to the library. Daddy said she was bright, witty, and "a formidable opponent when she had an opinion that was different from yours."

Granny Lee was just about the smartest woman I'd ever known. She shared her travels to mysterious lands and introduced us to exciting characters along the way. When she caught me frowning, she would remind me that "a smile is an easy way to improve your looks." Or when we talked about why some people seemed happy and others didn't, she would say, "Everyone wants to live on a mountain but most of the happiness and growth comes while climbing it." I tried to remember all her sayings and would write them down as soon as I had pen and paper.

She put on her bonnet and walked with us to the garden to do some weeding and staking. Granny Lee took long strides when she walked and, even though her hair was white as cotton, she didn't look like someone almost seventy years old. Mother, who considered Granny Lee one of her best friends, said, "She has a regal bearing that shows she came from fine stock."

Walking back to the house, Wes told Granny Lee about the incident with Slowfoot at the cave and wondered if she would mind telling us what she knew about his family.

"John Menloe said you'd be asking me about that. We'd better get out of this sun, get us something cool to drink, and sit a spell if I'm going to tell you that story," she said, removing her bonnet and apron.

Wes and I sat in the swing sipping lemonade. Granny Lee settled into a wicker rocking chair with her knitting needles and a ball of yarn, and began relating the tale.

"His name is Lonnie Jackson and he came from a rich family; well, rich at one time, anyway."

Granny told how Lonnie's grandparents moved from New Orleans sometime around 1878, a few years after she was born, and built a large mansion about five miles down the road. "It was in the style of those old antebellum houses built before the Civil War. It seems that Mr. Justin Bove—they pronounced it Bo-vay—made a lot of money in oil and invested most of it in the stock market."

Granny Lee paused to sip some tea before continuing.

"They were rather peculiar folks. Justin's wife, Lorene, was an attractive lady, but town folks thought her to be snobbish. Their daughter, Maribelle, attended a fancy school in the east but came home before graduating. The Boves had their own way of doing things and most folks thought they were out of place in Adairsville. They brought their servants with them from New Orleans and built a small house in the back of the mansion for them," Granny Lee said, as she motioned for us to help unravel her ball of yarn.

"That mansion was one of the finest houses in this part of the country; almost as fine as the Cherry Mansion across the river," she said, pointing eastward.

According to Granny Lee, the house had two floors and a large balcony decorated with wrought iron. "Just like New Orleans," she explained.

"The Boves had a few milk cows, some goats, and the best Tennessee walking horses money could buy. He had two fine carriages shipped up from New Orleans and, if you happened to be out here on a Sunday afternoon, you might see them dressed in their finest store-bought clothes, riding in a carriage drawn by one of those horses.

"Later Justin bought a Model A Ford touring car and a flatbed truck. He sold one of the carriages and kept the other stored in his barn. For some reason, they did most of their trading in Savannah and that didn't set too well with the local store owners.

"After Maribelle came home from college, rumor was that she was going to have a baby. My father wondered about that because he didn't recall ever seeing another white man living at the mansion. Justin put out the word that the father was a Captain Jackson who had been killed in the Spanish American War. They even told it that Captain Jackson had fought side by side with Teddy Roosevelt and was a distant relative of Andrew

40

Jackson. I don't think anyone ever believed those stories but they continued to be told," Granny Lee said with a smile.

"This was the beginning of a lot of bad luck and sorrow for the Boves," Granny Lee continued.

Her mood was somber and her voice revealed sadness as she told how Lorene Bove had died mysteriously soon after Maribelle's child was born.

"The gossip was that she had taken her own life but no one knew for sure. She was embalmed in Savannah, laid out in a fine bronze casket, put on a train, and sent to New Orleans for the funeral and burial. Justin never married again. He traveled some, but mostly stayed at home and took care of Lonnie and Maribelle."

"And Miss Maribelle's baby was Slowfoot?" Wes asked, wide-eyed.

"Yes, and one of the midwives told Daddy that he was a strange-looking baby," Granny Lee said.

"Did that have anything to do with why Miss Lorene killed herself?" Wes asked. Granny Lee said that no one really knew and the family never talked about it.

Lonnie finished sixth grade and then went away to a private school atop the Cumberland Plateau in East Tennessee.

"I think the name of the school was St. Andrew's Academy, but I'm not sure. He only stayed a few years and soon after he came home, he fell out of the hayloft and hit his head on a rock. Justin took him to a hospital in Memphis for treatment and they kept him there for several weeks, but Lonnie was never the same after that. He stayed pretty much to himself and only went into town when he was with his granddaddy or one of the servants. I would see him walking down the road toward the river and wave at him, but he never waved back.

"When the stock market crash came in 1929, Justin lost just about everything he had. He couldn't keep up the house and all but two of the servants left and went who knows where. Ruby, one of the colored girls, actually more white than colored, was Maribelle's maid and was very loyal to Justin. She and her mother stayed on to help take care of Maribelle until after the fire; then they went back to New Orleans.

41

"Everything just went to seed," Granny Lee said sadly. "The paint peeled off the mansion and weeds grew where flowers and grass had thrived. That beautiful ironwork on the balcony became coated with rust. People were afraid to go near the place and some suggested it was haunted. Mr. Justin died of a heart attack in 1931 and was buried alongside his wife in New Orleans, so we were told."

"So Slowfoot and Miss Maribelle lived alone in that old house?" Wes asked.

Granny Lee paused as she watched a car kicking up dust on the road in front of her house. "My nose has been itching so much lately, I thought that might be company coming."

As the car continued down the road, Granny Lee returned to the story.

"For the next four years, they got by somehow. I know they sold their cars, the carriage, and the horses and that probably gave them enough to live on. Several people offered to help, but they were proud folks and wouldn't take any kind of charity."

Granny Lee then told about the night of the fire.

"I could see the blaze from this porch," she said, pointing toward the sky. "That old house just went up like kindling soaked in kerosene. Lonnie was on his way home from the river when the fire started. By the time he got there, everything was gone, including his momma."

Wes and I knew the place. The only reminder of the house was a brick chimney standing defiantly among the ruins. The barn in the pasture had no roof and the two remaining sides were leaning toward the ground.

Granny Lee paused for a moment and scratched her head, as if trying to remember something. She then told how after days of going through the rubbish, Lonnie just walked off and as far as anyone knew, he never returned to the place.

"For a while I lost track of him. Sightings were rare and rumors about him unreliable. Then one day he showed up in town pulling a cart made of old barn lumber and bicycle wheels. That was right after the servant's house burned on Halloween night. Most people figured vandals set the fire," Granny Lee said as she wiped her glasses.

"Parker told us that Slowfoot built a house over by the Ridges, but nobody ever got a close look at it," Wes said.

"That's what I've heard. He probably used some of that lumber from the old barn," Granny Lee said.

We asked if she knew where he got the money for goods and other things.

"There were people who believed that old Justin had hidden lots of money in the house because he didn't trust banks after the crash. Some folks think Lonnie knew about the money and that's what he was looking for in the rubbish."

"What do you believe?" Wes asked.

"It's possible, but I personally think he was penniless. He had too much pride to live like a pauper if he didn't have to and that's reason enough for me," she said with finality.

"Who owns that land now?" Wes asked.

"I'm not sure," Granny Lee said. "Everything burned and I'm told there's no record in the court house about the deed. I suppose Lonnie could claim it if he was of a mind to, but he's not, and no one else seems to have any interest in it. A lot of people think there's a curse on the whole place."

Parker's wife agreed with Granny Lee. She told us later not to go near that place. "That old house had haints in it and the ground it stood on has been cursed by the devil and that's why nobody wants anything to do with it."

Some people thought the chimney stood as a monument to the curse.

"I think it's best if you boys stay away from Lonnie and don't ever tease him about his foot or the way he looks," Granny Lee said as a warning and as a consideration for Lonnie's feelings.

"Well, all I know is he saved our lives," I said.

"We could've killed that snake if you could throw straight," Wes said laughing. I was a little hurt but said nothing. Wes would tell me later that he was just joshing.

After that day we decided there was no need to fear Slowfoot anymore, but agreed that if we ever saw him again, we'd call him Mr. Jackson.

4

We arrived home with Daddy around 4:00. After fetching Moo Moo and putting her in the pen, we went to the back porch to wash up. A hand pump that pulled up the water from a spring-fed well, and forced it through a corroded copper faucet into a bucket, generated our water supply. There were many people in Adairsville who still had cisterns or wells in their backyards. Buckets, tied to ropes looped through pulleys, would haul up the water. Girls believed rainwater was better for their hair, so they used barrels to catch the water as it ran off the roof. I think they read that in a magazine at the beauty parlor.

I was hungry, so I went to the garden and pulled up some green onions and plucked a tomato off the vine. After finding a couple of biscuits left over from breakfast, I sat down at the table and washed down my snack with a glass of cold buttermilk. The table, with its white melamine top and shiny chrome legs, played a big role in our family life. We ate all our meals at that table. Between meals, it was a place for a Monopoly board, jigsaw puzzles, and where Mother cut out her patterns. Late at night, Daddy wrote his sermons there. Rue wrote letters and did her homework, and in December, we addressed Christmas cards at the table. On Sundays, Mother covered it with a white tablecloth for dinner. It sat at the edge of the kitchen near the large opening where you entered the living room. The chairs were also made of chrome and had cushioned seats covered in red plastic.

I was on my way to find Wes when I heard Rue yelling something as she hurried down the road toward the house. Mother was sitting on the porch darning. We ran to the front yard just as Mother came off the porch. She was straining to hear what Rue was saying.

"Daddy's bringing home a mule," we thought she said.

Just then, Mother could see a man who resembled her husband walking down the road holding onto a rope tied to a mule.

"Lord have mercy," she said as she moved closer to the road.

"It's a horse!" I said excitedly as I ran toward Daddy.

"It's no horse," Mother said as she adjusted her glasses to get a better look.

She was right; it was no horse. In fact, it wasn't even much of a mule. It looked like it hadn't eaten in weeks.

"Why, you can see the ribs almost coming through the skin," Rue observed.

Daddy tried to ignore the people who had come out of their houses to watch him pass. "Good afternoon, Brother Turnage," one neighbor said, smiling. "Is that one of your new converts?"

Daddy laughed and said, "Well, Melvin, this wouldn't be the first jackass to get religion."

Mother was shocked to hear him talk that way and said, "Lord have mercy," again.

I was now walking with Daddy and holding onto one of the ropes dangling from the mule's neck. It suddenly occurred to me that God might have heard my prayers after all but thought I asked for a mule instead of a pony. Daddy said in sermons that if you have enough faith, God will hear and answer your prayers. Every Christmas, I would pray that God or Santa would bring me a pony. I believed that if I prayed hard enough, did all my chores, and didn't say cuss words, God would reward me with a pony. Every Christmas morning, instead of running into the living room where Santa had left our toys and candy and nuts, I would run to the back door and look for my pony; but there was never a pony. My eyes would fill with tears and I would wonder why this was such a hard task for God. It's not that I was asking for a lot of money or a big house or even a new bicycle; just a pony, that's all I wanted and I wanted it more than anything I had ever wanted in my life. After each disappointment, I had doubts about my father and about God. For some reason, I never blamed Santa Claus. But I got over it because I knew there would be another Christmas and, like that mustard seed Daddy talked about, I would let my hope and faith grow for another year.

By now, Daddy was leading this mangy creature up the driveway and into the back pen, where Moo Moo was bellowing loudly in protest. Mother and the rest of us followed and waited for the mule to be tied to the fence inside the pen.

"Now, Milton, if it's not asking too much, would you please explain where that mule came from and what we're going to do with it?" Mother said, with hands on her hips.

Daddy was usually not timid about talking, but he was having a hard time finding the right words.

"You see," he finally said, "the Grange had an auction today, up near the lumber yard, to raise money to buy some paint and repair the steps. They asked me to be the auctioneer since I'm used to speaking in front of people." We waited for him to finish his story.

Charlie Parsons, a man not known for his charity or his love of preachers, had donated the mule for the auction. He had spread the word to let Daddy make the opening bid and then no one was to raise it. That would leave "the preacher owning a worthless mule." Daddy was not in on the ruse. Sure enough, he made an opening bid of three dollars. The silence that followed was heard all over Adairsville before the day ended. The Turnages were now the proud owners of a mule so skinny, it could never support a rider, and certainly couldn't pull a wagon.

Wes and I went out to the pen to move him away from Moo Moo, who was not happy with her new roommate. The mule stepped on my foot and I didn't even feel it. Uncle John sent Parker over to take the mule to his barn. He told Daddy that he would keep it there until the people from the glue factory in Savannah picked it up. When asked, Uncle John explained that there was a rendering plant across the river that used the hoofs, bones, tendons, ligaments, and cartilage from old horses and mules to make glue. Although he explained that the glue was used mostly for heavy furniture, I quit licking stamps.

Rue, Wes, and I all agreed that the only jackass at the auction that hot summer day was Charlie Parsons. Wes and I would figure out a way to get even with Old Man Parsons.

After getting Moo Moo calmed down, Wes went to the backyard to soften some clay, and I headed to the living room to listen to the Cardinals play the Giants. We owned an RCA Victor table model radio with push button dials. It was made of dark mahogany and the speaker was covered with a piece of brocade decorated with flowers. Daddy said it was a much finer radio than the old Crosley he had a few years ago. Mr. Macgregor and Uncle John had fancy floor model Motorolas, but their sound was not any better than ours, so we said.

The radio was a very important part of our lives. Daddy liked to listen to the news read by Gabriel Heatter or H. V. Kaltenborn, and he never missed one of President Roosevelt's speeches. Before Pearl Harbor, Daddy was a pacifist, and often preached that war was evil and unnecessary, but the Japanese attack changed his mind. He now preached that we were justified in fighting the Germans and Japanese, who were "as evil as Satan himself," he would say.

Daddy practically worshipped President Roosevelt. He quoted him often and once built an entire sermon around the State of the Union Address of 1941. *The Clarion Standard* printed the entire text of Daddy's sermon. Mr. Fesmire, the druggist, had the print shop design a poster listing the four freedoms of democracy made famous by that speech, and placed in every store in town. The poster read:

"THE FOUR FREEDOMS OF DEMOCRACY

1. Freedom of speech and expression—everywhere in the world.
2. Freedom to worship God in his own way—everywhere in the world.
3. Freedom from want—everywhere in the world.
4. Freedom from fear—everywhere in the world.

But the radio was also our main entertainment at night. The silliness of *Fibber McGee and Molly* and the *Burns and Allen Show* brought delight to everyone. There were dramas like *First Nighter*, *The Shadow*, and *Lux Radio Theater*. Mother listened to a soap opera called *Stella Dallas* and singer Kate Smith, who had a strong, throaty voice but couldn't read music according to an article Mother had read in a magazine.

One of my favorites, *Major Bowes' Original Amateur Hour*, aired on Sunday night. If church ran late, I would have to dash home to get there before the end of the show. Sometimes, through the open windows of homes along the sidewalk, I would hear Dick Contino playing "Flight of the Bumble Bee" on his accordion. That was my clue that I had missed most of the program, because, being a winner for thirteen straight weeks, he was always the last contestant.

I loved to listen to Cardinal baseball. I used a piece of cardboard from the print shop to write down the starting lineup, and then I would keep score inning by inning. I kept those score cards the whole season and knew the batting averages of every Redbird player and the stats on each pitcher. Wes liked all the programs, but he was always drawing or sketching while he listened to the radio. Miss Ross, the art teacher at the school, told Mother that Wes had talent that needed attention.

The heat was stifling, and the humidity made it hard to breathe. On days like this, the outdoor privy would emit putrid odors. Rue was in her room trying to decide about a dress for a date with a new boyfriend who was coming to pick her up in a couple of hours. She liked this boy better than the others she had dated and wanted to make a good impression.

Daddy and Mother were sitting on the front porch talking about the three dollars for the mule. Mother was still upset and said some nasty things about Charlie Parsons.

Daddy said that Charlie meant no harm. "It was just a little prank and I happened to be the victim," he said without conviction.

Suddenly Mother said, "Milton, what's that strange odor?"

Daddy turned up his face and sniffed. "Something unusual about that," he said.

They both got up and went around to the back of the house, and as they got closer to the privy, the odor intensified.

"It's coming from the privy, Grace," Daddy said as he opened the door. I also realized that there was something putrid in the air.

Rue came out and started to cry. She admitted that she had been so concerned with what her boyfriend would think about the smell emanating from the outhouse, she took a bottle of Mother's Apple Blossom perfume and poured it into the privy.

When her boyfriend arrived, Rue refused to come out of her bedroom. Mother knocked on the door and told her to come out immediately.

"I'm going to count to . . . no, I'm not going to count to anything. I'm telling you, Ruth Ann Turnage, to come out this minute and start acting your age."

Dabbing at her eyes and still sniffling, Rue came out.

"Now, you go dry those tears, put some powder on your face, and go make that boy feel welcome," she said in a voice filled with irritation.

Her boyfriend knew something strange was going on, but he didn't look like the kind of fellow who would ask.

I think everyone in Adairsville got a whiff of a very strange fragrance that Saturday afternoon, and for days we held our noses when visiting the privy. Mother said that if Rue wasn't so all grown-up, she'd put her over her knee and spank her. Rue worked hard selling popcorn at The Dixie Theater to make enough money to buy Mother another bottle of perfume.

It was getting close to supper time and Mother was in the kitchen cooking. I moved to the porch after the Cardinal game ended, and was sitting on the steps reading a comic book. Daddy was thumbing through the *Saturday Evening Post* when J. C. Macgregor drove up in his pickup truck. In the back was a bicycle. Mr. Macgregor walked to the porch where Daddy met him. They exchanged a few pleasantries and then Mr. Macgregor said something about the bicycle. Wes had come around the side of the house and was standing next to the bed of the truck.

"I want the boys to have Junior's bicycle," Mr. Macgregor said slowly. Wes and I were speechless.

We looked at each other in stunned silence. We had been saving for three years to buy a Western Flyer and now we were being given a Schwinn Roadmaster with deluxe balloon tires, a floating saddle, and adjustable seat post. Unlike the cheaper models, this one also had a horn and battery operated lights mounted on the handlebars. It was beyond anything we had ever imagined.

We weren't sure what to say. Mr. Macgregor, taking the bicycle out of the truck, said, "You boys were good to Junior and I appreciated it. He used to tell me how you would take up for him and let him play ball with you when the others didn't pick him for their team. He'd want you to have this bicycle."

"You don't know how happy you've made these two boys of mine," Daddy said as he shook Mr. Macgregor's hand.

"We'll take real good care of it," Wes said.

"We miss Junior," I sputtered and could not finish.

"Oh, and one more thing," Mr. Macgregor said as he reached into the front seat of the truck. "I won't have any need for this sack of marbles. You boys can use them, I'm sure. And don't wear out your knuckles," he said, smiling and patting Wes on his head.

"Gosh" was about all I could get out.

We thanked him again and waved as he backed down the drive. It was like Christmas morning. There was no pony, but something even better: a bright-red bicycle that was as good as new. Mother had a hard time getting us in for supper. We took turns riding the bike up and down the road until Daddy threatened to take it away from us if we didn't come in. We were allowed to put it on the back porch where it would be safe. After supper, in the darkness, we sat on the porch and wiped it with an old towel and thought about tomorrow's adventures. Of course, we had forgotten that tomorrow was Sunday and most of the day would be spent in Sunday school, church, Epworth League, and church again. But that would be okay because we were feeling good about our parents, God, and Mr. Macgregor. And we both had good thoughts about Junior.

During the summer, Daddy preached revivals in small churches in remote rural areas. He looked forward to them and it was another source of income for the family. The churches would take up an offering every night during the revival and give it to Daddy at the end of the week. He would bring it home and on Saturday morning the contents of the brown bag would be poured onto the kitchen table for counting. Wes and I were allowed to count the pennies, nickels, and dimes. Daddy counted the larger coins and bills. The count usually totaled up to $20 or $30, which was put into an empty butter crock and saved for special things. The churches also sent Daddy home with sacks of corn, green vegetables, jars of pickles, fresh fruit, and always, a watermelon.

Daddy liked to tell about experiences he had at revivals. One of the stories he told over and over to us and anyone who would listen was about a revival he preached for Brother Caldwell in Hickory Hollow over by Bolivar. At the beginning of the week, Brother Caldwell talked to Daddy about Sol, a farmer who claimed to be an agnostic. His wife was very active in the church and wanted her husband to become a Christian.

"We're gonna bring old Sol to Jesus this week," Brother Caldwell had said.

"Just how we were going to do that, he didn't say," Daddy said, smiling.

Since Sol didn't show up at the nightly services, Daddy and Brother Caldwell decided to call on him at his house. Sol was cordial and his wife gracious as they served some iced tea and sugar cookies. Afterward, Sol took Daddy and Brother Caldwell out to show them his farm. They looked at the tall, green corn, the cotton stalks loaded with bolls ready to burst open, and the cows grazing in foot-high clover. There were two large barns and a brick silo. Sol was obviously proud of his farm and talked about how much a successful farmer needed to know about soil, weather, erosion, and chemicals. Sol said a farmer had an obligation to nature not to exhaust the soil, erode the land, and deprive wildlife of their refuge and habitat. Daddy was so impressed, he quoted Sol in a sermon.

They walked over to a large melon patch where Sol pointed out a huge watermelon he planned to take to the county fair. Daddy said it looked like it might weigh as much as seventy-five pounds.

"There's nothing quite like the luscious juiciness of a watermelon cut fresh from its stem and split open in the field," Sol said with fervor.

Finally, Daddy, in a moment of inspiration, raised his hand toward the horizon and moved it from one side to another, and said, "Sol, you are very fortunate to have all this. Just look at what God has given you. He has blessed you with rich land and abundant crops."

Sol pondered the thought for a moment. He then stuck his thumbs in the bib of his overalls and without much emotion said, "Well preacher, you should've seen it when God had it by himself." With a wave of his hand, he turned and walked toward the house.

Daddy laughed every time he told the story.

"What a sight," he said, "an agnostic got the best of two preachers and left them standing in the middle of a watermelon patch speechless."

5

In mid-August, we returned to school and my anxiety about going into sixth grade increased when I met my new teacher, Miss Willie Maude Sellers, who was tall, skinny, and unpleasant. She had just graduated from a teachers' college in Nashville and was sent to practice on us.

On enrollment day, I wrote "Vance" on my card.

"That's not your real name, now is it, Mr. Turnage?" she asked sarcastically. She sent me to the blackboard and instructed me to write in bold letters my full name: Luther Vincent Turnage. There was snickering in the room and Miss Sellers did nothing to stop it.

It's not that I didn't like my name; it's just that I liked my nickname better. Mother once told me that Daddy wanted to name me Martin Luther, but she thought that too pretentious. Her grandfather was a Vincent and Daddy agreed to use the name as long as he could keep Luther. Wes started calling me Vance when I was about two years old and it stuck.

Miss Willie Maude was the homeroom supervisor and taught English and spelling. Other teachers were brought in for history, math, and science. One of my favorites was Miss Ross, who taught music and art, and led the school choirs.

"She plays the piano by ear," Mother told us.

I said, "Boy, she ought to be in a carnival if she can do that."

Wes impatiently explained that it meant she played without reading musical notes. "Once she hears a piece of music, she can just sit down at the piano and play it," Wes said.

She would come to homeroom three times a week and teach us songs and encourage us to take music lessons. One of the songs almost drove me and everybody else nuts.

Mares eat oats and does eat oats,
And little lambs eat ivy.
A kid'll eat ivy too, wouldn't you?

We sang it like it sounded to us:

Mairzy doats and dozy doats and little lamzy divey
A kiddley divey too,
Wouldn't you?

I loved Miss Ross, but I couldn't get that tune and those words out of my mind for weeks. I woke up at night thinking about it. I hummed it, whistled it, and muttered it until I got on everyone's nerves.

"Stop it, you've got me doing it," Wes would say.

"If I hear that song one more time, I'm gonna put tape on your mouth," Rue warned.

I asked Miss Ross to teach us another song so I could get that tune out of my mind. She did and the new tune that took control of my mind went something like this:

Would you like to swing on a star, carry moonbeams home
*   in a jar,*
And be better off than you are, or would you rather be a
*   mule?*
A mule is an animal with long funny ears, he kicks up at
*   anything he hears,*
His back is brawny and his brain is weak, he's just plain
*   stupid with a stubborn streak,*
And by the way, if you hate to go to school, you may grow
*   up to be a mule.*

In other verses, she substituted "fish" and "pig" for "mule." The refrain was also very catchy.

All the monkeys aren't in the zoo, every day you meet quite
*   a few,*
So you see it's all up to you,
You can be better than you are,
You could be swinging on a star.

It was quite unforgettable.

Wes started eighth grade and got the meanest teacher in the school. His name was Willie Butterfield, but some of the parents and a few brave students called him "Button" because he was only five feet tall, very thin, but strong as an ox. His hair was a yellowish-brown, and he wore vested suits with a white shirt and striped tie. His lips always seemed to be in a pucker, as if he had just sucked a lemon. Mr. Butterfield was also the elementary school principal and pastor of a rural Baptist church over by Shiloh.

He had a violent temper and everyone in his class was afraid of him. Someone had carved a large paddle for him out of a one-by-four and engraved it with the words: TO BROTHER BUTTERFIELD, WHOM GOD HAS CALLED TO DISCIPLINE WAYWARD CHILDREN.

It had holes about the size of dimes to increase the pain. Wes was not looking forward to a year in the same room with Brother "Button" Butterfield, but he was looking forward to being in the same room with Mary Beth Shipley. He wouldn't admit it, but we all knew Wes had a crush on her.

We whiled away recess time with tongue twisters, like "My brother Esau said he saw the first saw that ever sawed in Arkansas."

"Bet you can't say that one fast," I would tease.

There was also one about Peter who picked a peck of pickled peppers, but I couldn't say it, so I forgot it. The younger girls played jacks and skipped rope. The older boys shot baskets or tossed a baseball.

Our classroom was dingy and smelled of chalk dust, sweaty boys, and cheap toilet water worn by some of the girls. The teacher's desk was placed up front with a large blackboard behind it. The student desks were worn from use and penknife carvings, and had hinged tops that hid a space for storing books, pencils, tablets, and spitballs. The poor lighting cast a dusky gray over the room. All twelve grades met in this red brick building that had an unfortunate shortage of windows. Except for a fifteen-minute recess and thirty minutes for lunch, we sat for long hours at our desks, suffering through stifling heat in summer and numbing cold in winter.

Wes and I were more fortunate than the kids in the county who had to get up at dawn to catch a school bus. We walked to school in summer and winter. The yellow school buses would pick up the white kids first, take them to school, and then make the rounds picking up the colored kids. They were taken to a frame school in the southwestern section of the county. I never gave any thought as to why we had separate schools any more than I thought about why white people believed they were better than colored people. I never heard Mother and Daddy say anything bad about the Negroes, but they never explained why our skin color made us so different. And if Wes thought anything about it, he never mentioned it to me.

After school, Wes and I would hurry through our chores so we could ride our bike. One hot afternoon, we decided to ride out to the Cox farm. Mr. Hannibal Cox grew some of the best watermelons in the county and had won prizes at the county fair. All the churches used his melons at their picnics and revival dinners. Wes and I thought this was a good day to sample the cool, red meat of a blue-ribbon watermelon.

As we headed down the highway, Wes thought of a way to justify our mission. "Let's pretend we're inspectors sent by the county fair judging committee to test these watermelons."

"Good idea, Wes," I said innocently.

We turned off the highway, and after riding a mile or so down a dirt lane, we parked our bicycle by a tree and walked across a wooden bridge that spanned a small creek. There was a large field covered with long green vines and huge watermelons. Soon we found several fine specimens and carried them back to the bridge. We busted open two of the watermelons, ate the hearts, and threw the rinds into the creek. We had decided that these were not blue-ribbon quality. Just as we opened the third melon and started testing it, we saw Mr. Cox fast-stepping it across the field.

From the other direction, a man carrying a black book and dressed in a white suit walked briskly down the dusty road toward the bridge. It was The Reverend Hezekiah Lacy. We were so scared we couldn't move, so we just sat on the edge of the bridge holding pieces of watermelon in our laps and wondering if we should jump into the muddy water. Looking up at Reverend Lacy and Mr. Cox, we both knew we were in big trouble.

"And what may I ask are you boys doing?" Mr. Cox yelled.

Before we could say anything, he shouted, "And look here, Zeke. You see what they done. They deliberately ruined three of my prize melons. Those were some of the ones I'd marked for your church picnic Sunday."

He picked up a stick and we thought he was gonna hit us; but he didn't.

I looked at Wes and said, "Aren't you going to tell them we're watermelon inspectors?"

Wes forced a grin that slowly turned into a frown and said, "They'll never believe us, Vance."

At that moment, it occurred to me that Wes might not be as smart as I thought he was.

"I know you boys and I know your father. You'll have hell to pay when he hears about this," he said, throwing the stick into the creek.

We begged him not to tell our father and promised to pay for them or work for nothing during harvest. Mr. Cox was not inclined to be charitable.

"Now, now, Mr. Hannibal," the reverend said. "There are plenty of good melons left for me to choose from. I know these boys and I'm sure they're most eager to repent of their waywardness and seek your forgiveness—and God's—so that they can return to their righteous ways." Holding out the black book, he said, "The Bible says we must forgive those who do evil and trespass against us."

Mr. Cox said he didn't think the Bible was talking about trespassing on private property and stealing watermelons.

Reverend Lacy held the Bible in the air and said, "No, the good Lord didn't give us specific guidance for the disposition of melon thieves, but He did say that he who forgives will be blessed and rewarded. So I think this unfortunate situation calls for a measure of leniency and a full cup of compassion."

"That's right, Mr. Cox, we're really sorry for what we did and won't ever do anything like this again," I said pleadingly.

"Well, if you were my boys, I'd give you a thrashing you'd never forget," he said, motioning for us to get off his farm.

Knowing his two boys, we thought that was a good idea, but it wasn't the right time to mention it.

We gathered up our shoes, ran to our bicycle, and rode home as fast we could. Doing something that stupid and getting caught taught us a lesson we never forgot. And we lived with the dread that Mr. Cox would tell Daddy.

The news we heard when we got home took our minds off watermelons. The sheriff had been by that afternoon to tell Daddy that all the evidence pointed to a sad fact. It seemed that Junior had been hit on the head with a blunt instrument and was dead before he was thrown into the river. Daddy explained to us that the sheriff and his deputies had been working with the F.B.I. office in Jackson to review the findings.

We were shocked and terrified thinking about it. At first, we couldn't speak; then the questions wouldn't stop.

"Why would anyone do that to Junior?" "Who did it?" "Was he killed at the river or somewhere else?"

Daddy didn't have answers to our questions, but said the sheriff believed that Junior either went to the river with someone who killed him or he was caught by surprise by the killer. When we asked how they knew he didn't drown, Daddy explained that the autopsy showed there was no water in his lungs.

"If he had been alive when he went into the river, his lungs would've been filled with water," he explained thoughtfully.

Mother had listened quietly and then said, "Boys, you're going to have to be more careful where you go and what you do."

Daddy added, "That's right, no more trips to the caves or the Ridges unless Parker goes with you."

I asked why he mentioned the caves and Ridges. "They don't think Slowfoot had anything to do with it, do they?"

"Nobody's under suspicion at this time. A lot of work has to be done before the sheriff can start making arrests. Until then, you have to let us know where you're going and when you'll be back," Daddy said with urgency in his voice.

On Sunday, Daddy said in his sermon that "Adairsville has lost some of its innocence and we need to pray that in time we'll regain it."

Wes and I lost some of our innocence in Daddy's eyes when Mr. Cox told him about the watermelon incident. We knew it was coming when we saw Mr. Cox briskly walking over from the Baptist Church toward Daddy.

I had seen Daddy angry but never like this. He was furious as he told us how disappointed he was and how he had taught us that stealing and damaging other people's property was wrong.

"How can I preach to others about honesty and good behavior when I have two boys going around stealing and wasting produce that comes from another man's labor?"

A spanking would have been much less painful than the look of disappointment on his face. We were forbidden to ride our bicycle for a week and had to be in our room every night by 8:00. I told Wes that I'd never eat another watermelon as long as I lived.

But I soon realized what a dumb promise that was and I got over it.

6

October brought the World Series and the closing of school for cotton picking. We kept our ear to the radio, listening to the World Series between the St. Louis Cardinals and the New York Yankees. Daddy even broke his rule of "no baseball games on Sunday" in order for us to hear all the games. When the Cardinals beat the Yankees four games to one, there was a lot of celebration in our house.

October also gave us a break from Miss Willie Maude and Button Butterfield. Since we didn't have to save money for a bike, we happily anticipated what we would do with the money earned picking cotton. The *Sears and Roebuck Catalogue* replaced magazines and comic books as our nightly reading material. Our wish list was growing.

Early every morning, Daddy would drive us in his brown 1936 Plymouth, which he bought from Mr. Shipley for $275, out to Mr. Parsons' farm. Daddy always needed extra money for Christmas, so two or three days a week, he picked alongside us. When the cotton is in full bloom and ready for picking, the fields are white like snow. The dew in the early morning sparkles in the rising sun, creating a canvas of rainbow colors.

"People live and die by their cotton crops," Uncle John reminded us.

It was the most important cash crop in the South. If it rained at the wrong time or stayed dry too long, it would damage the crop. Insects could ruin a good field of cotton in just a few days.

When cotton was ready for picking, farmers had to have workers in the field as soon as weather permitted. Sometimes it was hard to find enough local pickers, so farmers hauled them in from other counties. Mr. Parsons made sure that all his pickers were in the field when the cotton was ready. Booker, one of his "Nigra hands," as he called him, went over to Crump one night just before cotton picking time, and got into an argument with a man over a crap game. After a few missed punches, Booker stabbed the man and killed him. He was charged with murder and put in jail. Mr. Parsons went to Savannah and talked the sheriff into letting Booker out on bail until after the cotton had been picked.

"I'll see that you get him back," Mr. Parsons promised.

We picked alongside Booker and wondered if he might have killed Junior.

Daddy said not to worry about Booker. "He won't do you any harm."

Booker liked to sing while he picked. We could hear his deep bass voice bellowing, *"Swing low, Sweet Chariot, coming for to carry me home."* Seth said, "He's not likely to be singing when the sheriff comes to carry him back to jail."

But Booker had something else in mind as he chanted:

I looked over Jordan and what did I see,
Coming for to carry me home,
A band of angels coming after me,
Coming for to carry me home.

On the last day of the picking season, Booker collected his wages and disappeared. A week or two later, his wife and children left town. The sheriff dropped the charges and everyone forgot about Booker.

When we first started picking cotton, Wes and I wore Cardinal baseball caps. Other pickers laughed and kidded us about our city hats and said, "They ain't gonna protect you out here."

After a few days, Daddy took us to the dry goods store and bought us wide-brimmed straw hats and long-sleeved cotton shirts. The hats were to protect us from the hot sun and the long sleeves protected us from the strange insects that liked to eat flesh.

When we got home, we decided that the straw hats were not to our liking. The crown of the hats was of the Hopalong Cassidy and Gene Autry style. We thought Hoppy was a sissy cowboy and Gene was a singing cowboy, which we rightly believed were not the kind of cowboys we wanted to look like. Wes was convinced that we could change the hats to look more like the Johnny Mack Brown flat top worn by real cowboys.

I was not sure, so I made Wes fix his first. He pushed the top of the hat down to a square and flattened it to the style he liked. It wouldn't stay down so he used his teeth to bite around the rim until the stubborn straw stayed in place. I watched anxiously as he put it on his head, tilted it a few times to check different angles, and, with a glint in his eye, said, "Now, that's the way it's supposed to look."

I agreed, and let him fix mine the same way. The next day when we went to the cotton field, Daddy studied the hats and just shook his head. Our cotton-picking buddies kept their thoughts to themselves.

Cotton-picking wasn't as hard as hoeing, but it wasn't something I was eager to get out of bed for.

"I'd rather be swinging on a star and carrying moonbeams home in a jar," I would sing off key as we walked to the field.

"And be better off than you are," Wes would answer.

For his age, Wes was one of the best cotton-pickers around. He filled his sack quicker than most and was constantly checking on how Seth was doing.

Most cotton was picked by pulling the fiber out of the boll and putting it into a long sack made of heavy cotton ducking. The cotton bolls had sharp edges and could cut the fingers to the bleeding point. In addition, one of the worst things was those dreaded stinging worms—long furry creatures that hid under the leaves, just waiting for the right moment to sting whatever exposed flesh it could find. Every picker got stung three or four times a day. Granny Lee knitted us some wool mittens and cut the fingers out so we could pull the cotton and still have some protection on our hands.

If you picked in the tall cotton near the bottoms, you might see a snake scurrying between rows. "Muley" Pickens was bit

by a cottonmouth several years ago and died before they could get him over to Doc Townsend's office.

The sacks were three to fifteen feet long and had a wide strap that was placed over the neck and rested on the shoulder. When the sacks got too heavy to drag, you picked it up, tossed it on your shoulder, and carried it to the wagon. Mr. Parsons would hoist the sack up and hang it on the scales. Most farmers used the balance type scales hung from the propped-up tongue of a wagon or from a tripod. An iron weight called a "P" looked liked a bell with a hook attached. The weigher moved it along the ridges of the metal arm until the scale balanced. The point of balance indicated the number of pounds in the sack. There was a small P for short sacks and a large P for longer sacks.

A marker, usually Mr. Parsons, kept a record of the pounds each picker brought in, and, at the end of the day, the worker was paid one dollar per one hundred pounds.

I thought being a marker would be better than picking, so I asked Mr. Parsons about it.

"When you learn how to pick cotton and grow a few feet, we'll talk," he said with his usual charm.

When the marker decided there was enough cotton for a bale, he hitched a tractor or truck to the wagon and drove it to the gin. A large vacuum tube sucked the cotton from the wagon and sent it into the ginning mechanism. A bale of cotton, after ginning, usually sold for about fifty dollars. Some gins would process the cotton free in exchange for the seed, but if the farmer wanted to keep the seed, ginning was about five dollars. Uncle John told us that cottonseed was excellent feed for cows because it produced milk with a sweet flavor.

Most of the pickers brought their lunch to the fields unless they lived close by and could walk home for dinner. Some workers built fires to boil coffee in large pots and warm up rabbit or squirrel stew. The cotton sacks made a good soft seat for eating and resting.

There were two large water buckets near the wagon with a dipper hanging on the side of each. One bucket and dipper was for whites; the other for colored. Since the pails had to be filled several times during the day, I thought about asking for the job of water boy, but I didn't want any more of Mr. Parsons' sarcasm.

The contest between Wes and Seth was something to watch. On a good day, Wes could pick up to 200 pounds. Some of the older pickers picked five or six hundred pounds. After the first day, Wes and Seth were about even. I was about two hundred underweight.

I not only hated picking cotton, I hated Mr. Parsons.

Daddy said, "Son you don't have to like Mr. Parsons, but you can't hate him. Hate will make you sick."

I thought not hating him would make me sicker. I much preferred working for Uncle John, especially when I learned that he didn't like Mr. Parsons either.

"He's got a real mean streak, that one has," he would say, talking about "Old Man Parsons," as we got to calling him.

Uncle John was one of the first farmers in Adairsville to own a tractor; a Farmall International that had cleats on the wheels. When Mr. Parsons saw the tractor, he went out and bought a Fordson with rubber wheels. Uncle John traded his Farmall for a green John Deere with rubber tires and a cushioned seat.

The tractors made life easier for the farmer, but many still plowed with mules and horses. As Mother often said, "John Menloe is a gentleman farmer." That meant he didn't plant cotton and didn't have to live off the land. And, although she didn't come right out and say it, she meant that Uncle John was not a redneck farmer like Mr. Parsons.

Uncle John grew alfalfa for hay and corn for feed and prepared pastures of clover for his premium Jersey cows. His hogs came from Hampshire stock, not the Duroc Jersey, or Poland China, or the Ohio Pig raised by some farmers. He received premium prices for his hogs and beef at the stockyards in Memphis.

Uncle John could be just as ornery as he was kind and generous. He hated regulations and regulators, especially when it involved those "gol darn slick fellows in linen suits out of Washington and Nashville."

The "Cattle Dipping Law" was one that caused the veins in his neck to almost pop. The legislature had passed a law requiring all cattle to be dipped in a prepared solution to kill ticks. Uncle John was even angrier when his farm was chosen as one

66

of the places for a dipping pit. Miss Loretta, his wife, warned him about keeping his blood pressure under control.

Wes and I helped Parker build the vat according to the guidelines sent out by the farm agent. The vat was usually constructed by digging a trench six feet deep and twenty feet long and lining it with cement. It was then filled with a mixture of water and a solution provided by the Farm Bureau. The cattle were pushed into the vat until they were almost submerged, and then forced to swim to the other end. Farmers were so angry about the program that the tick inspectors were afraid to come around without being armed. The farmers complied, however, and the ticks soon disappeared.

After about three weeks, all the cotton worth picking had been picked, ginned, baled, and sent off to the mills. It had been a good crop throughout West Tennessee, and farmers were grateful. Wes had out-picked Seth and made more money than last year. I made less.

For the next six weeks, the United States Post Office would be our ally—a friend we trusted and depended on. At breakfast, we would scan the back of cereal boxes for special items like Dick Tracy wrist radios, rings with secret compartments, magic kits, and Buck Rogers ray guns. Two box tops, a dime, a three-cent stamp, and the constancy of the post office were the ingredients of many happy experiences. The same was true when ordering from the Sears and Roebuck Catalogue.

Daddy and Mother put their orders in first, then Rue, Wes, and I added items. One year I ordered a whole box of multiflavored Lifesavers that caused Mother to frown and Wes to scowl, but Daddy said it was my money and he guessed I had a right to squander some of it. We watched for the mail carrier and anticipated the arrival of our orders with growing intensity and excitement. We were never disappointed. The postman, carrying large, brown-wrapped packages, brought us the rewards of our hard work. It was also the first sign of Christmas.

Every year at this time, Mr. Shipley gave Daddy a roll of tickets to the Dixie Theater. Daddy allowed us one movie a week. Wes and I usually chose Saturday afternoon because we thought we got the most for our ticket. If a Shirley Temple movie played during the week, we gave up our westerns for her. I think I saw *Little Miss Marker* two or three times.

We saw almost all of the main cowboys, but our favorites were Johnny Mack Brown and the Cisco Kid. We also liked *Red Ryder* and *Little Beaver* serials because every week they ended with a cliff-hanger and the promise "to be continued."

Mother and Daddy went to the movies infrequently and only if there was something special showing. They saw *Gone with the Wind*, but wouldn't let us see it because they thought it was too violent and had a curse word in it. Mother liked *Wuthering Heights* with Laurence Olivier and Merle Oberon, and said she would see any movie that had Olivier in it. Daddy said he didn't mind watching Merle Oberon.

The Dixie Theater was located in the middle of town on Main Street. It had a marquee used for naming the features; a glass ticket booth; and a lobby filled with the smell of fresh popcorn. Many Saturdays, Rue worked the popcorn machine and sold candy. It was a small theater filled with narrow folding seats with armrests. The screen was streaked with either age or some kind of silver coating. The upstairs balcony had a separate outside entrance and was reserved for the colored. It was called the "chicken roost."

One of my Saturday chores was picking up the Sunday bulletin from the print shop. Mr. Crowe, the owner and operator, suffered from sinus problems, which caused him to sneeze constantly and blow his nose into a red bandanna handkerchief. He was unshaven and wore a dirty apron that hung down around his knees.

Cletus Brimley, the full-time typesetter, reeked of sweat and tobacco. He was capable of spitting four or five feet and incapable of hitting any of the spittoons placed around the room. The shop was so full of trash and wooden trays it was hard to walk. The noisy press and the clacking sound made by the linotype machines made it difficult to talk.

What I liked about going on Saturday was seeing Johnny Fesmire, a part-time linotype operator and Rue's current boyfriend. Johnny was a senior in high school, a star basketball player, and the son of the owner of the drugstore. Sitting in an old armless chair in front of a huge machine that looked like an oversized typewriter, he carefully followed the rules outlined in a stained manual attached to the machine. A molten pot of lead, heated by a gas burner, was on the left side of the machine. Scraps of lead, cut from the letters, were raked into the pot and used to form slugs.

Johnny warned me to stay away from the pot because it often got too hot and spewed molten lead that fell on your legs.

Johnny said, "Wanna see what hot lead can do if you're not careful?" He would then pull up his pants leg and show me scars from burns.

I liked Johnny and thought he was funny and tough. As he set his type, we talked about the St. Louis Cardinals and basketball, and sometimes we talked about Rue.

"What does your father say about Rue and me?" he asked with a devilish gleam in his eye.

"Well, he'd rather Rue dated a Methodist instead of a Presbyterian," I said, teasing him.

"If Rue and I get married, I'll become a Methodist. You tell him that."

Then he asked, "Heard anything about Junior's murder lately?" I said I hadn't.

"Don't be surprised if you read something in *The Clarion Standard* about Junior soon," he said.

"If you don't tell me, I'll say some bad things about you to Rue," I said.

He just shook his head, radiated a disarming smile, and said, "You don't know anything bad about me, and besides, your Daddy will know what I'm talking about."

When I got home, I asked Daddy if he knew what Johnny was talking about. He just shrugged it off saying, "Just more gossip, son; don't pay any attention to it." I took him at his word and soon forgot about it.

I found Wes sitting in the swing drawing. It didn't take much persuading to get him back to our marathon Monopoly game.

"I'll trade you three railroads for Park Place," I said.

"You must've sniffed some of Mr. Brimley's snuff if you think I'm that stupid. Spin the wheel."

The game was on.

7

In November, the farmers turned their attention to the *Farmer's Almanac* and listened carefully to the weather reports on the radio. It was hog-killing time and picking the day depended a lot on the weather. It had to be cold enough to keep meat from spoiling, but not so cold it would freeze the carcass. Uncle John and his neighbors, who would bring their hogs to his barnyard for butchering, sat around the stove at Taylor's grocery and picked the day. They usually chose a Saturday so the school kids could help out.

It's hard to imagine how anything so gruesome could be considered festive, but it was. Just about every farmer raised hogs to sell for additional income and to slaughter for a winter supply of food. Pork provided about half the food staples eaten by country folk. A well-fed sow could produce two litters of pigs a year and each litter birthed from eight to twelve piglets.

A lot of preparation and planning went into hog-killing. Fire pits were dug; knives sharpened; dry wood stacked; iron kettles, washtubs, and steel barrels were put in place; jobs were assigned; and the ladies got together to plan for the food.

Large sacks of salt were stacked in the barn. Lye and slaked lime and sausage seasonings were purchased and put where it would be easy to get to when needed. Tripods or other contraptions had to be built for hanging the hogs.

Usually there were five or six families bringing one or two hogs each for butchering. By the time the women and kids arrived, there could be as many as forty people at one hog-killing.

The day arrived and, although we didn't like the gore and blood and smell, we looked forward to the excitement that came with this strange ritual. Uncle John acted as host, coordinator, and master of ceremonies. Around 4:00 or 5:00 A.M., several of the farmers and their boys met Parker at the barn to start the fires for the kettles and the barrels. They checked all the equipment before setting it up. Granny Lee and some of the wives prepared a large breakfast with several pots of strong coffee and hot apple cider. When the other farmers and their helpers arrived just after daybreak, the process had already begun.

The hogs, nine this year, were brought in pick-up trucks and placed in a hastily constructed pen covered with sawdust and hay. A two-wheel horse cart was moved to the edge of the pen and, since the smell of blood spooked horses, men pulled the cart. Parker was known as one of the best butchers in the county, and the others learned how to cut from him. He was constantly explaining and teaching anyone who would pay attention. We listened and learned more about hog-killing than we ever wanted to know.

When the time was near for killing the hogs, Uncle John would tell all the kids to move away from the pen. Parker and some of the men would go into the pen and, while two men held the pig on the ground, another would hit it on the head with the blunt end of an axe. That would stun the hog long enough for Parker to slit the throat so the bleeding could start. Some farmers used rifles to kill the pigs, but Parker believed the meat was better if the bleeding began before the hog died and "Besides," he said, "I don't want no bullet ruining those brains." He and many others considered hog brains scrambled with eggs a delicacy.

After allowing sufficient time for bleeding, several men would move the pig to the cart and haul it over to a metal kettle filled with boiling water.

Parker would say to anyone in earshot, "Gotta make sure this water is the right temperature, 'cause if it's too hot, we gonna scald this pig, and if it's too cold, it's gonna be hard to scrape all them hairs off."

Uncle John would laugh and repeat what he said every year, "That's right, Parker, can't be too cold cause if it is, then he who eats the most meat will get the most hair."

71

The carcass was lifted from the cart and dropped into water seasoned with slaked lime and fresh pine boughs. Parker believed this mixture made the hairs come off easier. The hog was then taken from the barrel and hoisted up by his hind feet and tied to the tripod. Sometimes they tied single trees to the hog's feet, and then pulled them up by a rope run through a pulley. Uncle John and Parker had enough places built for hanging three hogs at a time.

Parker would explain carefully how to get all the hair off the skin. "You gotta make sure your scraper is not too sharp and not too dull," he would say, as he pulled the knife down the skin.

While Parker washed up, another worker would clean the carcass with lukewarm water and a stiff brush. As this was being done, two other hogs were hit on the head, their throats cut, and their bodies dipped in boiling water and strung up.

We always watched in awe as Daddy joined in this unseemly ritual. It was the only time we saw him in overalls stained with blood. Mother refused to come, but would prepare casseroles and send them over at dinnertime.

There were many times when I felt like going behind the barn and throwing up, but I didn't want anyone to know this. The first hog-killing I went to, I got sick and ran home. Mother fixed a potion of vinegar and baking soda to settle my stomach. She stirred it until it fizzed, sending bubbles up my nose as I drank it.

"There, that ought to make you feel better," Mother said.

"That's as bad as castor oil," I said, washing out my mouth with water.

Wes and I had to keep the fires going and fetch water for the steel drums. During lulls, we would challenge Seth and Moses to a game of marbles or stick ball. Uncle John and Daddy would call out to us at times, reminding us that we were here to work.

Parker would yell, "You younguns get over here and put some wood on this fire, or we'll be here till Christmas."

Once the hogs had been suspended from the poles, the most important process began. Parker, the master carver as he was called, would take his special knife and slit the carcass down the belly from top to bottom. Tubs were placed under the hogs to catch the innards.

Parker would say with a dramatic flair, "Now, this is where you gotta know what you're doing."

He would then open the entire stomach cavity without puncturing the gut. If any bile was spilled, it could ruin the meat. Everyone watched the cutters carefully to make sure they didn't make a mistake. With one hand holding the side of the hog, he reached inside the carcass with the other hand and pulled out the intestines and the stomach and let them fall into the tub. Daddy then took over and extracted the heart, lungs, bladder, liver, pancreas, and kidneys, which were saved for further processing and cooking or discarded, according to the tastes of the farmer. The hogs were then cleaned and the process of cutting began. Using a well-honed butcher knife and chopping ax, the hogs were cut into sections. The head was cut off and put aside for use later. Sausage grinders and iron kettles were readied. Timing was important and Uncle John kept everyone busy.

Making lard was a very important chore and required careful attention. Small amounts of leaf fat from the gut cavity were put into the hot kettle and other leaf fat was added gradually. The skin of some of the fat was left on to make cracklins. As they rose to the top, they would be scooped out and put on paper sacks to drain. Cracklins were used to make cornbread or eaten as snacks.

Someone had to stir the fat constantly, and that usually meant one of the older kids. This was almost as bad as cotton-picking. I would pretend I was busy fetching wood or water, or helping Parker, but to no avail. I had to take my turn stirring the pot of lard. The temperature had to be kept at about 212 degrees, Parker would mutter to himself. I never knew how he tested the temperature.

The rest of the process was not quite as messy and gory. Carving tables had been set up by the barn for cutting. Hams and shoulders were removed and set aside for salting down before being hung in the smokehouses. Parts of the hog were put through the sausage grinder, seasoned, and pushed into thin cloth bags.

While the sausage was being made, everyone counted on Mr. Curtis to tell his annual joke.

"Two things you don't want to ever see being made: sausage and laws," he would say in a loud voice, and everyone laughed as though they were hearing it for the first time.

Slabs of bacon were carved from the carcass. Backbones and ribs appeared. Salt pork was made by cutting pieces of fat and placing them in a barrel filled with a brine solution of salt, vinegar, and sugar. Boards were placed on top and weighted down with bricks to keep the meat submerged in the brine solution. After a few weeks of curing the meat, it could be kept for a long time without refrigeration.

By the time three hogs had been cut up and put aside for processing, the ladies announced that dinner was ready. The tables, made by placing boards across sawhorses, were now laden with food. All kinds of vegetables, meats, bread, and dessert were washed down with hot coffee and warm cider. Although no one talked about it, it was common knowledge that some of the cider had been laced with a bit of rye whiskey. I guess that's why Daddy drank only coffee. Dinner was the highlight of the day and everyone brought hearty appetites to the table. Daddy blessed the food we were about to eat and the food we were preparing for the winter. After eating and resting for about an hour, we started the whole process over.

After lunch as everyone was going back to work, Sheriff Perkins drove up and stopped at the gate. J. C. Macgregor and a man dressed in a blue suit, white shirt, and tie were with him. The sheriff waved at everyone as he stopped by the gate. Daddy and Uncle John knew they were being summoned. They walked over to the gate and the men talked for about twenty minutes.

As the sheriff was leaving, he yelled to Parker, "When's that aviator son of yours coming home, Parker?"

"Be home Thanksgiving, I reckon," Parker said, smiling.

"Bring him 'round. I wanna get a good look at him in uniform. Mighty fine boy, that Euclid," he said as he walked away.

Parker grinned from ear to ear and saluted the sheriff. Daddy and Uncle John talked quietly to each other before returning. Wes said he heard Daddy say, "They've got the wrong man, John."

Wes and I were curious about why the sheriff had come out and who the stranger was, but we knew we would have to wait until later to find out. It was back to work for everyone.

There was no waste with a hog.

Uncle John said, "When God created the hog he had his hat on straight." He meant that the hog was just about perfect because of what it produced.

Even the hog's head did not go to waste. It was boiled along with the ears and nose and scraps like skin, bones, tongue, and heart. It simmered until the meat fell from the bone and the skin could be pierced with a finger. The skin and the meat picked from the bones were run through a meat grinder. After adding spices like red pepper, garlic powder, marjoram, and savory, the mixture was boiled, cooled, and poured into pans. This gelatin-like mixture was called souse or head cheese and served with turnip greens and vinegar. Wes said he would just as soon pass on the souse.

I thought eating the head of a hog was bad enough until I learned about chitterlings, called "chitlins" by most folk. Chitlins were the intestines of the hog. They were cut out, washed several times in buckets of briny water, then run through with long reeds to finish the cleaning process. Everyone knew that the colored folks liked chitlins, but they didn't know that the Methodist preacher and some of his friends were chitlin-lovers too. A week or so after hog-killing, Daddy and a group of men would get together at Sheriff Perkins' house and cook chitlins. They cooked them outdoors in a pot of boiling water heated over a fire pit. Mother told us that the odor from cooking chitlins was strong and unpleasant. That's why she never allowed chitlin dinners at the parsonage.

Although store-bought soap was cheap and preferred over handmade, some people still made their own soap. Strong lye was used with the fat of the hog to make cakes of soap. Sometimes lavender and other herbs were added to provide a pleasant aroma.

By the end of the day, after all the hogs had been butchered and the processing completed, farmers gave portions of their share to the coloreds as payment. We were given an ample supply of bacon, sausage, ribs, souse, cracklins, and yes, chitlins.

Uncle John would put a ham and shoulder in his smokehouse for us to eat after the curing process. All the other meat was stored in buckets, tubs, boxes, and flour sacks and put into the back of the trucks. The hams, bacon, and some of the shoulders would be put in the smokehouses that day.

The cleanup process was hard and just as important as the early morning preparation. While they were finishing up, there was talk about the arrest of Lonnie Jackson.

One farmer was heard to say, "I thought all along he might be involved. He's a strange fellow and mean as a bull in heat, I'm told. Don't know why it took the sheriff so long to figure that out."

Wes and I looked at Daddy and Uncle John, but they said nothing.

Granny Lee kept her thoughts to herself, but the frown on her face revealed concern. We were in a hurry to get home and talk to Daddy and find out if he really thought Slowfoot was guilty.

Uncle John finally spoke a kind of benediction. "It's been a long day and I know we are all tired. Just want to thank everybody, and especially the ladies for the food that sustained us. Let's go home with thanksgiving in our hearts for all our blessings."

Everyone said, "Amen."

"Race you home," Wes said, as we ran ahead of the caravan pulling out of the barnyard.

8

A week after we'd killed the hogs and a few days before Thanks-giving, we learned about Lonnie Jackson's arrest. Between what Daddy and Uncle John had told us and what we read in *The Clarion Standard*, we understood why Slowfoot had been "de-tained," which was what the sheriff was calling it now.

On the morning of the day he was killed, Junior had been seen with Lonnie walking down Saltillo Road, just a mile from the river. When the sheriff questioned the ferryboat operator, he told him that Lonnie often brought his cart down to the land-ing and crossed the river for supplies. "And sometimes there was a boy with him," he had added.

When the sheriff and his deputy didn't find Lonnie at his shack, they started looking around. They found some things that belonged to Junior and others that came from the hardware store. When asked later, Mr. Macgregor couldn't remember sell-ing them to Lonnie and didn't know how he got some of Junior's stuff. The bicycle wheels on the pull-cart were from an old bike Junior had stored in his garage. Behind the shack, the deputy found a crowbar that appeared to have blood on it. He sent it to the FBI office in Jackson. After determining that it was blood, they sent it to Washington, along with a sample of Junior's blood that Doc Townsend had saved from the autopsy.

The Washington Bureau could not make a positive match and *The Clarion Standard* quoted Doc Townsend saying, "The reason they couldn't make a match was because the blood on the crowbar was contaminated."

Wes looked the word up in the dictionary but still didn't understand what it meant.

The Sheriff told Daddy on the phone the night of the arrest, "It's not much but it's enough to bring him in for questioning."

The sheriff figured that Junior might have accused Lonnie of stealing and "Lonnie probably got angry and scared, so he killed him," the sheriff had said.

When Daddy asked about Lonnie's house, the sheriff told him that the place was small, but neat, and had a wood-post bed with a straw mattress, a stove for heating and cooking, two chairs, a few pots and pans, and a cupboard made of apple crates for storing food and staples. There were all kinds of tools and animal traps. A rifle was hanging on a hook over the door. The Sheriff described the rifle as a rare Winchester 94 model with a .30–30 caliber.

"This is a classic lever-action rifle that's hard to find in these parts and a favorite with hunters," the sheriff said.

Daddy and Uncle John didn't think the crowbar and bicycle wheels on the cart were enough evidence for Lonnie's arrest.

"We're just talking to him," the sheriff said, defensively.

"But you're talking to him while he's in jail," Uncle John said accusingly.

"It's for his own good," the sheriff said, "and besides, he's getting three hot meals a day and a soft bed to sleep in."

Daddy wasn't convinced but let it go for the time being.

Daddy said we had to put these things aside in order to get ready for Thanksgiving. There were some people in Adairsville who didn't have much of a family and others who had none. Daddy thought the church ought to provide a family setting, so he started a tradition of having Thanksgiving dinner in the church basement and inviting people to bring dishes of food to share. The Shipleys and Fesmires provided the turkeys and some of the ladies went down early to put them in the oven.

Every year, fifty to seventy people came to sing hymns, listen to a brief homily, and share the usual Thanksgiving fare with all who came. Most of the people were Methodists, but it was open to everyone in the community. Granny Lee brought some of her Presbyterian friends, her rhubarb pies, and a green bean casserole. Robert Earl was there with his mother and sister, but was sulking and didn't say much. Wes overheard him telling Mavis Butler that his father was teaching him to drive.

There was only one thing that spoiled this special day for us—a visit from Uncle Jarman and Aunt Minnie, and their three girls. As much as we loved our mother, we didn't care for this sister and her family. Uncle Jarman was a braggart and show-off. He had made a lot of money selling medical supplies to hospitals and was eager to tell you how much everything cost. He drove a black LaSalle made just before President Roosevelt stopped the production of most cars. Aunt Minnie wore a fur coat even when it wasn't cold and had a ring on every finger. Bonnie Sue, their youngest girl, was a biter. She bit people anywhere she could plant her teeth. After every visit, I had teeth marks on my hands and arms. The only good thing about their visit was they didn't spend the night.

After they left late in the afternoon, I suddenly realized that Bonnie Sue had not bitten me once all day.

I asked Mother about it and she said, smiling, "When I visited them in Memphis last spring, I told Minnie about a remedy for biting and she used it."

"What was it?" I asked.

"I told her to fill an atomizer bottle with a mixture of vinegar, castor oil, and water and every time she bit someone, Minnie was to spray this potion in her mouth and not let her wash it out."

"And that worked?" Rue asked, looking up from her magazine.

"She's not biting anymore, is she?" Mother said triumphantly.

About mid-morning on Friday, Daddy got a call from Uncle John inviting us over to visit with Parker's son, Euclid. Mother and Rue couldn't leave because they had clothes ready to hang on the line, but Wes and I went with Daddy. Private Euclid Browne stood tall and straight as he shook Daddy's hand and winked at us. The only time I'd seen him was at Shipley's garage, where he'd worked as a mechanic. His deep tan uniform, adorned with braids and bronze buttons, made him look like the pictures of pilots in magazines. Only one thing was different; we'd never seen a picture of a colored soldier in any of the magazines.

Parker was beaming as he showed off his son. Seth and Moses just grinned as they stood at their brother's side.

"Euclid, I declare," Daddy said, "you sure have grown since I saw you last. Now let's see what this inscription is," he said, as he looked at something pinned on his coat.

On a cloth badge were printed the words: 99TH FLIGHT SQUADRON OF TUSKEGEE. Another one read, UNITED STATES ARMY AIR CORPS.

"So you're going to be a pilot?" Daddy asked.

"I hope so, Brother Turnage. Right now I'm just a technician and mechanic, but they're training me to be a real pilot," Euclid answered.

"In that uniform with those things pinned to his chest, he looks like an officer to me," Uncle John said.

Parker answered, "Not yet, Mr. John, but he won't be a private long."

"Now, Papa, don't you go and 'barrass me," Euclid said, with a smile that made him look just like Parker.

Uncle John said, "Well, we're mighty proud of you and all the others who are protecting this great country."

We wished Euclid well and said our good-byes. We didn't know that this was the last time we would see him alive.

That night, we learned that Daddy and Uncle John had been meeting at the hardware store with Mr. Macgregor and the sheriff to talk about Lonnie Jackson. After we went to bed, we heard Mother and Daddy whispering and knew that Daddy thought the sheriff was wrong.

Once when Daddy was answering a question raised by Wes, he said, "Well, we're going to have to wait and see what comes of this. In time we'll know the truth."

I blurted out that we already knew the truth and said something about Slowfoot saving our lives. Daddy was more than interested in this confession and Wes was livid.

"You moron," he said.

We told the whole story and Daddy listened patiently. "You should've told me about this a long time ago," he said sternly, and gave us that dreaded Turnage look. Nevertheless, we could tell that he was pleased with what he'd heard because it was another reason to believe Lonnie.

On Saturday morning, before Daddy had finished his second cup of coffee, the phone rang. It was Sheriff Perkins. He apologized for calling so early, but said it might be urgent. "Lonnie Jackson wants to talk to you," he said.

"Why on earth would Lonnie want to see me?" Daddy asked.

"All I can tell you, Milton, is when I asked if he wanted to talk to a lawyer, he said, and these are his exact words, 'No, but I would like to talk to that preacher Turnage.' " Although it was an unusual request, the sheriff saw no reason to deny him.

When Daddy arrived at the courthouse, a deputy escorted him to the sheriff's office, where Lonnie Jackson was waiting.

"Roy, can't you take those things off?" Daddy said, motioning to the handcuffs.

The sheriff hesitated for a moment before unlocking and removing the cuffs.

Daddy then said, "Before we get started, I just want to thank you for helping my boys over at the caves with that snake. They wanted me to tell you that."

Lonnie sat very still staring at Daddy with those narrow, black eyes, but said nothing. Daddy had an uneasy feeling as he leaned back in his chair and waited for the sheriff to proceed.

Finally, Lonnie put his hands on the table and began to talk. He spoke out of one side of his mouth and had a slight stutter.

"Preacher, I didn't kill that boy and I think you know it. Junior once told me that if I ever needed help of any kind, I was to ask for you. He liked your boys and he trusted you. I think you can look at a man and tell whether he's good or bad."

"Afraid I don't have that kind of power," Daddy said, smiling.

Lonnie continued. "Me and Junior were friends, Preacher. He's the only real friend I had in this town, and that's why I wouldn't hurt him."

Daddy looked over at the sheriff as though he was about to ask something. Instead, he turned back to Lonnie and said, "Tell me about your friendship with Junior."

Lonnie told Daddy and the sheriff how he and Junior met several years ago while fishing down by the landing and took a liking to one another.

"Guess we were a lot alike," he said.

Junior told him how mean some of the kids were to him and the bad things they said about him. Lonnie told Junior he understood cause people made fun of him, too. Lonnie related a story about how Junior helped him build the pushcart with barn lumber and the wheels from an old bicycle. He said that Junior would get him tools from the hardware store or from his father's workshop. "But I always paid for them," he quickly explained.

They fished together and rode the ferry across the river to get groceries and other supplies.

"We went to Savannah 'cause people over there knew my Pappy and didn't ask questions," he explained.

Junior helped him carry the supplies home and even cut firewood for the stove. "We did a lot of things together, Preacher, and I came to love that boy," Lonnie said, showing some emotion for the first time.

"Did you build that house of yours all by yourself or did Junior help you?" Daddy asked.

"No, that was before me and Junior became friends. You know the freight train has to slow down when it comes across that old trestle over the river, and sometimes it even stops on this side. Hobos jump off the train and live for a while in the caves. I got to know some of them and paid them to help me build the house. They were more than happy to work for a few dollars and some cans of food. They still use the caves over by the Ridges."

The sheriff listened quietly and looked as though he wanted to believe Lonnie. He finally moved from his chair and stood by Lonnie. "I have a very important question to ask you and I need a straight answer."

"I'll answer any questions you and the preacher have, and I'll tell the truth," Lonnie said, without appearing to feel threatened.

"Where did you get the money for food, clothes, supplies, and that Winchester rifle?" the sheriff asked bluntly.

Lonnie shifted in his chair and brushed a hand through his matted hair. "This is one of the reasons I wanted to talk to you and the preacher together," he said.

Daddy and the sheriff leaned forward and waited.

"I wanna ask you a question, Sheriff. Did you find a ten-dollar Indian head gold piece in Junior's pocket when you took him over to doc's office?"

The sheriff didn't have to think long before answering, "No. There were only a few small coins, a knife, some steel marbles in his front pockets, and a handkerchief stuffed in his back pocket. What's a ten-dollar gold piece got to do with Junior's murder?"

Lonnie asked if he could have something to drink. One of the deputies brought him a Coca Cola. As he started to sip it, Lonnie talked of things that surprised Daddy and the sheriff. He explained that his grandfather had bought gold coins before the Depression and kept them in a metal box in a closet in the mansion.

"Pappy, that's what I called my granddaddy, told me that these would be mine after he was gone. Kinda like a stake, he called it," Lonnie said quietly.

"After the fire, I went through the ashes looking for that box. I couldn't find it under all the burnt stuff and I figured that Momma must have moved it or spent it. Then I remembered that Pappy once told me he had a special hiding place in the barn under a water barrel. Every man needs a special hiding place, he said. I found it just where he told me. He had buried a metal box in the ground under some planks. There were a lot of $20 and $10 gold coins in the box and a wad of paper money tied together with a string. The papers at the bottom of the box looked kinda important, so I took them to a man over in Savannah who told me they were old stock certificates that weren't worth anything," Lonnie said.

"What else was in the box, Lonnie?" the sheriff asked.

He said there was a deed to his granddaddy's house and property.

Daddy thought for a moment and, pulling his glasses down to his nose, asked, "Did you ever know your father or anything about him, Lonnie?"

"No, I never knew him 'cause he died before I was born. I did see a picture of him that Momma had," Lonnie said, looking out the window.

"And where did you get the rifle?" the sheriff asked.

"It was Pappy's gun he bought in New Orleans. Momma wouldn't let him keep it in the house, so he kept it in the barn. That's why it didn't burn with everything else," Lonnie said.

The sheriff scratched his head and looked at Daddy for some guidance.

"So that's where you got the money for food and other things you needed?" the sheriff asked.

"Yes sir," he said, sipping the Coke. "I spent all the paper money first and then had to start using those gold coins."

Daddy asked, "Lonnie, do you still have some of those coins?"

"Sure, I do, preacher. I've got lots of them buried under the floor of my house in that old metal box. I did just what my Pappy told me; I had a special hiding place."

"Did you ever spend any of the coins in town at any of the stores?" the sheriff asked.

"No sir, I didn't, 'cause that would have started talk," he said.

He then explained that he had taken the coins to Mr. Ben Cowser at the bank and traded them for dollar bills.

"Mr. Cowser said that he wouldn't tell anybody about the coins as long as I traded only with him," Lonnie added.

That brought a frown to Daddy's face and a quick question from the sheriff, "Do you remember how many coins you traded with Ben Cowser?"

"Well, can't say that I remember exactly but we've been trading for more than two years," Lonnie answered.

"Did Mr. Cowser give you full value for the coins, Lonnie?" Daddy asked.

Lonnie was not sure what full value meant, so Daddy asked if Mr. Cowser gave him twenty dollars for every twenty-dollar gold piece.

"Yes sir, he sure did. He offered to help me with a loan so I wouldn't have to use the coins but I didn't feel good about that."

"You think Ben was fair with you, then?" the sheriff asked.

"I would say Mr. Cowser has always been more than fair with me and my family," he answered without hesitation.

The sheriff nodded and indicated he wanted to hear more about that.

"Well," Lonnie said, "after Pappy died, Mr. Cowser used to come out to the house and visit with my momma and help out with a lot of things, like selling the carriage and car for her. Momma always spoke highly of Mr. Cowser and said he was the only friend we had in town. They would sit on the porch and visit for long periods. Then one day I heard them arguing out back of the house and she was telling him she didn't want no charity. Mr. Cowser didn't come around much after that, but that was just a few months before the fire."

After a moment, he said, "Mr. Cowser did come out once to bring some things to me at my house by the Ridges. He drove in as far as he could, but couldn't get through because of that big rock and the blackberry bushes. That was before Junior and me cut them bushes back. I went out and he gave me a couple of boxes of food and some tools. I wanted to pay him, but he wouldn't let me. I didn't see him again until I went to the bank the first time to cash in some of the coins."

Daddy and the sheriff were trying to sort all this out. Daddy got up and walked to the window and then turned to ask Lonnie if he knew how old the coins were. "Do you remember the dates on the coins?"

"Well, I never paid much attention to the dates but they were old. And I do remember that the one I gave Junior was a 1907 Indian head with some fancy writing on the back. Mr. Cowser looked at them pretty carefully though, and wrote down something on a piece of paper every time I traded one," Lonnie answered.

"Could we see some of those coins if we promise to give them back?" Daddy asked.

"Sure, preacher, you can look at them if they haven't been stolen while I've been locked up. I know I can trust you," Lonnie said.

Sheriff Perkins told Lonnie he needn't worry about anyone getting into that house with that angry dog he had guarding it.

"You been feeding him, like you promised?" Lonnie asked.

"Yeah, we drive up and throw some food out the window because he won't let us get near the house," the sheriff said.

Remembering something Lonnie had said earlier, Daddy asked, "You said you always paid for the hardware Junior took from the store, but Mr. Macgregor can't remember selling you anything. How'd you do that?"

"When I needed things like nails, tools, a hammer, or whatever, Junior would get them for me and we would figure the cost and I would give Junior the money to put in the cash drawer at the store," Lonnie said.

"You know, Lonnie, we can check this out," the sheriff said sternly.

"I'm just telling you what I know and how me and Junior worked things out," he said, staring out the window.

Daddy looked puzzled and asked, "Why didn't you just buy them yourself at Macgregor's or in Savannah?"

"Cause Junior wanted to get them for me. He didn't even want me to pay for them, but I made him take the money. Later we quit doing that and Junior would go over with me to Savannah and get supplies," Lonnie said.

Daddy walked to the corner of the room and whispered something to the sheriff. Lonnie finished his Coke.

"Just a couple more questions, Lonnie," the sheriff said as he straddled the chair next to the table. "When did you give Junior that ten dollar gold piece and why did you give it to him?"

"I gave him the coin that morning on the day he was killed 'cause I wanted him to have it. It looked special because it had an Indian head surrounded by stars on one side and a bald eagle on the other. He didn't want it and said he wouldn't know what to do with it, but I had picked it out and I made him take it because he'd been good to me."

The sheriff was puzzled but went on to his second question: "How you figure blood got on that crowbar?"

"Easy," Lonnie said, "I use that crowbar to kill animals after I trap them. You know raccoon and possum put up a pretty good fight fore they die. I also killed a wild dog and a wart hog with that iron."

"Did you ever hit a human being with that iron, Lonnie? Your answer is going to be very important and we can't help you if you don't tell the truth," the sheriff said.

Lonnie hesitated and looked at the sheriff and then at Daddy. "I won't get in more trouble if I tell you, will I?" he asked, squinting.

"You'll be in a lot more trouble if you don't," Sheriff Perkins said.

Lonnie spoke without much emotion. "I hit one of those hobos when I found him rummaging around in my house. It wasn't hard enough to really hurt him; just enough to get his attention, but he bled a lot before he ran off across the Ridges. I never saw him again."

Suddenly the sheriff jumped up and asked angrily, "Did you ever use it to kill a boy?"

Daddy was startled by the question and the harsh tone.

Lonnie just sat there staring straight ahead, and after a moment, he looked at Daddy and said, "Preacher, you don't believe I did it, do you?"

Daddy said, "You know it's not up to me, Lonnie, but for what it's worth, I believe you and I'll do what I can to help." The sheriff frowned and said nothing.

Daddy and Lonnie shook hands firmly, and as he was leaving the room, Daddy suddenly remembered something. "Who else besides you, Junior, and Mr. Cowser knows about those coins, Lonnie?"

Lonnie thought a moment, and then said, "Unless Junior told somebody, not another soul knows." With that, Lonnie was led back to his cell.

As Daddy was mulling over what Lonnie had told them, the sheriff came back into the office. He threw the cuffs on the desk and said, "Now that's either the tallest tale I've ever heard in this office or we've got the wrong man locked up."

"You've got the wrong man locked up," Daddy said. "There's no way Lonnie Jackson could have made up those things and you know it. He's plenty smart but not that smart."

"Well, if he did give Junior a gold coin, where is it?" the sheriff asked Daddy.

"It now belongs to Junior's killer," Daddy said thoughtfully.

"You think that's why Junior was killed?" the sheriff inquired.

Daddy shook his head, indicating he didn't know the answer. "Could be that Junior was killed for the coin or maybe whoever killed him found the coin in his pockets," Daddy said.

The sheriff sat down behind his desk and started shuffling some papers. His forehead was wrinkled and a frown was clouding his face. Suddenly he asked Daddy, "Why did you ask about the dates on those coins, Milton?"

"Just a little curious about what their real value might be. That's why we need to see those coins," Daddy said.

"I'll arrange it with Lonnie," the sheriff said as he walked out of the room.

Daddy picked up the phone and called Macgregor's Hardware Store.

"J. C.," he said, when Mr. Macgregor got on the phone, "this is Milton. Sorry to bother you on a busy Saturday afternoon, but I need to ask you a rather unusual question."

J. C. laughed and said, "That wouldn't surprise me."

Daddy smiled and thought about what a good friend J. C. was and how much he'd been through with the death of his wife and now Junior.

"If at the end of the day you had more cash in your register than you had sales receipts, how would you explain it?"

J. C. thought about the question for a moment and then answered, "Well, I wish I could say that happens often, but to answer your question, it would mean either my sales clerk or I had failed to ring up some items. We always try to make sure everything balances at the end of the day, but sometimes we're over and sometimes we're under."

"In the past two years, as far as you can remember, have you been over a number of times?" Daddy asked, hoping for the right answer.

"Well, now that you mention it, there were days, mostly Saturdays as I recall, that we took in more money than we had sales receipts. We never could figure it out, but since it was over and not under, I didn't worry much about it. Guess I'm not gonna know what this is all about, Milton?"

"I'll tell you as soon as I can make sense of it myself. You've been helpful, though, and I appreciate it. See you in church tomorrow," Daddy said as he put the phone on the cradle.

He then dialed the number of Ben Cowser. The maid answered and said Mr. Cowser was out of town.

After Daddy told the sheriff about his conversation with J. C. Macgregor, the sheriff phoned the FBI office in Jackson and talked with the agent who was helping with the case.

When he hung up, he said, "At least, one thing is now clear: the tainted blood was due to the mixing of human and animal blood."

The agent suggested that the sheriff wait until Monday to release Lonnie so he could be there when they opened the box and looked at the coins. "You don't want him running, Roy," the agent had warned.

"Roy, you tell him he's going to be free to go on Monday just as soon as you can finish the paperwork," Daddy said, more forcefully than he intended.

"I'll do that, Milton. Now you go on home and write a good sermon. And, by the way, we need to keep this whole story to ourselves for a while."

"I understand and I promise I won't even share it with my family," Daddy replied. The sheriff said good-bye and walked toward the jail.

When Daddy came home, all of us were in the living room waiting to hear about his meeting with Lonnie.

"I wish I could tell you something, but the sheriff and I agreed not to share this with anyone until there can be some further investigation. Just be patient and you'll get the whole story at the right time," he said, with sadness in his voice. "All I can tell you is that Lonnie Jackson is a lot smarter than most people think."

After Daddy went to the back porch to wash up, Mother explained. "He doesn't want to burden us with something we have to keep secret. We can't tell what we don't know. That's why it's better we don't know."

We understood and knew that in time we would hear the details about what Daddy, the sheriff, and Lonnie Jackson said to each other on that Saturday.

9

As Sunday school superintendent, it was Ben Cowser's responsibility to open the assembly with a hymn and a prayer. On the Sunday following Daddy's meeting with Lonnie, Ben was absent and had not asked anyone to fill in for him, which was strange for a man who was always prompt and reliable. Ben's wife and children were also absent.

Monday morning when Daddy called the Cowser home, Mrs. Cowser told him that Ben was still in Memphis and wouldn't be home until late that night.

"Is everything all right, Mildred?" Daddy asked.

She assured him that it was, but Daddy was not convinced.

The sheriff picked up Daddy around ten o'clock in the morning. It was a cloudy, cold day, which seemed appropriate for the occasion. Special Agent Barry Timmons, who was providing assistance at the request of the sheriff and county prosecutor, sat in the backseat. Lonnie, who wore a faded wool coat and his usual brown felt hat, sat quietly next to the agent and stared out the window. They drove out to the Ridges, toward Lonnie's house.

"Watch out for that rock, Sheriff!" Lonnie warned, as they approached the narrow path to the house.

"I know, Lonnie, I almost took a fender off getting in here last time," the sheriff lamented.

As he steered his car through the opening between the rock and thorn bushes, he sensed something was wrong. Lonnie was the first to see his dog lying on its side near the iron fence.

"Oh my Gawd," Lonnie exclaimed, "my dog's dead."

The sheriff stepped out of the car and motioned the others to follow. Lonnie ran to his dog and knelt beside him. Tears came to his eyes.

After looking closely at the dog, Agent Timmons said, "From the looks of his mouth and eyes, it was some kind of poison, maybe arsenic." There was a small amount of meat on the ground, which the agent picked up with his handkerchief and put into a bag.

Daddy and the sheriff walked through the rusty iron gate and entered the house. It had been ransacked. The straw from the mattress was strewn across the floor. An overturned wooden crate had littered the room with food. The stove was lying on its side among scattered ashes and a metal stovepipe was dangling from the ceiling. Planks on the floor had been plied loose.

"What a mess," the sheriff muttered as he carefully stepped over some broken glass.

The agent said nothing as he walked around studying the scene.

"What do you make of this, Roy?" Daddy asked.

"Looks like somebody knew about the coins and figured that with Lonnie in jail, it would be a good time to steal them."

"They didn't find them," Lonnie said angrily. "They're under the planks where the bed was."

"They planned it carefully," the agent said, "the poisoned meat and all."

The sheriff added, "I can tell you for sure, that's the only way they were going to get past that dog."

Lonnie was in the corner using a poker to pry loose some boards. "There she is," he said, as he pulled the metal box from under the floor and placed it on top of an old chest.

"Let's have a look," the sheriff said with anticipation.

Lonnie opened the box and everyone except Lonnie stared unbelievingly at its contents. It was filled with shiny gold coins and some faded documents that were tucked against the side.

"My gracious sakes alive, that's a sight I never thought I'd see," the sheriff said.

The agent ran his fingers through the coins and expressed disbelief. "These must be worth hundreds of dollars," he said.

"Probably more than that," Daddy said, after examining some of the coins. "Some of these go back to the eighteen-hundreds. Look, here's one dated 1874."

Later, they would learn that the oldest coin was a Carson City double eagle dated 1852.

Lonnie had left the room and was out seeing to his dog. He was walking toward the back of the shack carrying a shovel.

Daddy said, "Let's take care of Lonnie's dog first, then we can check out these coins."

They pulled their coats up around their chins, put on their gloves, and helped Lonnie dig the grave and put the dog in it. Daddy said a few words about a dog being man's best friend and offered a brief prayer.

While the agent was searching the area and Lonnie was putting stones on the crude grave, Daddy and Sheriff Perkins talked quietly over by the car. They were concerned about finding a place for Lonnie to live.

"It's obvious he can't stay here with no heat and everything torn up," Daddy said.

"And it might not be safe now that someone knows about those coins," the sheriff added.

The agent, standing by the rock at the entrance, motioned for Daddy and the sheriff to come over. "This rock has been scraped and there seems to be some paint on it," he said, rubbing the area with his hand.

"Do you think that whoever tore up this place ran into that rock?" the sheriff asked.

"That would be my guess, and it might be an important piece of evidence," the agent observed.

He took out a pen knife and a piece of plastic wrap and scraped shards of paint from the rock. Carefully folding the samples into the plastic, he put it in his overcoat pocket, explaining that he would send the sample to Washington where they might be able to tell the make of the car and even the year it was built.

"Sheriff, you might want to have your deputies start looking for a dark red or maroon car with a dent in one of the fenders and some scratches on the side."

Uncle John offered to let Lonnie live in a small house over on Jarvis Lane that once was the home of Uncle John's mother.

She died about six years ago and Uncle John rented it out for a while, but closed it up after a tenant did some damage to the property and left town without paying the rent. Lonnie had said he didn't want charity and could pay his own way. Without explaining what he meant, the sheriff told Uncle John that there were funds to cover the rent. Uncle John said it didn't matter to him about the rent, he was just glad he could be of help.

Two deputies went out that afternoon with Lonnie to get his personal things and tools and move him into his new home. The house was small but neat and had a warm morning wood stove that heated the four rooms. There was a two-burner electric stove and a small Frigidaire in the kitchen. A pump for water was just off the back porch and worked well except when it froze. Not far from the back step was Lonnie's cart that he planned to paint and print something special on the side come spring.

Mother and Mrs. Menloe stocked his pantry with jars of beans, corn, applesauce, pickles, sauerkraut, tomatoes, and Muscadine jelly. Lonnie showed his gratitude by tipping his hat and saying "Much obliged," but it was hard for him to admit that this place was any better than the shack out by the Ridges.

The sheriff assured Lonnie that the coins would be kept in a safe place until they found Junior's murderer.

"Someone knows about those coins, Lonnie, and soon everybody in town will know. We need to put them where they can't be stolen."

He told Lonnie that they would have Molly, "who has worked in this office for ten years and is as honest as the day is long," make a list of all the coins, their dates, and denomination, before they were put in the safe.

Molly insisted that someone else be present when she counted the coins for the inventory. Daddy was chosen and Lonnie approved. The agent gave Sheriff Perkins the name of a coin expert in Memphis who could come to Adairsville and assess the value of the coins.

He groaned and said, "I don't have a budget to pay for experts to come all the way from Memphis just to look at some coins."

"You'll figure out a way to do it," Daddy said unsympathetically.

The sheriff was apprehensive about talking to Ben Cowser.

"I've known Ben and his family for a long time and thought a lot of his father and mother. I don't want to do anything to hurt our friendship," he said, frowning.

"I know how you feel, Roy. He's not only my friend but he's Sunday school superintendent as well. Maybe there's a good explanation for what Lonnie told us about the coins. You know, Ben is innocent until proven otherwise," Daddy said, with a frown to match the sheriff's.

"I'll talk to him just as soon as he gets back, but I want you there with me," the sheriff said to Daddy.

"Are you sure that's a good idea, Roy? After all, this is police business, not church business."

"It would mean a lot to me, and I think to Ben, if you could be there," the sheriff pleaded.

Daddy reluctantly agreed but with the condition that Ben understood that they were not there to interrogate him.

The sheriff nodded, got up from his desk, put his hand on Daddy's shoulder, and thanked him for his help. "You're the best friend I've ever had, Milton. In spite of my peculiar ideas about the church, you've always been there for me. I just want you to know that I appreciate it."

Sheriff Roy Perkins needed a friend the next day when the editor of *The Clarion Standard* called.

"Roy, you know I don't try to tell you how to do your job, but I'm in the newspaper business and that means I print news—not day-old or week-old—but current news. I know something is going on and you're not keeping me informed. Now Roy, I don't want to have to print an editorial that says the sheriff of this county is withholding news from the voters who elected him."

Sheriff Perkins took that as a threat. He drew a few deep breaths before he replied. "You know I've always been up-front with you about everything that's going on, and I intend to continue to do that, but you've got to understand that I'm dealing with some very delicate matters, and I don't want people to get hurt just because I can't keep my mouth shut."

"I understand what you're saying, but you have to appreciate my position. I know you not only released Lonnie Jackson, but you moved him into a house on Jarvis Lane. Everyone was led to believe he was your prime suspect and now he's out of jail and getting free board," Jacob Yancey said with a little fire in his voice.

"We didn't have enough evidence to hold Lonnie and we moved him into town for a reason which I'll explain in detail as soon as I can. Jake, I'm working with the FBI on this case, as you know. They're advising me about certain matters and I need to listen to them. As soon as I can release more details, you'll be the first one I call. Just be patient and give me a little slack on this one," he pleaded.

"Okay, but don't keep me on a string too long, Roy. Patience is not one of my virtues," the editor said.

"I promise to give you everything I know just as soon as I can, and you know my word's always been good," the sheriff said, as he hung up the phone and sighed.

"Milton," the sheriff said when Daddy answered the phone. "I just heard from Jake and he's fuming about not being told what's going on."

"It won't hurt him to fume a few days, and you know you can't let this get out until you've talked with Ben," Daddy said.

There was a long sigh before the sheriff responded: "Yep, that's the only fair thing to do. I'll hold off Jake until we can hear Ben's side of this."

Daddy hung up the phone and a frown furrowed his brow as he thought about what might turn out to be a messy affair.

Wes was coming home every day with new stories about Button Butterfield's temper and his conduct in the classroom. Several boys had been taken to the principal's office and spanked with the now famous paddle. Most of them didn't return to class until a few days later. Wes had always liked school and made good grades, but he told Mother he was having bad dreams and hated school.

Mother said, "Wes, you have nothing to be afraid of as long as you show respect for your teachers and don't misbehave."

Wes said, "I know, Mother, and I'm trying not to do anything that will make him mad at me."

Wes told me that this experience with Button was one of the worst things he'd ever gone through. I could tell because he didn't eat much and stayed in the bedroom more than usual. I would find him sitting by the window drawing pictures of a man with horns holding a paddle that looked like a pitchfork. Other times, he was sketching a face of a girl that looked a lot like Mary Beth Shipley.

Ben Cowser agreed to meet with the sheriff and Daddy on Thursday.

"It's the best I can do, Roy. I've got these pesky auditors in for the next two days. You wanna tell me what this is about, or do I have to wait until Thursday?" Ben said with a lilt in his voice.

"Nothing serious, Ben, and it can wait until Thursday. Okay if we come to the bank and meet in your office?" the sheriff asked.

Ben said he would arrange to have the boardroom available at ten o'clock Thursday morning.

Ben Cowser was one of Adairsville's most prominent citizens. He was always smartly dressed in dark suits, white shirt, and silk tie. His black hair and mustache were sprinkled with flecks of gray and accentuated his handsome face and tall frame. He had a swagger to his walk. He was highly thought of by everyone, but especially by the farmers and merchants who depended on his bank for long- and short-term loans. He treated everybody fairly and, even during the rough years following the Depression, he made an effort to avoid foreclosure or calling in loans that were past due.

Ben's grandfather, Captain Charles Earl Cowser, a Civil War hero, was killed during the Battle of Shiloh while serving under General Albert S. Johnston. He briefly took command when the General was hit with a Minnie ball that severed an artery in his leg. Johnston could have been saved if he had not sent his surgeon off to care for wounded Union prisoners. Later that same day, Captain Cowser was killed near the sunken road. Ben's father, Melvin, was born in 1862, the same year his father was killed.

Mr. Webb, the history teacher, taught a special course on the Civil War for the eighth grade class, and Mr. Melvin Cowser was the source of many firsthand stories. He told of the famous Battle of Pittsburg Landing, later renamed the Battle of Shiloh because of its proximity to the Shiloh Church, a meeting house built by a Methodist preacher in 1850 and located nine miles from Savannah on the west bank of the Tennessee River.

The small, simple church had one window and two doors and stood at the top of a sloping hill near Owl Creek. On both sides were camps of Ohio regiments. Another Union army unit occupied ground in the peach orchard nearby.

"Shiloh is a Hebrew word meaning 'place of peace,' and the church stood as a contrast to the harsh reality of war," Mr. Webb explained.

He told how the church had no furniture before the battle because a Confederate General named Cheatham had removed the pews and pulpit to use in his camp. At one time, it was converted into a hospital and guarded by soldiers. Later, the boards were ripped from the floor and used to build coffins for Union soldiers. After the battle ended, the church was vandalized and every log removed, leaving only the foundation.

Mr. Webb told his class that this battle was one of the bloodiest of the war, with more than 25,000 Union and Confederate casualties. When Daddy would take us to Shiloh Park, we always visited the sunken road where the Confederate Army fought off General Prentiss in the battle that came to be known as the Hornet's Nest because, as one soldier described it, "the bullets buzzing through the saplings sounded like a hornet's nest."

A pond near the peach orchard was a gathering place for the wounded on both sides. They came to bathe and drink the water. Most never left. It was known as the Bloody Pond. When I read the historical marker, I tried to imagine what it was like on that gray dawn morning in April of 1862.

After the Battle of Shiloh, General Grant, who had his headquarters in the Cherry Mansion in Savannah, arranged for the burial of bodies from both armies. Later the cemetery was designated as a national memorial, and gravestones were erected and marked. Once the war ended, the Shiloh Church was rebuilt and again became a place of worship for the people of that community.

Melvin and Lottie Cowser chose to live in Adairsville because it was close to the Shiloh battlefield. Melvin opened a dry goods store on Main Street and set up a loan office in the back. When the loan business outgrew the dry goods business, Melvin opened the Farmers and Merchants Bank in a small building just off Main Street. His bank grew along with his reputation for honesty and fairness. When Ben turned fifteen, he began working in the bank as a janitor sweeping floors, emptying wastebaskets, and dusting the desks and tellers' cages.

Through Melvin's good management and the strong rural economy in West Tennessee, the bank came through the Depression without defaulting on any of its obligations to customers or the state banking authority. Melvin built a large two-story house on Main Street just a few blocks from the bank. When Lottie died of cancer after a long illness, Ben and his young family moved in with Melvin.

Ben attended Auburn University, graduating with honors. When he returned to Adairsville, he married Mildred England, the daughter of Kennesaw England, a successful merchant in Florence, Alabama. He began as a teller in one of the side cages. Melvin was happy to have his son working at the bank but gave him no special consideration. Ben came up through the ranks by working hard and learning the business from his father. When Melvin retired in 1931, Ben was named president of the bank. Two years after retiring, Melvin was raking leaves on a hot summer day and suffered a fatal heart attack. The church was not large enough to hold all the people who came to pay their respects.

Ben carried on in the same tradition as Melvin and the bank's assets continued to grow, making it one of the leading banks in West Tennessee. The Cowsers were active in the church, involved in civic affairs and, although Robert Earl was a troubled child, they showed great pride and affection for both their children. Besides being Sunday school superintendent, Ben was president of the local Rotary Club, a member of the school board, and as a Master Mason attained the 33rd degree, the highest achievement in Scottish Rite Freemasonry.

Daddy, along with just about everybody else in Adairsville, considered Ben to be one of its finest citizens.

When he talked about the meeting scheduled with Ben on Thursday, I heard him tell Mother, "I hope and pray that nothing comes out of this meeting that will change my feelings about Ben Cowser."

Mother said, "Ben Cowser is probably thinking the same thing."

10

Thursday morning, Daddy, Sheriff Perkins, and Ben Cowser sat around a large table in the boardroom of the bank. Ben had his secretary prepare a pot of coffee and place it on a cart in the corner. They sipped coffee and talked about the latest news from the war front. Sheriff Perkins asked Mr. Cowser about the car he recently purchased from Curtis Shipley. Ben was excited and eager to talk about it.

"It's a 1940 Cadillac Fleetwood V12 series with fender wells, tire covers, wheel discs, and white sidewalls. Curtis said they were hard to find but he located one over in Montgomery and had someone drive it up. It runs like a top—a real beauty."

Daddy, who wasn't much interested in cars, said, "I saw it the other day and it looks like you need a chauffeur."

When Daddy once remarked that Ben liked fine cars, Mother added, "He likes everything that's fine."

"What color is it, Ben?" the sheriff asked.

Ben, thinking the sheriff was just making conversation, said, "It's dark green."

"Guess you gave it a good test run on your trip last week," the sheriff noted.

"I wanted to, but Mildred and the children drove over to Florence to visit her sister over the weekend. I think she just wanted to show off that new car."

"So you drove the pickup to Memphis?" the sheriff asked.

Mr. Cowser said, "No, I decided to take the train. I wasn't sure that truck would make the trip."

After five or ten minutes of what appeared to be small talk, Sheriff Perkins explained the purpose of the meeting and carefully went over every detail of what Lonnie Jackson had told them last Saturday. Daddy made a few comments, but otherwise sat quietly and observed the reaction of Mr. Cowser.

When the sheriff had finished, he directed his full attention to Mr. Cowser and asked, "Did Lonnie tell us the truth or is there something he might have left out?"

Ben warily eyeballed the sheriff, shifted uneasily in his chair, and fiddled with his empty coffee cup before answering.

"Well, I have to say that Lonnie has a good memory for details. That's about the way it was; just as he told it."

"What did you do with the coins?" the sheriff asked bluntly.

"Oh, they're still in a lockbox in the bank. I tried to tell Lonnie there was no need for him to give me the coins. I would have given him whatever money he needed, but he insisted I take the coins. I just treated the money as advances on a loan and considered the coins as collateral. I figured that one day Lonnie would want them back and we would work something out."

Daddy asked, "Ben, do you think the coins are worth more than their face value?"

Ben was uncomfortable with the question, but answered without looking up. "I really don't know, Milton, I've not had them appraised or even discussed their value with anyone."

"Lonnie told us how good you've been to him and how much you helped his mother before the fire. He wanted us to know that you had been about the only friend they had," Daddy said.

Mr. Cowser gave a nod of appreciation, but said nothing. The sheriff poured another cup of coffee and sat on the edge of the table.

"Your father also befriended Maribelle and Lonnie, didn't he?" Later, Daddy said the question puzzled him.

Ben was quick to respond. "He did what he could to help after Mr. Bove lost everything. He tried to arrange loans for him and offered to buy some of his land, at reasonable prices mind you, but Mr. Bove rejected his help and continued to do all his banking, what little there was, over in Savannah. My father got to where he'd go out to the house to visit with Maribelle and Lonnie only when Mr. Bove was in New Orleans or Savannah."

"I'm curious, Ben," the sheriff said, "why did your father feel the need to help the family when it was obvious Mr. Bove didn't welcome his friendship?"

Ben rose from his chair, walked over by the window, and gazed down at the movement of people and cars on the street below. He seemed to be putting a lot of thought into his answer.

Finally, he turned and said, "I'm not sure I can answer that, Roy. All I can tell you is that before my father died, he called me to his bedside and instructed me to be attentive to the needs of Maribelle and Lonnie Jackson. I could tell it was very important to him and I made a solemn promise to carry out his wishes. I think I've kept that promise."

Daddy pushed his glasses up on his forehead and scratched his nose. "That's very commendable, Ben. I know your father would be pleased with what you've done for them and be proud of you for what you've done for this community," Daddy said with sincerity.

The sheriff stood up, shook Ben's hand, and said, "That's about everything we need at the moment. Thanks for your cooperation and your time. I know this is a busy time for you."

Daddy shook hands with Ben and patted him on the shoulder and said, "I expect to see you leading that assembly on Sunday."

"I'll be there, Milton, and I'm sorry about last Sunday. I just plain let it slip my mind about getting a replacement."

They started to leave when the Sheriff stopped and said, "Oh, by the way, Jacob over at *The Clarion Standard* will want to talk to you for a story he'll be running. I promised him I'd give him all the details as soon as I wrapped up a few loose ends. It might be a good idea, though, not to mention anything about loans to Lonnie. Just tell him that you cashed the coins in for paper money so Lonnie could trade without creating suspicion. We're going to make it clear that Lonnie's coins are being kept in the jail safe."

"I'll be careful when I talk to Jacob. I know he's wily as a fox and one of the best at getting information that people don't wanna give," Ben said, as he walked with the sheriff and Daddy toward the door.

The Sheriff later learned that Ben had gone to his office immediately and called J. Leonard Driscoll, Attorney at Law.

On the sidewalk outside, the sheriff was not happy and said to Daddy, "Don't you think it strange that the Cowsers had such an unlikely arrangement and alliance with the Boves?"

103

Daddy didn't agree and said it's not unusual for someone to befriend another. "Your job has made a cynic out of you," Daddy said, waving over his shoulder as he walked away.

Sheriff Perkins went to his office, sat down at his desk, and began writing something on a piece of paper. When he finished, he examined what he had written, placed it in an envelope, and addressed it to: Special Agent Barry Timmons, Federal Bureau of Investigation, Federal Building, 200 Main Street, Jackson, Tennessee.

On his way home, Daddy stopped by for a visit with Lonnie, who seemed to be stuttering more than usual, but Daddy thought it was probably because of stress.

As he drove us to the park to deposit our flattened tin cans in the collection bin, he told us about the meeting and seeing Lonnie. Once a month a $25 war bond was given to the kid who collected the most cans. Wes and I shared the prize two months ago and were working hard to win another one. The metal from the cans were recycled and used in war production. We also saved old newspapers and even the smallest pieces of tinfoil from gum wrappers.

The Friday afternoon edition of *The Clarion Standard* had the story on the front page. Daddy read it carefully and said it was a fair account. The story quoted Lonnie, Ben Cowser, and the sheriff and explained in detail why Lonnie was no longer a suspect. It closed by stating that the case was still open and the investigation was continuing. There was very little said about Ben Cowser's friendship with Lonnie and his mother and nothing was said about Melvin Cowser. Also omitted from the story was the break-in and damage to Lonnie's shack. Later, Johnny Fesmire told me how he and Cletus Brimley stayed up most of the night setting the type for the newspaper story.

Uncle John just frowned and scratched his head when Daddy told him what Ben had said about his father asking him to care for Maribelle and Lonnie. His tone was not critical, but he said, "I agree with Roy on that one. It's way past peculiar."

Daddy shrugged it off and said he hoped we could make it through the Christmas season without more unpleasant surprises. I, too, wished for the same thing.

11

Saturday morning, as I returned from escorting Moo Moo to her pasture, I saw Wes and Daddy waiting by the car for our annual trip to find the perfect Christmas tree. We always looked forward to the adventure and to the challenge of finding a tree as good as or better than last year's. Daddy headed out Highway 64 toward Crump and took Highway 22 to Caney Branch Road, where he picked up the highway that led to Locust Point Christmas Tree Farm on Snake Creek Loop near Shiloh. The owner knew Daddy from the time he had preached a revival at the Shiloh Methodist Church and had invited him to come to the farm and cut his tree. We had come every year since then. As soon as we got out of the car, he led us to a plate of fresh gingersnaps and filled our mugs with hot cider.

At the tree farm you could harvest one of the white or Virginia pines, which we always did, or you could purchase one of the pre-cut balsam firs or blue spruces. We trudged through rows and rows of trees of all shapes and sizes, remembering that Mother had instructed us to find a tree that was full on all sides and had branches that spread out. She had also reminded us not to forget the wreath and swags. After searching for almost an hour, we found a Virginia pine that looked perfect, and Daddy sawed the tree as close to the ground as he could. We tied the tree to the top of the car, put the wreath and swags in the trunk, and drove home.

Late in the afternoon, we placed the trunk of the tree in a bucket of wet sand, and Mother put a skirt, made of an old bed sheet, around it. We opened the large box full of decorations that had been carefully put away the year before and laid them out on the floor.

105

Decorating our tree was not a job for the impatient. We slowly wound the colored lights around the tree until they covered it from top to bottom. Ornaments were removed from tissue paper and, as we talked about where they came from and how long we had had them, we hung them on the branches of the tree.

Our ornaments were not showy or flashy, but each one carried some special meaning. There was a crèche carved out of balsa wood by an old man in Gatlinburg; a rocking horse made of molded plastic given to us by a neighbor in Memphis; angels with wings crocheted by Granny Lee; five small Christmas trees made from clay by Wes and engraved with the names of each family member; pine cones I had collected and painted red and blue and silver; several small bells covered with tin foil made for us by an uncle; and our favorite, a brass star from India given to Daddy by a missionary.

Rue had baked gingerbread cookies with a hole near the top for the hanging ribbon. It was anyone's guess as to whether the cookies would still be on the tree on Christmas. With a needle and thread, we strung popcorn and raw cranberries into garlands and hung them loosely around the tree. Wes and I always got the assignment of untangling the thin strips of tinsel, which we called icicles, and hanging them on the outer edges of the branches. Daddy put the star on top of the tree and plugged in the lights. We gave a sigh of relief as the lights in the connecting strands lit up.

Mother was busy putting the finishing touches on the wreath and hanging it on the outside of the front door. The swags were wrapped around the two posts on the front porch and secured with tiny nails. She came over when the lights were turned on and said, "That's the prettiest tree we've ever had." We would have been pleased, except we remembered she said that every year. With Mother and Rue keeping us on key, we sang one verse of "*Silent Night, Holy Night*." It was a special time and a reminder that in three weeks we would once again experience those magical moments that make up Christmas.

After dinner, Daddy was sitting with his ear close to the radio listening to Edward R. Murrow report from London. He was frowning and mumbling something about the bombings. On Saturday afternoon at the Dixie Theater, we had learned about blackouts, blitz bombings, and had seen pictures of goose-stepping German soldiers with raised stiff arms uttering "Heil Hitler."

Wes was in his room sketching and I was engrossed in the latest Captain Marvel comic book. Rue was out on a date with Johnny and Mother was busy with one of her knitting projects. The phone rang and Daddy answered it as he motioned for me to turn down the radio. We could tell by the sound of his voice and the look on his face that it was not good news.

"Papa is dead," Daddy said, as he hung up the phone and walked over to embrace Mother. We had known for a while that Papa was very feeble and sickly. Daddy's sister had moved him to her house where she could look after him. Mother and Daddy had made several trips to visit with him over the past few months. It was a sad ending to what had been a wonderful day.

Two days later, the family drove to Giltedge, to the house where Daddy grew up and had felt the call to the ministry. The frame house was built on log stilts and open all the way around. We could crawl under and sit on the dirt without our heads touching the floor beams. It was a good place for building roads for our homemade wooden cars, exchanging stories with our cousins, and testing our rubber guns. With the help of Papa, we took a good piece of wood, carved it to look like a rifle, but left the top flat. We would notch out several places in the flat part of the stock and attach a leather strap on top, folding it into the notches. We cut an old inner tube into rubber rings, attached one to the end of the barrel, and stretched it down until it fit into the notch and over the leather strap. We usually made three notches so we had three shots with our rubber rings. When we were ready to fire, we lifted the strap, causing the rubber rings to fly toward their target. When they hit uncovered flesh, they caused some pain and often left welts on the face.

When we got stung by a wasp, as we often did, Grandmother would put her finger in the corner of her mouth, pull out some wet snuff, and put it on the sting. It wasn't pretty, but it worked.

Papa had been Sunday school superintendent for thirty years at the New Hope Methodist Church, and opened every Sunday morning assembly with the hymn, *"We're Marching to Zion."* He was a wonderful grandfather who liked having us trail along as he fed the hogs, milked the cows, pitched hay over fences, and tended to the garden and crops. At night, he sat by an oil lamp and read Zane Grey novels and puffed on a brown pipe filled with Sir Walter Raleigh. Daddy said his father was not much for a lot of talk, but "when he did engage in civil conversation, he had sufficient knowledge of his subject that others thought it worth their time to listen."

Our grandmother, who had died several years ago and was like a second mother, often teased Papa by saying, "He's often wrong but never in doubt." As we sat in front of a stone fireplace listening to the crackling of burning wood, she would tell stories of her childhood and then tuck us into a feather bed warmed with heated flatirons.

Daddy had two brothers and a sister, each with large families. Wes and I had spent many happy weeks visiting our grandparents, uncles, aunts, and cousins in this small rural community. These memories came back to us as Mother tucked us into that warm, fluffy featherbed the night before the funeral.

The next morning, I went outside and walked across the muddy yard trying to find stepping stones to keep from getting red clay on my polished shoes. The fruit orchard, just across a wire fence, was where we picked rusty pears, wiped the dust off on our pants, and chewed them to the core.

People from around the county came to see these strange-looking pears covered with what looked like freckles. About a year ago, I said to Papa, "Aren't you proud of your funny-looking pears? In the Bible this would be called a miracle."

Papa smiled and with his usual modesty, said, "No, Vance, it's not a miracle. It's what's called cross-pollination and anyone with a little patience and know-how can do it."

Grandmother used her cooking talent to turn this strange fruit into preserves that won blue ribbons at the county fair. The jars were decorated with bright bows and given to friends and family at Christmas time.

As I looked at the wooden swing that Papa had built and hung with rope from a gnarly limb, I thought of Bobbie Jo, my cousin. She didn't seem to have any playmates or friends, and even her brothers wouldn't have much to do with her. She would sit for hours in that swing and sing the same song over and over again:

Farther along we'll know more about it,
Farther along we'll understand why.

I would get angry with her and yell, "Why don't you learn a new song? You're driving us out of our cotton-pickin' minds."

She'd stick out her tongue at me and sing louder.

Cheer up my brother, live in the sunshine,
We'll understand it all bye and bye.

Sometimes Wes and I would sneak up behind her and pop her with a rubber band on her backside. She'd tear off running down the road crying, and we'd chase after her, saying: "Now, there's no reason to cry and go tattle to your Mama. It was just a little 'ole rubber band. It couldn't hurt much."

Her mama would tell Grandmother what we'd done and Grandmother would say, "If I were your mother, I'd go out and cut me a good willow branch and swat your backside." That would have been better than the lectures and pinching our ear lobes.

That's about as close as Grandmother ever got to spanking us. She was a very gentle person and wouldn't hurt a fly except when it came to chickens, and then she was downright mean. When she needed chicken for dinner, she'd grab one and start swinging it round and round to wring its neck. Feathers would fly everywhere and the poor hen would give out a cackle that sounded like a scream. When it fell to the ground, it flopped around until it died.

I thought this was cruel but not much worse than the way Daddy did it. He'd put the chicken's neck on a block of wood and chop off the head with a sharp axe. It would jump around spewing blood on everything in sight. It was quicker and maybe less painful than Grandmother's way, but not a pleasant thing to watch.

I once asked Parker if he didn't think there was a better way to kill a chicken. He thought about it for a while and said,

"Well, I don't know whether there is or not, but there's one thing for sure: you can't eat a live chicken." He laughed and slapped his knee once or twice.

Knowing that Wes was smart about a lot of things, I asked him if he had any ideas about how a chicken would prefer to die.

Frowning and slowly shaking his head, he said, "Sometimes I worry about you, Vance."

Bobbie Joe had died last year. She came down with a chill that turned into pneumonia and she stopped breathing. She was only a year older than me, and it made me sad thinking about her sitting under this oak tree, singing that hymn. I wished that I hadn't teased her and snapped her with rubber bands.

I sat down in the rickety swing and pushed my feet against the ground to move it back and forth. Suddenly, I started to sing softly.

Farther along we'll understand why,
Cheer up my brother, live in the sunshine.
Farther along we'll understand why.

A tear rolled down my cheek and settled at the corner of my mouth. I looked up and Wes was standing nearby. He smiled and sat down in the swing and began to hum the tune.

After a few moments of silence, he said, "Maybe we will. Maybe we will."

"Will what?" I asked.

"Maybe farther along we'll understand about Bobbie Jo, Junior, Slowfoot, Papa, and . . . " His voice trailed off.

The pews in the small frame church were filled with family and friends of Papa's. The chrysanthemum wreaths and bouquets of white roses that decorated the front of the sanctuary were pretty and colorful, but their pungent odor tickled my nose.

A former pastor, who had known Papa well, talked about his life of service to the community and the church. The new preacher at the church read passages of Scripture and concluded his remarks by reading a poem that Mother didn't seem to care for. After the funeral and graveside service, we went back to the church to visit and eat food provided by ladies in the church.

Before leaving town, we made one last visit to the cemetery, where we walked over to the Turnage family plot. A winter snow had dusted the granite headstones and whitened the ghostly mounds of the cemetery. Mother knelt down and placed a bouquet of flowers on a tiny gravesite. On the small headstone were the words:

IN LOVING MEMORY

PETER FRANCIS TURNAGE

AUGUST, 1926–DECEMBER, 1926

And inscribed at the bottom: A CHILD SHALL LEAD THEM.

The firstborn son of Mother and Daddy had died of pneumonia when he was five months old. Wes and I often talked about what it would have been like if he had lived.

Wes looked down at the grave, put his hand on my shoulder, and said, "Wish you were here, Peter. We would've been like The Three Musketeers."

Not much was said on the long drive home. Wes and I watched for Burma Shave signs but read them silently.

12

It was the day before Christmas and the ground was covered with snow. It would be the first white Christmas I had ever seen and all because of Bing Crosby and a new song we'd heard for the first time a week ago. Mother had the radio on one night listening to Christmas music when the announcer introduced Bing Crosby to sing his latest hit, "I'm Dreaming of a White Christmas."

When the snow came, Mother said, "Well, looks like we won't have to dream about it."

Parker sent word by Seth for Wes and me to come over for a sleigh ride. We covered our long-handle underwear with corduroy pants, wool shirts, and parkas and put on high-top boots. Mother caught us at the door long enough to wrap scarves around our necks and pull toboggan caps down over our ears. Parker was hitching up the lines of one of Uncle John's horses to a single trace attached to the sled.

Uncle John had two horses: one, named Ben, was gentle as a lamb, but could run like a racehorse; the other was called Hur and was mean and ornery. General Lew Wallace, while living in the Cherry Mansion in Savannah after the Civil War, wrote a book called *Ben Hur*, which Uncle John read. He thought these were good names for his horses "that were surely as sturdy and frisky as one of those Roman stallions."

Some folks liked to remind him that Wallace was a Yankee General, but Uncle John just shrugged it off and said, "He might have been a Yankee, but he was also a gentleman and a fine writer."

The flat bottom of the sled was built by nailing wide boards across two runners that had been shaped in the front like skis.

It was large enough for five or six people. Parker had blankets ready to cover us before we started our trek across the back pastures. As we glided through the new snow, Parker led us in singing "Jingle Bells." We scared the crows out of the trees; saw deer scurrying for cover; passed strutting turkeys with their goggle-eyed brown heads; teased jackrabbits as they ran ahead of the sled; and watched for a sighting of the mysterious eagle that came and went at its pleasure. When we returned to the barn, Uncle John was pouring cups of hot chocolate with tiny marshmallows swimming on top. After gulping down the sweet mixture, we wished Parker and his family a Merry Christmas and headed across the orchard to get ready for the visit from Santa Claus.

I can't remember when I first learned the truth about Santa Claus, but I continued pretending to believe.

"Why give up a good thing?" Wes had said.

Although we changed as we got older, and outgrew Tinker Toys, scooters, whirlybirds, and Lionel trains, and I quit praying for a pony, the excitement of Christmas never changed. The ritual of Christmas Eve and Christmas morning was always the same.

Before going to bed, we would select a special spot—a chair or corner of a couch—where Santa was "instructed" to leave our toys. Rue said she was too old for Santa and refused to claim a space.

"It's her loss," I said.

"And maybe our gain," Wes added.

The excitement was so intense; sleep was always difficult. When we were younger, we were afraid Santa would arrive too early and the noises in the living room would spoil the surprise and anticipation. Now, we tried not to listen to the noises our parents made as they played Santa.

Christmas morning was electric and began anywhere from 3:00 A.M. to 5:00 A.M. I would usually wake first and shake Wes, saying, "Santa's come."

Wiping sleep from our eyes, we'd stumble through the darkness to the living room, groping for the light switch. Wearily, Daddy would come in, dressed in pajamas and a robe, and plug in the Christmas tree lights. Hearts pounding a little faster, the light revealed a beautiful sight: gifts, candy canes, oranges, apples, nuts, and raisins still on the vines. And sometimes there would be a big hairy coconut for each. Later, we would take an ice pick, punch holes in the eyes of the coconut, and drink the milk. A substantial stomachache usually followed.

It was always a mystery to me how my parents were able to put together these assortments time after time. Over the years, we would wake up to cap pistols, cowboy hats, footballs, dominoes, Lionel trains, and a Monopoly set with the dice missing. Daddy did not like dice because they were used for gambling, so we replaced them with a spinning wheel. In a good year, there might be a coaster wagon, a sled, or a B.B. gun.

On this Christmas, Wes got a set of oil paints with a pallet and brushes, and a large pad of sketch sheets. I got a knapsack, made of soft leather with pockets inside and out, large enough to carry my books and lunch to school. The big surprise was a Cardinals baseball glove for me and a catcher's mitt for Wes.

If the hour was especially early, Mother and Daddy would patiently persuade us to go back to bed for a few more hours. Sleep never came but it gave us time to think about our presents and to anticipate the day's festivities.

While Mother and Rue were preparing a big breakfast, Wes and I were out back in the snow trying out our new gloves. After breakfast, Daddy always insisted that all the beds were made, the dishes washed and dried, and the house swept before we could open the presents under the tree. At a very young age, I had noticed that the presents under the tree were different from those brought by Santa. We got things like socks, underwear, handkerchiefs, and pencils. Wes did get a book on famous painters and I got a watercolor set, which I took to be a suggestion that I needed another hobby.

Rue, Wes, and I had pooled our money and bought Daddy some black leather gloves and a striped tie, chosen by Mother, of course. We gave Mother a neck scarf and a tea set, chosen by Rue, of course. Rue got a blouse, slip, some jewelry, and, much to her surprise, a red wool coat she had seen in a store in Savannah.

She exclaimed, "How did you know this was the one I wanted?"

They always seemed to know. Daddy and Mother exchanged their gifts. Daddy got a Parker pen and a red-letter edition of the *New Testament*. Mother got a sewing kit housed in a double-weave basket woven from river cane by a Cherokee Indian. Granny Lee had sent over five beautifully wrapped presents and Daddy had hidden them behind the tree as a surprise. There was a hand-woven table runner for Mother, a wool scarf for Daddy, and a cotton one for Rue. Wes was given the book *Gunga Din*, by Rudyard Kipling, and I got Robert Louis Stevenson's *The Strange Case of Dr. Jekyll and Mr. Hyde*.

As usual, Christmas was full of surprises and filled with a special kind of joy that's hard to describe.

It had become a tradition to go across the street to the Menloes' for Christmas dinner. Mother and Rue prepared dishes of sweet potatoes, string beans, corn pudding, and a macaroni-cheese casserole, and for dessert, they made mincemeat and pecan pies and a coconut cake. Uncle John baked a fresh country ham and Mrs. Menloe prepared other dishes. Lucy, who was home from Southwestern College in Memphis, was busy setting the table and arranging serving trays on the buffet counter. Granny Lee and Mother uncovered dishes of food while Rue put several pans of homemade rolls in the oven.

Sheriff Perkins came in wearing a dark suit, one of the few times I had seen him when he was not wearing his uniform. The men were in the living room discussing politics as they examined the new grandfather clock Uncle John had bought in Atlanta. He was a collector of new and antique clocks and had a very old water clock, two cuckoo clocks made of wood from the Black Forest of Germany, an eight-day mantel clock, and several others that chimed on the hour. Mrs. Menloe complained that she would prefer clocks with less activity and noise.

"Just one that goes tick-tock," she said, smiling.

Uncle John got everyone's attention and announced he was about to tell an interesting story. The local town gossip, who remained nameless, kept sticking her nose into other people's business and, although most people were unhappy with her activities, they were afraid to say so.

"She made a big mistake, however, when she accused Joe Ledbetter of being drunk after she saw his pickup truck parked in front of the local pool hall and bar," Uncle John said, laughing.

She confronted him and said seeing his truck there would tell everyone in town what he was doing. Joe, a man of few words, stared at her for a moment and then walked away. He didn't try to explain or defend or deny; he said nothing.

"Later that evening," Uncle John continued, "Joe parked his pickup in front of her house and left it there all night."

Uncle John slapped his knee and laughed loudly along with everyone except Mrs. Menloe.

"You should be ashamed, John, telling a story like that in front of the children and on Christmas Day of all things," she scolded. It was a perfect time for her to lead everyone into the dining room.

We stood around the table holding hands as Daddy offered the blessing. After some small talk, Uncle John changed the conversation to the war and some "unpleasant things going on." Mrs. Menloe seemed uncomfortable with his tone and the subject.

"I don't agree with what we're doing to Japanese-American citizens," he said as he pointed his fork in the air. "Why, just the other day over in Memphis they closed a Japanese bakery and took all its assets and posted guards outside. And did you know that the chairman of the city park commission announced the destruction of the Japanese Gardens in Overton Park?"

No one commented, so Uncle John went on. "That commissioner also said they were going to fill in the lake to form a sunken garden. *The Commercial Appeal* said if the government considered the garden offensive, they should just call it a Chinese Garden. They look about the same, the article said. Now, I hear out in California they're putting Japanese men, women, and children in camps surrounded by barbed wire. They call them relocation centers, but it sounds like prison to me. It's not right, I tell you. It's just not right."

Finally, the sheriff spoke up and said, "Well, I don't agree, John. We're at war with Japan and we don't know whether these Japanese are with us or against us. Maybe their loyalty is with their country."

"This is their country, Roy. They're citizens and most of them were born here," Uncle John declared raising his voice and ignoring Mrs. Menloe's effort to calm him.

Lucy surprised everyone when she spoke up and said, "What about the Italians and Germans? We aren't persecuting them, are we?"

"That's a good point, Lucy. We aren't putting them in concentration camps," Uncle John said.

"Well, that depends on where you live," Granny Lee said, "I read about a German family in Chattanooga who was accused of having a two-way radio used for contacting German U-Boats. They were arrested and detained until a Jewish lawyer persuaded the judge to release them. The lawyer pointed out that he didn't think there were any submarines cruising around Chattanooga."

I was watching Daddy and waiting to hear what he would say. The sheriff must have felt the same way, because he turned to him and asked, "Well, Milton you've been mighty quiet about this and that's not like you. What about it?"

Daddy was thoughtful as he said, "I have to agree with John on this one, Roy. There's a church in Memphis named 'The Rising Sun Baptist Church,' near where I used to serve. I was told that the people in city government tried to force them to change the name. That kind of antagonism and prejudice isn't right. After all, we're fighting to protect this country and our rights as citizens, and if we don't protect the rights of all citizens, then none of us are safe."

The sheriff said, "Well it might be easy for us to say that since we don't have any Japanese living here."

"It doesn't matter where they live," Uncle John said, "they still have the same rights as you and I do and I intend to write Boss E. H. Crump, that unelected and self-appointed mayor over in Memphis, and tell him so."

Mrs. Menloe tapped her fork against a glass and said firmly, "Now that's enough talk about that. This is Christmas and we don't need our dinner spoiled with disagreements."

Uncle John started to say something, but he got a look from his wife that made it clear that she meant what she said.

117

The conversation turned to things more personal and local, but not one word was said about Lonnie, Mr. Cowser, or Junior. There was, I guessed, some interesting talk when Daddy, the sheriff, and Uncle John wrapped themselves against the chill and took a long walk through the orchard. It also gave the sheriff the opportunity to smoke. Mrs. Menloe didn't allow any "foul-smelling cigar" in her house.

All Daddy told us when we got home was, "The sheriff said he's putting some things together and will be getting a report from the FBI soon. Other than that, there's nothing else that can be done."

I wasn't sure we were hearing everything Daddy knew.

Late in the afternoon, Rue said if we would get a big bowl of clean snow, she would make snow cream. Finding clean snow in our yard wasn't easy, but we succeeded by staying away from the chicken coop, the privy, and the cow pen. Rue mixed evaporated Carnation milk with sugar and vanilla extract, and gradually added the snow until it became smooth and firm, like the ice cream we made in the summer in our wooden freezer.

Wes and I spent the rest of the day building a fort and having snowball fights with friends. During the fights, we thought of how Junior would love to be there throwing snowballs filled with walnuts.

Except for thoughts about Junior, it was a day I would remember as one of the happiest.

13

The snow had melted, we were back in school, and the New Year was three weeks old. The war news was not good and pre-sliced bread was banned because the steel from bread-slicing machines was needed for guns, tanks, and other war supplies.

On New Year's Eve, we had fired Roman candles, watching them explode against a dark sky, and shot tiny firecrackers scaring the cow, the chickens, and Mother. We were allowed to stay up until someone in New York told us the New Year had arrived and Guy Lombardo played "Auld Lang Syne."

New Year's Day we sat close to the radio listening to the Rose Bowl game between Georgia and UCLA. We still hadn't gotten over last year's game when Oregon State beat Duke 20 to 16. This year we were rooting for Georgia but knew it wouldn't be easy with All-American Frankie Sink out with two sprained ankles. We didn't have to worry, however, because his replacement, a sophomore named Charlie Trippi, rushed for 130 yards and was voted Most Valuable Player. Georgia beat UCLA 9 to 0 with a safety and a touchdown. It was one of the most exciting games in Rose Bowl history. Soon after the win, Charlie Trippi joined the Army Air Corp.

Since Christmas, Wes had been painting almost every day. He had taped a sheet of his sketch paper to a piece of heavy cardboard and placed it on an easel that he made from pieces of a wood crate given to him by Mr. Wenzor at the appliance store. He kept the easel set up by the window in the bedroom and I watched him dip his brushes in little jars of paint and thoughtfully move them across the paper. I tried imitating him with my watercolors and tablet paper, but soon realized I wasn't meant to be an artist.

When he finished the painting, he proudly showed it to me and then to the rest of the family. It was a picture of a large clay pot surrounded by two apples, an orange, and a pear. We were surprised and impressed by the vivid colors and the nearly perfect shape of the pot and fruit. It was clear to everyone that Wes had a special talent.

A few days later, Wes and I went to the print shop and talked Johnny into making some block letters that we pasted in an arc at the top of the picture. They read: CLAY IS LIFE. Underneath the bottom of the clay jar, Wes wrote in small letters, JWT. Miss Ross tacked the painting to the bulletin board at school for a week and when Wes brought it back home, Mother found a frame for it and hung it on the wall in the kitchen.

After seeing how good Wes was, I talked him into drawing a comic book. Wes had taken a special interest in the war and sought out information from Daddy, Mr. Webb, and Uncle John, who read two papers a day and listened to all the radio broadcasts about the war. Uncle John told stories about what was happening on different fronts of the war and how navy pilots flew their planes off huge ships and sank several German U-Boats. Out of these stories, Spin Hawk was born. Wes, thinking about how many gold stars hung in the windows of Adairsville homes, wanted to create a hero who was helping win the war.

Spin Hawk was a twenty-one-year-old Navy Lieutenant J. G. who had enlisted as a seaman recruit, gone through boot camp in San Diego, and eventually passed the exam that allowed him to become a Navy Hell Cat Flyer. I listened to Wes describe his hero and knew I wanted to be involved in the writing of the book.

For the next several weeks, Wes spent most of his spare time drawing the frames of Spin Hawk and his gunner, Fuzzy. I would check every page and give Wes my opinions about his drawings and whether I thought the story seemed real. Wes described how Spin and Fuzzy flew off the deck of the USS *Oriskany*, a mighty naval aircraft carrier, and was hit by anti-aircraft fire while attacking a large German battleship. They landed on the beach of an island occupied by the Germans.

The rest of the book was about Spin and Fuzzy surviving and planning sneak attacks on the Germans at night. When Wes had his doubts about Spin Hawk killing so many Germans, he would notice another gold star going up in a window reminding us that another son or husband had become a casualty of the war, and decide that it was okay for his heroes to kill as many of the enemy as possible.

Wes finished the eighteen-page comic book and drew a cover with the title "The Adventures of Spin Hawk." At the bottom, he printed the words, "Written and Drawn by J. Wesley Turnage." After some discussion and a little anger on my part, he agreed to put the words "Ideas by Vance Turnage" on the inside cover. It was almost better than nothing.

Late one evening, a knock on the door startled us. Daddy answered quickly. Uncle John had come to tell us that Euclid had been killed. Daddy turned pale and Mother put her hand over her mouth and said, "Lord have mercy."

"How did it happen?" Daddy asked.

"All I know," Uncle John said, "is that there was a plane crash in Alabama and Euclid and the pilot were killed. Parker was in such a state he could hardly get the words out when he came over tonight."

Uncle John explained that the sheriff's office received a telephone call from the War Department and they asked the deputy to go out and tell the family. Daddy was irritated with the way the news had reached Parker's family.

"Maybe it's better than a telegram," Uncle John said.

Daddy went to the bedroom to change his clothes while Mother fixed some hot tea for Uncle John. Rue had heard us talking and came out of her room. Wes and I thought about Seth and Moses and remembered how proud they were of Euclid when he came home on Thanksgiving in his starched uniform and highly polished shoes. I couldn't imagine how they were feeling. It would be awfully hard to get over the loss of an older brother that you looked up to.

Daddy came out of the bedroom dressed in a white shirt and tie and was putting on his coat. "John and I are going over to see Alva and Parker. They're going to need some comforting and a lot of prayer."

"I already called Roy to send someone out to tell Reverend Lacy. He'll be meeting us there," Uncle John said.

"Anything I need to do?" Mother asked.

"Not just now, Grace, but tomorrow you might want to visit with Alva."

On the inside of the cover page of *The Clarion Standard*, the editor wrote a lengthy story about Euclid and the Flight Squadron of Tuskegee, Alabama, and for the first time in anyone's memory, the paper printed a picture of a Negro. When Daddy read the story out loud, we understood why Parker and his family were so proud of Euclid.

Euclid had enlisted in the Tuskegee Experiment, as it was called. He was trained as a mechanic and technician and assigned to the 99th Flight Squadron, an all-Negro unit, which later became known as the "Red Tails." The story explained that this experiment was the first time the government had paid for flight training for coloreds and had challenged the discrimination and segregation practices of the War Department. Many of the pilots had been killed while flying missions over Germany. *The Standard* reported that Euclid was going up with a regular pilot, Lieutenant Rayford DePriest of Detroit, to test a recently rebuilt engine. The pilot lost control of the plane just after takeoff and it crashed into Soughalaschoe Creek in Alabama, killing both of them.

The body arrived in Adairsville after traveling from Tuskegee to Nashville by train, and then transported from Nashville in a hearse furnished by the local funeral home. The service was held at The New Salem Missionary Baptist Church on a cloudy, damp Sunday afternoon. The paper had run an announcement about the funeral and said everyone would be welcome.

Reverend Lacy said he knew Parker would be pleased if Uncle John and Daddy attended. "And bring those two boys with you," he said to Daddy. I don't know whether I was just getting used to funerals or what, but I wanted to go with Daddy and Wes.

Reverend Lacy had reserved places for us in a pew just to the right of the pulpit. Sheriff Perkins came with Curtis and Carl Shipley and sat with us. Congressman Murphy usually attended the funerals of soldiers killed in the war from his district, but for Private Browne, he sent a message of condolences, which was read by the mayor.

New Salem Church was a white frame structure with tall windows and plank floors. The benches were made of rough wood with slats for backs. Behind the pulpit was a raised floor with folding chairs where the choir, wearing maroon robes, sat. In the corner, opposite the choir, was an oil heater which replaced a coal-burning stove that once heated the building when it was a one-room schoolhouse. The smell of coal smoke still lingered.

While the choir hummed softly, a somber hush fell over the congregation as six men, two in uniform, carried the casket, draped with an American flag, up the aisle, and placed it in front of the pulpit.

In a strong voice Reverend Lacy read part of the 23rd Psalm, and by putting special emphasis on certain words, he gave new meaning to this familiar passage.

The Lord is my shepherd; I shall *not* want.
He *maketh* me to lie down in green pastures,
He *leadeth* me by still waters,
He *restoreth* my soul,
Yea though I walk through the valley of the shadow of Death, I will fear no evil. For *thou art with me*; thy rod and thy staff *they* comfort me. Surely, *goodness and mercy* shall follow me all the days of my life and *I will dwell in the house of the Lord forever.*

The choir sang all the verses of "The Battle Hymn of the Republic."

Master Sergeant Fred Jefferson rose to bring a message from the 99th Squadron. He spoke in a soft voice:

"Our unit is like a family and we stick together as a team. It made no difference about rank or education or where we came from; we knew there was something special about our unit. Private Euclid Browne loved to ride with the pilots on test flights and looked forward to the time when he would fly in the pilot's seat. But he also loved to work on planes and when he wasn't hitching rides with pilots, he was servicing planes. We depend on our mechanics to keep our planes flying safely. If Private

123

Browne didn't have the right parts to fix the plane, he would find a jeep or a truck and go to the nearest supply depot or to another base to find them. He had many friends, both enlisted and officers, and he served his country with honor and distinction. You can all be proud of Euclid Browne."

"Amens" and shouts of "Praise the Lord" could be heard.

Reverend Lacy came to the pulpit and began preaching with conviction and in a voice that betrayed some anger. Uncle John would say later that "Reverend Lacy was in fine form today." But the sheriff was concerned about some of the things the reverend had said and the way he said them.

"He was a fine soldier who loved his country even though his country did not always love him back," he said as he began to raise his voice. "That's right" and "Amens" were shouted. Reverend Lacy paced as he continued to preach.

"He served his country, though his country did not always serve him. He believed in defending democracy though democracy did not always defend him. He obeyed the laws of this land, though those laws did not always protect him. He praised the name of Jesus, but few praised the name of Euclid. He was a beloved son, a fine brother to look up to, and a man respected by all who knew him. He was God-fearing and peace-loving and courageous. He spoke no evil of others. He just wanted to be a good pilot and maybe God Almighty in His mercy will see fit to reward him for his deeds." He paused to take a sip of water, wipe his brow, and then continued.

"But today, in honor of Private Euclid Browne, we put away anger and resentment; we remove from our hearts the bile of bitterness; we purge ourselves of animosity. Let us remember that Jesus said, 'Blessed are ye when men shall hate you and when they shall separate you from their company and shall reproach you.' He commanded us to love our enemies and do good to those that persecute us. And, brothers and sisters, as hard as that might be at times, we must obey the word of God."

The congregation continued to shout words of agreement and approval.

Reverend Lacy then turned to Daddy and asked if he would come forward and offer a prayer.

124

Daddy prayed with fervor: "Lord, we know there are many mysteries in this life and we don't always understand why things happen. But we trust in Your mercy and love and comfort. We know war is evil and killing is wrong, but by your word, we know we sometimes have to fight evil with force. We ask your forgiveness for failing to work harder for peace, so young men like Euclid will not have to die. Give us wisdom to find the road to brotherhood and the courage to lay down our sword and shield and study war no more."

The people responded enthusiastically. The congregation stood and sang, "I am bound for the Promised Land."

Reverend Lacy concluded by saying, "Yes, our brother Euclid died in the early morning of his life and did not enjoy the warm sun of mid-day and the hot breezes of late afternoon, and the cooling shadows of evening. But in his mercy, God will not allow this young man's life, snuffed out so early, to die in vain. God will keep his promise to reward the righteous, for as He said, 'I am the resurrection and the life, and he who believes in me shall never die.' Brothers and sisters, these are the most important words the tongue has ever spoken and the ear has ever heard. They are an everlasting reminder of the power of the soul to outlast the changes of earth and rise victorious over the bondage of death. Hallelujah and everyone say Amen!"

The congregation responded and clapped their hands.

Without any introduction, a large woman with a voice to match, stood up in the choir loft and sang:

Sometimes I feel discouraged, and think my work's in vain,
But then the Holy Spirit revives my soul again.

The congregation joined her:

There is a balm in Gilead, to make the wounded whole,
There is a balm in Gilead, to heal the sin-sick soul.

As they sang more verses, the congregation began to sway back and forth and some held their hands above their heads. I looked across the aisle and caught a glimpse of Seth. He was not singing. His eyes were lowered and focused on the floor, and, as far

125

as I could tell, he had not shed a tear. Parker clung to the back of the pew in front of him and sang loudly as tears ran down his cheeks. I could not see the other children or Alva.

The service closed and, as the casket was carried down the aisle, the choir sang a rousing song I hadn't heard before. Burial was in the colored cemetery about a mile from the church.

On the way home we asked Daddy about the service and why Methodists didn't clap and shout and sing like the people at New Salem.

"It's just a difference in our culture and upbringing," he said. Then he added: "Sometimes I think we need a little of that spirit in our church. Maybe it would liven things up a bit."

Uncle John laughed and said, "Why, Milton if anyone said 'Praise the Lord' during one of your sermons, one of our ushers would shush him and tell him that we don't do that."

Daddy laughed along with Wes and Uncle John, but it took a while before I caught on. The laughter brought a sense of relief and replaced the ache for just a brief moment.

14

Although it was a school night, Daddy and Mother had agreed to let us go to a basketball game with Rue. It was one of the big games of the year. Adairsville was playing Selmer, its major rival and most feared opponent. Johnny Fesmire played forward and was the highest scorer for the Adairsville Wildcats.

The old gym was filled to capacity with local Wildcat supporters and Tiger fans from Selmer. The bleachers on both sides ran from the playing floor to the ceiling and the noise was almost deafening. The opposing players and coaches, separated by a scorer's table, sat on backless benches at the edge of the floor. The cheerleaders on both sides led the crowd in partisan cheers.

The game lived up to everyone's expectations. When the timekeeper sounded the horn to signal halftime, the game was tied at thirty-three all. The players and coaches headed for the locker room to plan strategy and give the usual pep talks. I headed to the bathroom and then to the concession stand for a cold Orange Crush and peanuts.

I rejoined Wes and Rue in the bleachers. We were sitting about halfway up in the center section and had a bird's-eye view of what happened in the next few minutes.

Clovis Blanchard, a slightly retarded man in his early twenties and strong as an ox, was obviously drunk and looking for a fight. Clovis had a harelip and cleft pallet that caused him to slur his speech even when he wasn't drinking. He wore tight shirts to reveal his huge biceps, mixed his moonshine with Coca Cola, and carried several bottles with him wherever he went.

Wes told me that people around town said that the cleft pallet "allowed the corn likker to go straight to Clovis' brain."

During the first half, Clovis had been shouting curse words at the Selmer players and referees.

"He can curse like a sailor," Uncle John once said. I didn't understand why sailors were such good cursers.

Tensions were running high, and Randy Woods, a graduate of Selmer High School and now a resident of Adairsville, was fed up with the Clovis' rantings. While the teams were still in their locker rooms and people were busy visiting the refreshment stand, Clovis pranced up and down the floor taunting the Selmer fans.

Randy was sitting at the top of the bleachers with his head against the wall, watching the spectacle.

Finally, he shouted at the top of his voice, "Get your drunken ass off the floor and go home to your mother, if you have one!"

Rue got up to leave, but Wes pulled her down as she muttered something to herself.

Clovis froze in his tracks and looked up to where the sound came from. His faced turned red as a beet and his eyes focused on Randy Woods.

With an empty Coke bottle in each hand and one stuck in each of his back pockets, Clovis began his unsteady climb up the bleachers toward Randy. Moving one riser at a time, he cursed Randy and waved the Coke bottles in the air. Randy responded with obscenities, calling Clovis a name that I was not allowed to repeat.

"Here comes the village idiot who gets his courage from 120-proof corn liquor in a Coke bottle," Randy said loud enough to be heard by those sitting in the upper bleachers.

Again, Rue thought we should leave but Wes and I weren't budging.

When Clovis reached the seat just below where Randy was sitting, he lunged toward Randy. Randy braced himself against the walls, lifted both feet in the air and forcefully pushed two big brogans into the middle of Clovis' stomach. Clovis began falling backward down the bleachers, forcing fans to jump out of his way.

As he was tumbling down the risers, he let fly his missiles, the coke bottles. I watched the whole thing and still couldn't believe that he could throw those bottles while completely off balance and falling. Not one, but all four bottles flew through the air and crashed against the wall, missing their intended target. The people in the stands were horrified, but made no effort to stop the fight.

The fall of Clovis finally ended as he hit his head on an iron rail and tumbled helplessly until he was lying flat on his back on the hardwood floor. He was dazed and unable to move.

Randy was not finished. He picked up a piece of the broken coke bottle, scurried down the steps, and, leaping over the iron rail, he landed on top of Clovis. Before anyone realized what he was about to do, Randy shoved the jagged edge of the bottle into Clovis' mouth. Blood spewed from his mouth and nostrils as he begged for help.

Two county deputies arrived, wrestled Randy away from Clovis, and handcuffed him. Randy was taken to jail and later released. Clovis went to the clinic where Doc Townsend sewed up the cuts in his mouth and gave him a tetanus shot. Both were given warnings, but no charges were filed.

Randy continued to come to ballgames and sit in his seat at the top of the bleachers. Clovis never attended another game. A few months after the incident, he was converted at a tent revival in Selmer and became a Pentecostal street preacher. Some wondered how he could preach with such a severe lisp, but most were just happy to hear that Clovis had given up drinking and now "lived for Jesus."

Adairsville beat Selmer by two points in overtime. Johnny scored sixteen points, including the final field goal that won the game. Except for the halftime rhubarb, it was a good night for the Wildcats. And, although I would never admit it to anyone, I thought it was just about the most exciting thing I'd ever seen.

When Rue told Mother about it, she put her hand over her mouth and said, "Lord have mercy!"

Daddy was also unhappy. "What is the world coming to when something like that happens at a basketball game?"

It was a question he tried to answer in his sermon on the following Sunday.

15

March winds and unusually warm weather brought warnings of possible tornadoes, the only flaw in a West Tennessee spring-time. We were sitting on the steps of the back porch talking about the State High School Basketball Championship and la-menting Adairsville's loss to Chattanooga Central in the semi-finals. Central had an undefeated season, winning thirty-three games, and beating their opponent in the finals by a score of forty-eight to thirty. Johnny Fesmire was the high scorer for the tournament and made the top ten All-Star Team. Rue got to go on the school bus to Nashville for the finals.

I was finishing building a kite out of old newspapers, round sticks, string, and homemade dough paste made from flour and water. Strips of an old sheet were tied together for the tail. There would be a kite-flying contest at the park in a few days and I wanted to be prepared.

Mother came out to the porch and sat down on a stool next to the butter churn. She told us that she had just finished writing a poem and wanted to read it to us. We were surprised because she had never done this before.

"It's about the place where I lived when I was your age," she said.

A few months ago, when we went to Papa's funeral in Giltedge, we had stopped by to see Mother's older bother, who now owned the family farm in Burlison. He had moved out of the old home place and built a red brick house where one of the barns once stood. Mother had cried when she saw the house, where she had spent so many happy childhood days, now sur-rounded by weeds, broken windows, and doors off their hinges.

Her brother was using it to store bales of hay, apple crates, and cider barrels.

With sadness in her voice, Mother read us the poem she called "The Old Home Place."

I went back to the Home Place
After years of being away,
To find it all deserted
Where children used to play.

The window panes were broken,
The floor had fallen in;
There were no glowing embers
Where the fireplace once had been.

No ticking on the mantle piece
Of the clock once so dear.
Nor could I hear the creaking
Of my father's favorite chair.

I stood in amazement
To see it all so bare.
What many years and nature
Can do when no one cares.

Rue took the poem to the print shop and had Johnny set it in a special type. Several copies were made and mounted on heavy cardboard for framing. Later, these were given as Christmas presents to a few of Mother's friends.

Wes came home from school sick to his stomach and, after a dose of vinegar and soda, went to bed. Mother knew something was wrong, but waited until Daddy came home before talking to him. Daddy returned from a trip to Covington, where he had met with his brothers and sister to arrange for the sale of their family farm. He was tired and irritable and what he heard didn't improve his mood.

Daddy went into the room and sat on the edge of the bed. When Wes turned over, we could see that his eyes were red from crying. It took a while before he could talk about what had happened at school.

As Wes began, Mother came in and placed a glass of cold milk and a cookie on the bedside table. The story Wes told was another gust from that ill wind.

Eric Gustafson, a below average student, had passed one of Mr. Butterfield's math tests with flying colors.

"Button knew right away that Eric had cheated," Wes said.

He was determined to find out who helped him with the test. Red-faced and angry, he made Eric go to the blackboard and explain how he had solved the difficult math problem. Eric couldn't do it. He stood in front of the class with chalk in his hand and didn't move.

Mr. Butterfield asked him the name of the student who had helped him cheat. Eric was afraid he might look at that person so he just stared out the window and said nothing.

"This was one of the strangest things I've ever seen," Wes said as he continued.

Button reached into his desk drawer, took out a box of Arm and Hammer baking soda, poured himself a handful, and, as he shoved Eric against the blackboard, he pushed the soda into his mouth. Eric's lips turned white and he trembled as he stepped aside.

"Now tell me who helped you," Button demanded.

Eric moved toward Button and said defiantly, "I ain't gonna rat on nobody, Mr. Butterfield, no matter what you do to me."

Wes drank some of his milk and took a bite out of the cookie before continuing the story.

Mr. Butterfield left the room and went to his office. Shortly, he brought back the paddle that created terror in the hearts of every student. Mr. Butterfield, to the horror of the class, told Eric to bend over and grab his ankles. When he did as he was told, Button began to hit him with the paddle. Eric didn't defend himself or try to move away. After five strokes on the back of his thighs, he asked again for a name. Eric said nothing. Button continued to hit him on the legs and buttocks, and when Eric tried to protect himself, his hands took a beating. Wes said his hands were bleeding and one looked like it was broken. Once, when Eric straightened up, Button missed his backside and hit him squarely on the shoulders. When he refused to bend over again, he was hit across the head and blood ran down his face.

Finally, Mary Beth Shipley stood up and was sobbing.

"Stop it. Please stop it. I did it. I was the one who gave him the answers."

Eric started to say something, and then stopped. Button's face reddened and he said angrily, "Come up here, young lady. You come up here right now."

At first, Mary Beth didn't move; then she slowly walked to the front of the room. Mr. Butterfield was flustered and didn't know what to do.

He finally said, "I don't usually paddle girls, but I think you need to be taught a lesson."

Before another word was spoken, Eric stepped forward and, towering over Button Butterfield, said, "If you touch her, I'll kill you."

Wes said there was a gasp and it felt like the whole room was paralyzed with fear. Mr. Butterfield was stunned and a flash of fear came across his face, an emotion he had never revealed to his students. He stood motionless for a minute and finally placed the paddle on the desk and ordered Eric to go to the bathroom, wash up, and go home.

Mr. Butterfield told Mary Beth she was suspended indefinitely and must leave the school grounds immediately. After Eric and Mary Beth left, Brother Butterfield lectured the class on the sins of cheating and lying.

"He beat the living hell out of him," Ollie Gustafson said in his Swedish accent, when he reported the incident to Earl Ashby, the County School Superintendent.

Mr. Gustafson, a farmer who moved to Adairsville from Minnesota, had bought fifty acres of land from Mr. Parsons and just barely eked out a living for his wife and six children. Eric, the oldest, was almost as tall as his father. Because he had been held back in school in Minnesota, he was older and bigger than the other eighth-graders.

Mr. Shipley, who was also very upset with Brother Butterfield, called him a "little tyrant" and said nobody had a right to do what he did to Eric and "my daughter."

Uncle John said, "Old Button made two big mistakes: using that infernal paddle on a Gustafson and expelling a Shipley."

The town was surprised when they heard that Mr. Ashby would hold a hearing regarding the charges brought by Ollie Gustafson and Curtis Shipley. The majority seemed to side with Brother Butterfield; others, because of respect for the Shipleys, thought differently. *The Clarion Standard* carried a front-page story about the incident, but did not include all the details of the beating.

Sheriff Perkins was quoted as saying, "We can't tolerate students threatening teachers."

He said nothing about teachers beating students.

Daddy, while sitting on a nail keg at Taylor's grocery store was asked what he thought about it.

"Well," he said carefully, "I don't approve of cheating and I think a teacher must be allowed to use discipline, but I think this was excessive."

Daddy's casual remark got back to Mr. Butterfield and made him furious. "You can tell Milton Turnage that if he won't tell me how to run my school, I won't tell him how to run the Methodist Church," he said to Uncle John as he was picking up his mail at the post office.

Uncle John was on the phone as soon as Button left, and told Daddy what he'd said. That did it for Daddy. He was as mad as I'd ever seen him. Mother tried to calm him down, but all he could do was pace and let out his anger.

"That runt of a man, who thinks he's a spokesman for God, needs to be brought down a rung or two," he declared.

"Lord have mercy, Milton, I've never heard you talk about anybody like that before," Mother said as she pulled him toward a chair.

Daddy did not sit; instead, he went to the kitchen table and began writing on his yellow pad.

Daddy's sermon on Sunday was more passionate than usual. He quoted from I Corinthians about love; he reminded us that God said, "Vengeance is mine"; he warned that "Violence begets violence"; and then he gripped the pulpit firmly with both hands and delivered the clincher. His final words startled many in the congregation, including his wife and three children:

134

"You know I'm not one to meddle in the affairs of those in positions of responsibility and authority, but my conscience importunes me to speak to this issue of corporeal punishment in our schools. While I believe in discipline and teaching compliance with rules and respect for those who must enforce them, I do not believe in excessive punishment whether it's in the home or the school. Students must obey their teachers, live by the rules, and respect their elders, and teachers must use every means at their disposal to discipline without resorting to punishment that is cruel, demeaning, and harmful. All of us must learn to temper our anger with love; to regulate the heat of our passions; to bring a proper measure of self-discipline to our actions; and to remember that physically abusing someone in the name of discipline is not a measure of strength but of weakness."

He concluded by quoting from Ephesians 6:4, " . . . provoke not your children to wrath; but bring them up in the nurture and admonition of the Lord."

All Wes could say was, "Boy, oh boy, oh boy. I can't wait till old Button hears about this."

I looked at Mother. She was pale and was doing what she always did when she was nervous; she twisted her handkerchief into knots. I had never been more proud of my father.

There were many comments after the sermon, some good and some critical. The one Daddy quoted when he got home made us all smile.

"Brother Turnage, this morning you quit preaching and went to meddling," Mattie Malone said.

Among the calls that afternoon was one from Sheriff Perkins who had heard from Mattie about Daddy's sermon. It was one of the few times that Daddy and the sheriff disagreed.

The school board scheduled the hearing for the Grange Hall because they expected an overflow crowd and also because the superintendent thought it best if it was held off the school grounds.

They were right about the crowd. After all the seats were taken, people stood around the walls of the room. Mayor Shipley, the brother of Carl and uncle of Mary Beth, was a member of the school board but didn't participate because of what he described as a "conflict of interest." From the looks on their faces, the other seven members of the board would rather be anywhere but the Grange Hall that evening. Wes and I sat near the back with several of our friends and some older students.

The hearing lasted about two hours and sometimes things got out of hand. The chairman of the board had to pound his gavel for order several times.

During one speech that was critical of Brother Butterfield, a woman rose and shouted, "You'd better not use that paddle on one of *my* children!"

Another time, a large man jumped up and yelled, "Spare the rod and spoil the child; that's what the Bible says and I believe in the Bible!"

Daddy explained later that the quote was from the poet Samuel Butler and written in the 17th century. "It's based on a verse in Proverbs about sparing the rod, but the rod is a reference to a shepherd's staff that was used to lead and instruct, not as a stick for beating."

Mr. Gustafson, dressed in overalls and a flannel shirt, made a speech that made some people cry. In broken English and with a thick accent, he talked about Eric and what a good boy he was.

"He's worked hard all his life and caused me no trouble. He could be smarter if he hadn't missed so much schooling trying to help put food on the table. He meant no harm by what he did. He was doing his best at book-learning so he could finish eighth grade and go on to high school. It broke my heart when I saw him that day, and my missus cried all night. He'd be the first to admit that he done wrong, but he didn't deserve to be beat up like an animal in front of the class." His voice cracked and tears were running down his cheeks as he sat down.

Doc Townsend, who had treated Eric the afternoon of the whipping, described the welts on his buttocks and legs and winced as he told about having to set the broken bones in one of his hands. "Blood had seeped through his shirt and one of his sleeves had been ripped off."

Mr. Shipley spoke briefly, defending his daughter. "What she did was wrong, but she was only trying to help Eric because she felt sorry for him. She's a straight-A student and has never caused any trouble in that school. And there is good reason to believe that Mr. Butterfield would have hit her with that paddle if Eric hadn't stopped him."

When some of the students applauded, Button Butterfield turned quickly and looked around the room. Wes slid so far down in his chair, he almost hit the floor.

A few parents and teachers testified about Mr. Butterfield's character and agreed that he was a good teacher. One parent spoke against Button and said her son had been whipped with that paddle last year and had hated school ever since.

Showing no signs of remorse as he boasted of his record as a school teacher and principal, Mr. Butterfield spoke in his own defense. He talked about being an ordained Baptist preacher and how he read the Bible every night.

"God called me to be a minister of the Gospel and he's also given me the opportunity to fill young minds with knowledge and truth. I can't do that without teaching respect for God's law and obedience of rules. When a teacher paddles a child, he is carrying out his duty to instruct and teach. What I did to Eric will make it easier for other teachers to teach in an environment of order and civility. If you take away our right to discipline students, you take away our right to teach," he said as he lowered his body into the chair.

There was a smattering of applause. *The Clarion Standard* printed the entire speech.

After a fifteen-minute recess, the school board announced their findings. They reinstated Mary Beth Shipley and instructed that the suspension not become part of her record and they ruled that Eric could return to school after he apologized to Mr. Butterfield and the eighth grade class for his threat. Finally, they reprimanded Mr. Butterfield for using "excessive means of punishment that did not fit the infraction." Mr. Butterfield was also restricted from further use of the special paddle and from spanking students in public.

The superintendent had the last word. "Brother Butterfield, we respect you as a person and as a teacher, but you must take the actions of this board seriously. If anything like this happens again, you will be discharged from your duties as principal and teacher."

With a scattering of applause and a few groans, the meeting was adjourned.

Mary Beth returned to class and continued to make top grades. Eric Gustafson never went near the school again. About a month later, Mr. Butterfield was looking out his office window and saw flames shooting up through the roof of his house. He sprinted across the schoolyard and arrived about the same time as the fire department. The fire was contained but the house was badly damaged. Although there were many rumors about the fire, no one was ever accused or charged.

16

A week after the Butterfield hearing, Daddy was at the church changing the hymn board at the front of the sanctuary when Sheriff Perkins came in with some bad news.

They talked quietly as they rode back to the courthouse to meet with Agent Barry Timmons who had driven over from Jackson. A few days ago, the sheriff received a report from the dealer in Memphis who came up to Adairsville to examine Lonnie's coins. He went over each one, giving careful attention to dates and condition.

"The reason it took so long," the sheriff explained, "is because some of these are so rare, it was hard to find an expert who knew their worth.".

Agent Timmons, who had read the report, remarked about what an unusual collection it was.

"There is an 1852 Liberty coin made in Carson City with a double eagle on one side and a liberty head on the other. The report says there's no telling how much that coin might bring at an auction."

Daddy summarized for the sheriff. "What you're saying is the coins are worth a lot more than their face value."

The sheriff nodded in agreement and added, "I guess it's about time we took a look at those coins in Ben's lockbox to see what they're actually worth. And let's just hope we don't find a shiny ten-dollar Indian head gold piece."

Agent Timmons apologized for the delay in getting a report on the paint scrapings found on the boulder at Lonnie's place.

"I've learned to live with the way things get done in Washington although I don't like it. What is it they say about moving at a snail's pace? Well that's the way the FBI moves when it's not dealing with a John Dillinger or a Baby Face Nelson."

He then explained that the report said the paint was from a Chevrolet made between 1937 and 1940 and the lab technician believed it was a pickup truck. Daddy was not sure what all this meant until he saw the look on the sheriff's face.

"Spit it out, Roy," he directed.

The sheriff's frown told Daddy he wouldn't like what he was about to hear.

"Milton, Ben Cowser owns a 1938 maroon pickup truck."

Daddy, surprised by the implication, asked testily, "Is Ben the only person in the whole county who drives a maroon pickup truck?"

The sheriff pondered the question, then said, "I don't know about that, but I do know that back in December, Shipley's garage knocked out a dent in the back fender of that pickup and repainted it."

"And how did you come by that information?" Daddy asked.

"I told Curtis to check his records at the garage and tell me if he had done any repair work on a maroon Chevrolet truck. He said they had Ben's truck in the shop for about a week because Ben insisted that the match be exact. Curtis had to call a dealer in Memphis and have the paint sent up."

Agent Timmons said there was more bad news. "I've been in touch with federal bank regulators and they told me that the auditors have found serious irregularities in Ben's bank. They expect to make their findings known soon."

Daddy slumped in his chair and said, "Good grief! Are you telling me that Ben might be involved in bank fraud on top of everything else?"

The sheriff nodded and Agent Timmons continued, "That's what it looks like now, but he might have a good explanation when they confront him with their findings. Anyway, I'll let you know as soon as they tell me. And by the way, the poison that killed Lonnie's dog was the kind used to kill rats."

Daddy felt a wave of depression coming on and started pacing. The agent urged the sheriff and Daddy to keep this information confidential until the auditors completed their report.

"What about the coins?" Daddy asked.

"I think I'll wait on that too," the sheriff said. "No need to let Ben know about our suspicions until we have all the facts.

Let's just hope we get the truth before Jacob spreads some wild rumor across the front page of *The Clarion Standard*."

Daddy was on his way out the door when the phone rang. The sheriff answered and with a shocked look, said, "We'll be there in a few minutes. Don't touch him. I'll get Doc Townsend there as soon as possible."

He hung up the phone and said, "Lonnie's been shot."

The sheriff, Daddy, and Doc Townsend arrived about the same time and were met by a neighbor standing in the gravel driveway. Doc Townsend went immediately to Lonnie and found him lying face down in the grass with blood oozing out his shoulder. He turned him over and began an examination. The sheriff learned that the neighbor had heard a shot and at first didn't pay any attention to it, but when he went out to get in his car a few minutes later, he saw Lonnie lying on the ground. He yelled for his wife and told her to call the sheriff.

"Lonnie's a very lucky man," Doc Townsend said as he poured something into a handkerchief and held it close to Lonnie's nose. "He's been shot but the bullet appears to have gone right through his body without slowing down."

"That's the darndest thing I've ever seen, Doc," the sheriff said as he leaned over to get a better look. "There's a hole in the back and one in the front. Guess we'd better look around for that bullet."

They found it lodged in a tree not more than twenty feet from where Lonnie was hit. The sheriff couldn't tell for certain what kind of bullet it was but he was already guessing it came from a Winchester rifle. Sure enough, the rifle Lonnie had brought with him from the shack was missing. The deputies searched everywhere around the house and yard, plus a three- or four-block area near the house.

"You mean someone took that rifle, shot Lonnie, and just walked away with it?" Daddy asked.

"Sure looks that way," the sheriff answered.

Lonnie was awake and talking to Doc Townsend when the sheriff came over to question him. Lonnie explained that he had been over at the lumberyard getting some two-by-fours, and when he returned he went to the pump to wash up, but didn't see or hear anyone. The next thing he remembered was hearing a bang and feeling a burning sensation in his back. When he fell, he hit his head on one of the boards and was knocked unconscious.

Doc guessed that he was shot at close range, but "if whoever did it was trying to kill Lonnie, he's sure a poor marksman."

Doc bandaged up the wound and a deputy transported him to Doc's office where he could be examined further to determine if he needed to be sent to the hospital in Jackson. The sheriff and Daddy stayed behind to look around the yard and house. The sheriff kept rolling the bullet around between his thumb and forefinger.

"Can't imagine why anyone would want to hurt Lonnie, Milton. Can you make any sense of it?"

Daddy thought about it for a moment, then said, "Unless, of course, Lonnie knew something about Junior's murder that he hasn't told us."

"You know, Milton, when I was elected sheriff of this town ten years ago, my wife, Martha, God rest her soul, said, 'Roy, I don't know why you want a job where you have to deal with folk who have no respect for the law.' I told her not to worry because Adairsville was a peaceful town and I wouldn't expect I'd be locking up many murderers."

He paused and wiped his brow with a red handkerchief. "Sure, we've had some stabbings, fights, drunken brawls, and a few shootings, but nothing like this."

"And I'm afraid we haven't seen the end of it yet, Roy," Daddy said, frowning.

Daddy stopped by Doc Townsend's office to check on Lonnie.

"I've stopped the bleeding and can't find any indication of internal damage, but I'm going to keep him here overnight just to be sure," Doc Townsend reported.

Daddy went back to the church and said a prayer for Lonnie Jackson. He sat quietly in a pew, realizing that an unsuspecting community was about to face a scandal that would put a stain on its character and possibly ruin the lives of a highly respected family.

As he thumbed through a hymnal, he thought about what he could do to help both the community and the family of Ben Cowser.

17

It was a hot and humid day in mid-April when the strong wind caused the rain to fall sideways. The principals of the high school and elementary school instructed the teachers to send the students home. Around 1:00 in the afternoon, students started boarding school buses lined up in front of the school. Wes and I were walking down Main Street when we saw the dark clouds moving swiftly across a dusky sky. We ran the last few blocks and headed for the root cellar where Mother was waiting. Rue was not with us and Mother was very worried. Later, we learned that Rue's teacher had taken her class across the road to a storm cellar. Daddy was at the Selmer Hospital visiting the sick.

The stillness that came just before the storm was something I'll never forget. Hail the size of marbles pounded on the roof and turned the landscape into a white winter-like spectacle.

The tornado moved in from the southwest, criss-crossing the open fields and touching down at intervals to destroy everything in its path. The driver of one of the grade school buses pulled off the road and tried to lower the windows to eliminate pressure that can cause something like an explosion. Before he could get out of his seat, the tornado came across an open field and lifted the bus into the air, causing it to roll over many times before it landed on its top. Five children and the driver were killed; many others injured. *The Clarion Standard* reported that the bus windows were blown out and the wind sucked the shoes off the feet of the kids. Children were catapulted from the bus through windows and some of the bodies were not discovered for hours. Books, lunch boxes, and shoes were found as far as twenty miles away.

Cars on open roads were swept up like toys and hurled across fences into pastures. On New Shiloh Road, one of the hardest hit areas, two children were seen running down the road toward their houses. They would be listed among the missing. The roof of the cotton gin was blown away and large pieces of tin flew across the sky and lodged into cows and horses, killing five. The funnel clouds destroyed one house and then jumped over another without even breaking a window.

Many houses were either badly damaged or completely destroyed. Barns were left without roofs. Silos were toppled, sending grains of corn flying into the sky like rain pellets. Stories were told about pieces of straw being driven like nails into telephone poles and trees. Power lines were lying across fences and roads, causing the whole town to lose electricity.

The tornado destroyed the house and barn of Charlie Parsons and killed his wife, Millie. They both had gone to the root cellar before the storm came, but Mrs. Parsons thought she had time to return to the house and get some picture albums she treasured. She was found near the back door where her body had been crushed by a dresser that had fallen through the ceiling from an upstairs bedroom.

No one knew how extensive the damage was or how many had been killed until the sheriff and a group of volunteers drove into the countryside looking for the injured, the dead, and the missing. Uncle John drove out to check on Granny Lee. There were two large trees down in the back of the house; one had missed the log cabin by no more than a few feet. Uncle John said Granny Lee was unharmed but she was still trembling as she told of watching the tornado move across Highway 64 toward the river.

Daddy made it back from Selmer about an hour after the storm had passed through. There was little damage along Main Street. Only a few trees were uprooted but limbs were strewn across the streets. He came home to make sure we were safe and then drove straight to the school to find Rue. As he passed by the churches, he noted with surprise that the only damage was a few broken windows.

The sheriff sent word that they were setting up a temporary morgue in the gym of the high school, where the bodies would be brought for identification. Daddy spent the evening at the gym comforting families who waited to see if their missing loved ones were among the dead. Watching the body of a child or adult brought in and placed on the floor and covered with a heavy black tarp was like nothing he had ever experienced.

Daddy was standing near the entrance drinking his third cup of coffee when a tall man dressed in overalls, a cotton shirt buttoned to the top, and muddy brogans, approached him. He looked familiar but in the dim light provided by lanterns and oil lamps, he couldn't see the man's face clearly. When he spoke, Daddy recognized the accent and knew it was Ollie Gustafson.

"Brother Turnage, I'm looking for one of my boys." He was fighting back tears and his voice trembled. "My neighbor saw him running down the road with another boy just as the storm came. We've looked everywhere but we can't find them."

Daddy knew they had been found. As he started to speak, Eric came over and motioned for his father to follow him. Daddy took Mr. Gustafson's arm and led him to the corner where earlier he had seen the bodies of the two missing children. Mr. Gustafson shook with grief and sobbed loudly as he pulled back the tarp to view the battered body of his ten-year-old boy. Eric helped his father up and they stood arm in arm for a long time. Looking at the other body, Mr. Gustafson realized it was the boy who had been with his son. He instructed Eric to find the parents and let them know where their boy was.

Daddy stayed with Mr. Gustafson until the undertaker came over to arrange for the body to be moved. He watched as they put him on a folding cot and carried him out the door. As they were leaving, Daddy saw a Catholic priest, who had driven from Florence, praying with a young couple as they knelt beside a small form at the other end of the gym.

Just after 11:00 P.M., the last identification was made. The Reverend Hezekiah Lacy came in with a member of his church who was looking for his little girl. The father was the caretaker of the cemetery, worked at the gin during cotton-picking season, and did odd jobs around town. He lifted the cover and wept along with Reverrend Lacy. She was no more than seven or eight years old and the only signs of injury were the blood and mud on her white dress. With the help of Reverend Lacy and Daddy, they

145

wrapped her limp body in a blanket and the man took her in his arms and carried her out of the gym.

Daddy sat down on a bleacher, put his head in his hands, and wept openly. After a few minutes, he felt a hand on his shoulder. He looked up and saw Maggie Townsend smiling down at him.

"You've done all you can do here tonight, Milton. Go home and get some rest. There are a lot of people who will need you tomorrow."

As he wiped his eyes, he hugged her and then walked to his car, unaware of the pouring rain.

On the way home, the thought of the harshness of such unnecessary suffering caused him to question why a loving God would allow it. As he turned over puzzling questions in his mind, he knew he must be prepared to help his congregation make some sense out of such hopelessness and despair.

Sixteen people had been killed—ten children and six adults. The community came together like never before. The Grange Hall was converted into a place where homeless families could come for food and shelter. All the churches prepared hot meals in their kitchens. Collection containers for clothing were placed in stores, churches, and the school. The Red Cross sent in doctors, nurses, and other volunteers to assist the victims. A special bank account was opened and people made donations to be used for rebuilding houses and barns.

Daddy visited distraught families, preached two funerals on Saturday afternoon, and prepared for two more on Monday. Millie Parsons' funeral was held at the funeral home and Daddy, much to his surprise, was asked to conduct the service.

We could not imagine how he found time to write a sermon for Sunday but he did and it was one of his best. On the glass-covered board in front of the church, Daddy's sermon topic was boldly announced: CURSE GOD AND DIE. The title shocked many people and, just as some came to find comfort, others came out of curiosity.

The text came from the Book of Job. "Man born of woman is of a few days and full of trouble. He springs up like a flower and withers away; like a fleeting shadow, he does not endure."

Daddy told the story of Job, a righteous man who had done nothing wrong, but was inflicted with great pain and suffering.

"Job was so distraught, he wished he had never been born, and as he questioned the unfairness of the calamities that befell him, his distraught wife encouraged him to curse God and die."

Daddy compared Job's suffering to what had happened in Adairsville. "Like Job, we have done nothing to deserve this tragedy. It was not God's will that nature suddenly turned into an untamed and unrestrained beast that killed men, women, and children and caused such unwarranted devastation."

He reminded everyone that good can come out of bad and quoted St. Augustine: "For the Omnipotent God . . . would not allow any evil . . . unless he is able to bring forth good out of it."

He said, "Just as Job refused to give up on God, even in the darkness of his hour of suffering, and would not heed the advice of his wife to curse God, we, too, must not give up.

"We must not lose faith because of unanswered questions. We must not allow the feeling of unfairness to nullify our belief in the goodness of God. We must not allow this experience to drag us into the depths of despair. We must use the pain and anguish and travail to strengthen our faith and create a greater dependency on God's grace and the comforting presence of his Holy Spirit."

Daddy concluded with the words of Job, who declared in the end: "I know that my Redeemer lives."

Granny Lee, who was in no mood to hear anything about a "storm that was predestined," skipped the service at the Presbyterian Church and came over to hear Daddy's sermon. After the service, she embraced my father and told him it was the finest sermon on the subject of suffering she had ever heard. *The Standard* printed excerpts, and papers as far away as Knoxville carried quotes from the sermon.

The people of Adairsville would rebuild their houses and barns; broken bones and scars would heal; their grief would be dulled; and life would eventually return to normal. What they could not do was replace the lives snuffed out on that terrifying day in April.

18

In the three weeks since the tornado, President Roosevelt had rationed meat, butter and cheese, and Gabriel Heatter was reporting on the radio that German troops were battering American tanks and infantry in Africa. Daddy was suffering from depression and a bad cold, but couldn't stop to rest because of his duties. Chairing a committee responsible for providing financial help to the families of the tornado victims was too important. He also couldn't get his mind off Ben Cowser and Lonnie Jackson.

"It seems as though everything is unraveling for Ben and his family," Daddy told Mother late one evening.

Ben had told Daddy that Robert Earl was being sent to a military school in Virginia.

"He needs to be in a place where they can deal with his temper and anger. Mildred and I have tried but we just can't handle him anymore," he said.

Lonnie Jackson was recovering at home and seemed to be doing very well for someone who had come close to being killed. The sheriff had called several times in the past two days to tell Daddy that everything was about to "bust loose" and he should be prepared for the worst.

After school, Wes and I had been working with Parker and his boys repairing fences and building a new pigpen. Parker was not the same. He didn't talk much and never laughed. The least little thing annoyed him, causing him to speak sharply to Seth and Amos, who seemed to be doing okay. But Wes said it would take a long time to get over losing a big brother like Euclid. Uncle John told us to just be patient with Parker. "In time, he'll be his old self." I hoped he was right but I had my doubts.

The town of Adairsville was no more prepared for what happened in the next few days than it had been prepared for the tornado. On Friday, bank auditors closed the bank, sealed all the files, and sent the employees home. A few hours later, the sheriff, accompanied by federal marshals, arrested Ben Cowser and charged him with bank fraud. According to *The Clarion Standard*, Mr. Cowser, accused of embezzling more than $25,000, had tried to cover the losses with forged documents of unsecured loans. The sheriff informed Daddy that the lock box where Ben said he kept the gold coins was empty. A local judge issued a warrant giving the sheriff and the federal agents permission to search "any and all properties belonging to Ben Cowser."

No money or coins turned up, but while searching the pickup truck, they found a lug wrench wrapped in a towel and lodged under the seat on the passenger side. After a careful examination, Agent Timmons commented that the lug wrench was stained with what appeared to be blood. The sheriff called Daddy and told him he would bet his last dollar that the blood was that of Junior Macgregor. High on a shelf in the garage, they also found an opened box of rat poison.

Daddy asked if it would be possible to see Ben at the jail. "Only if you can get by Mr. J. Leonard Driscoll," he said.

Driscoll had been retained several weeks ago by Mr. Cowser and was at the jail preparing a bond hearing.

"I don't think you're gonna speak to Ben Cowser any time soon," the sheriff declared.

"What did Ben say when you arrested him, Roy?" Daddy asked.

"He had tears in his eyes and all he would say is 'I'm innocent.'"

Daddy called to see if he could go over and visit with Mildred Cowser, but she would not come to the phone.

The maid said, "I'm sorry, Reverend Turnage, but Mr. Driscoll told her not to talk to no one and for me not to let anybody in this house without his permission."

Daddy was exasperated and more than a little testy. He was Ben and Mildred's pastor and wanted to help them during this difficult period in their lives. To be shut out by a lawyer, even if it was Leonard Driscoll, was more than he could bear.

"Roy, I want to talk to Leonard right now if he's still there," Daddy said in a voice expressing outrage.

The sheriff informed Daddy that Leonard was on his way to the courthouse to ask the judge to set bail and release Ben.

Mr. Joseph Murray, the district attorney, read the charges of bank fraud to the judge. He also stated that evidence had been found at Mr. Cowser's home that might call for other, and perhaps more serious, charges. Mr. Driscoll offered a plea of not guilty on behalf of Mr. Cowser and asked the judge to consider the reputation of his client in setting bail. The local magistrate took about two minutes to consider the arguments and set bail at $1,000. *The Clarion Standard* let it be known that they thought the bail was too low for such a crime.

Mr. Driscoll called Daddy from the Cowser house and apologized for not letting him see Ben.

"We'll work it out where you can visit with him and Mildred after I spend a little time with Ben. These are serious charges, Milton, and since you've been working with the sheriff on this case, I have to know what my client has done and give him my professional advice as to what he can and cannot say."

Daddy said he understood and just wanted to be there as their pastor and friend, not as an interrogator.

"I'll get back to you, Milton, I promise."

Mildred's eyes were red from too many tears and too little sleep as she greeted Daddy the next day. Daddy hugged Betty Lou and shook hands with Robert Earl, who had come home from the school in Virginia. They talked quietly as they waited for Mr. Driscoll to usher Daddy into the library where Ben was waiting.

He was dressed in casual slacks, a sports shirt, and a light cashmere sweater. He had not shaved and his hair was tousled. Daddy said later that he had never seen anyone in such anguish and torment. He was not the same Ben Cowser Daddy had known for five years.

He didn't get up, but shook Daddy's hand and said, "Sorry you have to see me like this, Milton, but I'm glad you're here."

150

Leonard Driscoll said, "Milton, I'm making an exception to my own rules about allowing a client to talk to anyone but me before trial. I want you to understand that whatever Ben says to you can't be used in court and cannot be used in testimony against my client. I think that's what they call confessional law."

"I understand," Daddy said.

The confessional law warning was unnecessary. Ben didn't say anything that explained what had happened or why he was accused of bank fraud. He talked about how sorry he was for anything he might have done to bring shame to his family and the community. He offered to resign as Sunday school superintendent until he could clear his name. Daddy said they could talk about that later.

"I just hope I won't be a disappointment to you, Milton. You've been a good friend and I'm grateful for your support."

Daddy was about to ask him about why the coins were missing and if he knew anything about the lug wrench, when Mr. Driscoll stood up and indicated that the meeting was over.

Ben lifted his hand to stop Driscoll, and said, "I've done some foolish things, Milton, but nothing like what they're accusing me of."

Daddy walked over to where Ben was sitting, put his arm on his shoulder, and prayed. Daddy said his good-byes to the family and left, wishing he could wake up and realize it was just a bad dream.

J. Leonard Driscoll defending Ben Cowser, Daddy thought as he drove away from the house.

"Now, that's an unlikely pair," he said to Uncle John later that evening.

Driscoll had the reputation as a brilliant lawyer with one of the finest legal minds in the region. His appearance, however, was not as tidy as his mind. Even his friends said that he could wear the best tailor-made suits from the finest stores and they would look like he slept in them. He had a shock of gray hair with locks falling down over his eyebrows. His vest pockets held a chain with a gold watch attached to one end and a Phi Beta Kappa key from Vanderbilt to the other. He kept a pair of glasses in his coat pocket but used them only for reading fine print.

Leonard Driscoll had joined his father's law firm soon after graduation and, after his father's death, had attracted a number of eager young lawyers who subscribed to the kind of law he practiced. Eighteen years ago, Mr. Driscoll went over to Dayton, Tennessee, and sat through the entire "monkey trial." The famous lawyer, Clarence Darrow, defended John Scopes, a biology teacher who was charged with teaching Darwinian evolution in violation of state law. The local prosecutor was assisted by William Jennings Bryan, a former presidential candidate known for his "cross of gold" speech and his conservative religious beliefs.

Driscoll loved to tell stories of sitting in the Rhea County courthouse in Dayton and watching these two giants go head to head. After witnessing Darrow's defense of a simple schoolteacher against a "stupid law," he decided that's the kind of law he would practice. He often took cases that other lawyers refused, either because they were unpopular or unrewarding financially. Like Darrow, Driscoll was an agnostic who had no interest in religious tenets and deplored fundamentalism of any kind.

The Clarion Standard ran a story that described him as having "a facile mind and a convincing presence." They noted that his ability to recall vital documents and tidbits of information during cross-examination was a rare gift. "No matter who makes up the prosecution team, they will find a formidable opponent in J. Leonard Driscoll," the story concluded.

Daddy understood why Ben had hired him; he just didn't understand why Leonard Driscoll would use his time and talent to defend a bank embezzler.

"Unless, of course, he thinks this is going to turn into a high-profile murder case with a highly respected community leader as a defendant," Daddy said, in a voice heavy with cynicism.

19

Two weeks later, *The Clarion Standard* ran the following headline: BANK PRESIDENT CHARGED WITH MURDER. The story reported what many people already knew. The F.B.I. lab report stated that the blood on the lug wrench matched that of Junior Macgregor's. It also revealed that a dealer in Nashville admitted to buying gold coins from Ben Cowser and paying prices far above the face value. Among the coins was a $10 Indian head gold piece.

According to the article, the prosecuting attorney released the following statement: "There is a preponderance of evidence pointing to the guilt of Mr. Ben Cowser. The lug wrench with the blood on it; the ten dollar gold coin; the paint from the rock, traced to Mr. Cowser's truck; and the rat poison used to kill Mr. Jackson's dog, are indisputable facts supporting a strong case of homicide. We are also sure that the depositions from interested parties will provide corroborative evidence establishing motive and circumstance. We will be asking the judge to revoke bail and incarcerate Mr. Cowser until the trial."

An emphatic plea of "not guilty" was once again entered on behalf of Mr. Cowser, as Leonard Driscoll ridiculed the prosecutor's statement and accused him of trying his client on court square before he'd been charged.

Judge Abner Tyler, the local magistrate, was in a difficult position. He was a personal friend of the defendant and knew if he ruled in his favor, it might eliminate him from being appointed presiding judge in the most famous trial of his career. He pondered the dilemma during a short recess and then ruled that bail would be set at $25,000.

"Preposterous," Driscoll bellowed. "He's a prominent member of this community, with no record of any misdeeds, and all the evidence presented in this indictment is circumstantial. I ask that bail be reduced to fit the situation, your honor."

Attorney Murray was on his feet as soon as Driscoll sat down. "I agree. It is preposterous, your honor. The defendant has been charged with murder and should be held without bail."

The judge listened patiently to other arguments for and against his ruling but refused the pleadings of both attorneys. Looking down at his calendar, he announced that the trial would begin on Monday, May 10th, at 9:00 A.M. Driscoll asked for more time but Judge Tyler renewed his earlier argument that "an early trial makes for speedy justice." The judge rapped his gavel and adjourned the court, not knowing that it would be his last ruling in this trial.

Daddy, Uncle John, and Mildred Cowser, who had been observing the proceedings from the spectators' area, went up to see Ben. Driscoll left them alone to visit while he talked to the court clerk about arranging bail.

Ben asked about Lonnie and said, "Milton, he doesn't think I had anything to do with that shooting, does he?"

Daddy assured Ben that the thought never crossed Lonnie's mind.

Uncle John said something like, "We're all pulling for you. You gotta hang in there and stay strong for yourself and your family."

The acting president of the bank arranged a loan that was secured by pledging the Cowsers' house and farm as collateral. Before the day was over, bail was posted and Ben went home. The sheriff, standing on the courthouse steps, watched Ben drive away in his fancy car. He stubbed his cigar on the concrete pillar and walked back to his office.

While all this was going on, Wes and I were trying to make the best of our school situation. Mr. Butterfield hadn't spanked anyone since the hearing and Miss Willie Maude was pretending she enjoyed her teaching and her students. We worried about how long this good fortune would last.

Wes and I spent Saturday afternoon watching our double feature and a chapter of a Red Ryder serial. After picking up the bulletins at the print shop, we went home to recreate the

154

world we had seen on screen and imitate our heroes. I didn't know that I was about to become the victim of a cruel joke by Wesley Turnage.

I strapped on my gun belt, holstered my cap pistol, and headed for the root cellar. Wes followed, wearing his creased straw hat. The root cellar was full of all kinds of vegetables in Mason fruit jars and labeled with a black pen. Mother, who was known for her fine sauerkraut, had the top shelf filled with jars of her secret recipe.

Cabbage was an important crop in West Tennessee, and farmers who were willing to set aside enough land for truck-farming, found it to be profitable but risky. Last year, buyers at the packing shed started off paying $120 a ton. Most farmers cut their crops as early as possible to get the best price. In a few weeks, the market was flooded and prices fell sharply. The Bryant Brothers, who were the largest local buyers and shippers, were luckier than other brokers in the area. When the prices starting falling, most of their cabbage was already in iced-filled freight cars on their way to northern markets.

Farmers who were not so lucky quit cutting and let the cabbage rot in the fields, or gave the surplus to the schools for their lunch programs. They also fed tons of the cabbage to their hogs until neighbors complained about the sudden aroma of methane gas that was making life unpleasant for chickens and humans.

Mother decided this would be a good time to make a lot of sauerkraut and store it in the root cellar. Wes and I had to go with Daddy to the cabbage shed and load several bushels into the car and unload them at our back door. We washed, cut the cabbage into wedges, and put them through a mill to produce thick strands. The cabbage strips were put into a large churn and covered with salt. The salt extracted the juice from the cabbage and produced a briny liquid which turned raw cabbage into sauerkraut. Before the war, kraut was sweetened by adding sugar, but with rationing, sugar could not be wasted on sauerkraut; therefore, the kraut was more briny and more sour than usual.

Two of Daddy's communion glasses, which looked just like the shot glasses used by cowboys in saloons in western movies, had been placed on a pretend bar made by putting a board across two barrels. I was surprised that Wes would be so bold. The communion glasses were kept in a silver tray in the cupboard next to the pantry. Daddy only brought the tray home from church to have the glasses washed.

The hero usually didn't drink, but the villain would walk up to the bar and ask for a shot of whiskey. The bartender would pour a drink into a glass and the cowboy would gulp it down with one quick motion. He would wipe his lips on his sleeve and say in a scratchy voice, "I'll have another one." That might go on for a while until the cowboy ran out of money or had to be carried out of the saloon.

Wes opened a jar of Mother's famous sauerkraut and strained the juice into an empty R. C. Cola bottle.

Wes said, "Okay, we're two cowboys at the bar having our shots of whiskey after a long day on the trail. I'll be the bartender."

He poured two glasses of kraut juice and said, "Down the hatch."

I gulped it down just like Bart Taggert had done in the movie that Saturday afternoon.

"Let's have another," Wes said as he filled the glasses.

I adjusted my holster belt and emptied the glass. After seven or eight glasses, I started feeling sick. Wes didn't seem to be affected by the salty brine and I soon found out why. There was a puddle of liquid on the dirt floor beside one of the barrels. It suddenly occurred to me that Wes had been pouring, but not drinking. He had been emptying his drinks on the ground while I continued to fill my stomach with kraut juice.

I was angry and upset but all I could think of was water. I went to the back porch and pumped water into a pitcher. Not bothering with a glass, I drank straight from the pitcher. I knew then I would never be able to look at another cabbage or stand the smell of kraut. I also knew that it would be a long time before I trusted my brother. It occurred to me that I could get even with Wes by telling Daddy we had used his communion glasses in our little pretend game, but the thought of that Turnage look and one of his lectures persuaded me to seek another means of revenge.

20

Judge Matthew Bascom, who was appointed by the circuit court to preside over the trial of Ben Cowser, called the court into session and instructed the attorneys and spectators on procedures and conduct in his courtroom.

Judge Bascom was a surprise selection because he was not usually assigned to rural courts. *The Clarion Standard* wrote that he "possessed one of the best legal minds among judges in the region." He was known for his sense of humor and a wit that sometimes sounded like sarcasm, but those who had been in his court knew he would not tolerate disruptions or shenanigans by attorneys on either side. He believed in decorum and civility, and could not abide lawyers who came into his courtroom unprepared. The judge, in his late fifties, had a white goatee and sported bright red suspenders under his robe.

Another surprise was the appearance of Mitchell Hancock, the leading criminal prosecutor in the attorney general's office in Nashville. He was there at the request of Joseph Murray, the local district attorney. Mitchell Hancock, born and raised in Asheville, North Carolina, graduated from Duke University and the University of Chicago Law School. After settling in Nashville, he became a member of the Davidson, Baker & Markham Law Firm, specializing in corporate and tax law, which he soon found to be boring. He left the firm and joined the attorney general's office, where he quickly established a reputation as the best prosecutor in the state of Tennessee.

In his late forties, he wore the finest tailor-made suits Nashville had to offer. His ties and shirts came from New York, his shoes from Italy. As an active member of the Episcopal Church in Belle Meade, he could use religion and piety effectively when it served his purposes.

When Jacob Yancey of *The Clarion Standard* asked Mr. Driscoll about his opponent, he replied, "I'm honored to be in the same courtroom with Mitchell Hancock. He's a worthy adversary and that's the way it should be. When a man is on trial for murder, the defense needs to be challenged to give due diligence in winning a clear verdict of not guilty."

Blond knotty-pine paneling defined the décor of the courtroom. The light coming through the tall windows created prisms that were stark contrasts to the dull light provided by the hanging chandeliers. The elevated area where the judge sat in a high-back swivel chair was, according to some attorneys, intimidating to the defendants and the jury. The court reporter sat just to the left of the judge, and the lawyers and defendant sat at two tables in front of the bench. There was a wooden rail separating the officials from the spectators. The jury box was situated under large windows and to the left of the bench. The room filled quickly and those who could not get in waited in the hall.

The Memphis Commercial Appeal, The Nashville Banner, and *The Jackson Sun* sent reporters to cover the trial. At the beginning and the end of the trial, there would be reporters representing large newspapers from as far away as Atlanta and Montgomery.

Jacob Yancey occupied a front row seat and brought along an artist to sketch faces for his paper, and a secretary whose shorthand would be translated each day to enrich the stories that appeared on the front page of *The Clarion Standard*.

Daddy sat with Uncle John near the back. Granny Lee, with her knitting needles and a small basket of yarn, was a frequent visitor. Mildred Cowser and Robert Earl sat in the front row behind Ben Cowser and the defense lawyers. Ben and Mildred often conversed during recesses.

Sheriff Perkins appeared as often as his duties would allow. He usually had a frown on his face and had to constrain himself during some of the testimony. Mayor Shipley and his brother Carl made appearances several times a week. Doc Townsend would appear as a witness, but not as a spectator.

Judge Mathew Bascom rapped the gavel and announced to the attorneys and the gallery that the court was in session and he was ready to hear opening motions before jury selection began. Mitchell Hancock made several attempts to get the trial moved to another county, but the judge denied the motions. In anticipation of the prosecutor's motion, *The Standard* had printed an editorial arguing against a change of venue because "people in this town are responsible and fair and will do their sworn duty."

There was a lengthy discussion about the rules of evidence and the legality of searches. The judge listened patiently and considered each argument from both sides before ruling that the evidence found in the search of Ben Cowser's house would be admissible and information about the missing coins in the lockbox at the bank could be presented. The judge noted three exceptions by the prosecutors to his rulings.

Selection of the jury began in the afternoon and, after two days of questioning by judge and attorneys, twelve jurors were chosen. Daddy observed that the prosecuting attorneys couldn't rule out everyone who had accounts at the bank because that would exclude just about everybody in the county. They did object to persons holding current loans from the bank and, of course, any close personal friends of Ben Cowser and his family. Among the jurors was a railroad ticket agent, a high school English teacher, a carpenter, the owner of the lumberyard, a tractor salesman, a cook at Mason's Grill, the supervisor of a new fabric mill, and several farmers.

In addressing the jurors, Mr. Driscoll spoke eloquently about Ben Cowser's background and his reputation as an outstanding citizen for many years. He pointed out the role of the bank in the life of the community and its contribution to sustaining a healthy economy during hard times.

"The policies of this bank under the leadership of Ben Cowser made it possible for the farmers in this community to hold on to their land and for merchants to expand their businesses during those perilous years following the depression," Mr. Driscoll said, as he stood directly in front of the jury box.

Mr. Cowser was portrayed as a Christian, a Mason, a Rotarian, and a loving father and husband. His virtues were extolled with just the right kind of emotion and sincerity. Mitchell Hancock remarked to a reporter that "the only thing they left out was his halo."

Mr. Driscoll spent a considerable amount of time pointing out that all the evidence was circumstantial.

"You have to look at these accusations with a great deal of skepticism. Ask questions in your mind about how conclusive these bits and pieces of so-called evidence are."

In conclusion, Mr. Driscoll said, "Does this sound like a man who would steal money from his own bank, cheat a poor man out of his inheritance, use a lug wrench from his truck to kill an innocent boy, and then put the wrench back where it could easily be discovered? When you look at this man, his family, and his character, you will have no choice but to find him not guilty of all charges."

The Standard wrote that the opening remarks were persuasive and presented a challenge to the prosecutors to prove their case. Daddy agreed with that conclusion.

Mr. Hancock used his opening statement to go over the evidence against Mr. Cowser. He calmly pointed out to the jury that the report of the bank auditors made it clear that money had been embezzled and that Ben Cowser was the recipient of the missing funds. He accused the defendant of taking advantage of Lonnie Jackson by giving him less than market price for the gold coins and then attempting to steal the other coins from Mr. Jackson's house. He reminded the jury that the paint scrapings from the rock and the rat poison used to kill the dog were not circumstantial. As he placed the lug wrench on the rail in front of the jury, he pointed to where the blood had been, and stated that the FBI lab had made a positive match with Junior Macgregor's blood. "That's not circumstantial. It's hard evidence," he said. He picked up the $10 gold piece from the table and showed it to the jury.

"If Ben Cowser did not kill Junior Macgregor, then how did this gold coin, given to Junior by Lonnie Jackson on the day he was murdered, get into the defendant's lockbox and eventually into the hands of a coin dealer in Nashville?" Mitchell Hancock asked, as he placed the wrench and coin back on the evidence table.

161

His final remarks surprised many in the courtroom, including the defense attorneys and Daddy.

"My colleagues have attempted to build their case on the defendant's reputation and a lack of motive. Members of the jury, the motive is apparent: greed. Ben Cowser needed money, lots of money. He stole from his own bank and from Lonnie Jackson. The motive for this heinous crime will become apparent as you listen to the testimony of the witnesses we present. Don't be misled by words like 'honor' and 'reputation' and 'religion.' The noblest of men can commit crimes. Church membership and Free Masonry do not preclude a penchant for deception and hypocrisy. Like the Pharisees in the New Testament, a man who displays his piety in public may practice deceitful duplicity in private. In addition, tendencies toward theft and violence are not limited to the poor, the unheralded, and the cautious. We will present our case and trust the good judgment of this jury to render a fair and impartial verdict."

An eerie hush fell over the courtroom as Mitchell Hancock sat down. By the accounts in *The Clarion Standard*, the jury and the spectators were clearly impressed with the lengthy opening statement of the prosecutor. The judge adjourned the court until Monday morning at 9:00 A.M.

"His performance attested to his reputation," Jacob Yancey wrote in an editorial about Mitchell Hancock.

Daddy was distressed by what he had heard and Uncle John said he was beginning to have his doubts about Ben's innocence. "Let's not jump to conclusions yet," Daddy said without much conviction.

Mother wanted to call Mrs. Cowser, but Daddy thought it might not be a good time. They sat on the porch and talked late into the evening. Wes and I heard every word, even the conversations that continued past our bedtime.

Daddy said, "I just can't imagine a man like Ben Cowser, with his upbringing and his ancestry, doing the things he's accused of. That's not the man I've known for these years."

About ten o'clock, we quietly crept from the front door to our bedroom. We hated to miss out on the discussions, but we had a big day ahead of us tomorrow and needed a good night's sleep.

21

Granny Lee arrived promptly at 9:00 to pick us up for our outing. Mother and Daddy trusted Granny Lee but were a little concerned about her driving record. The 1939 Ford coupe was the third car she had owned in four years. Several years ago, she ran into a light pole, cracking the radiator on her Plymouth, and casting Adairsville into darkness for several hours. Another time, she hit a galloping mule on Highway 64 and caved in the entire right side of the car. According to Granny Lee, the mule was stunned briefly but quickly recovered and galloped down the road braying loudly.

"It sounded like a victorious bray to me," she said, every time she told the story.

When Wes first heard the story, he said, "If that had been Daddy's mule, it wouldn't have made even a small dent in that car."

In spite of their concerns, Daddy and Mother were always pleased when Granny Lee included us in her trips. Today was to be a special treat because we were making our first visit to the button factory and would have a picnic lunch on the banks of the river.

We drove out Highway 64, crossed the Tennessee River, and, after making a gas stop in Savannah, headed up Highway 128 and took the ferry over to Clifton. On our way, we asked Granny Lee some questions about the trial. At first, she was reluctant to talk about it, not wanting to "spoil this special day."

After thinking about it for a few minutes, she finally said, "It's a very sad time for our town. We've walked through some dark nights lately and come out of our journey stronger and more

163

united as a community. But this trial casts a kind of shadow over everything that's decent and it's hard to see how any good can come of it. A strong sense of greed seems to be pervasive in that courtroom."

Wes and I decided to let it go and concentrate on buttons and guessing what goodies were in that picnic basket.

Granny Lee was very familiar with the town of Clifton. She made trips to the button factory often to pick up supplies for her weaving and jewelry-making. As we drove through the community, she brought the town to life with her stories and historical recitations. She told us how settlers had first come to the area in the early 1800s. The town's first name was Ninevah, taken from the Bible, but later was changed to Carrollville. When the residents moved to higher ground after the big flood of 1853, they called it Clifton, "a town set on high cliffs."

"The Civil War had a devastating effect on this whole area," she said, motioning with one hand.

She explained that most of the communities in Wayne County were loyal to the Union, but many of the people in Clifton allied themselves with the Confederacy. "The town was caught in the middle, which led to an unfortunate turn of events. The Tennessee River was used by both sides to move troops and supplies. Early in 1862, Union forces moved into Clifton and established a fort near where the ferry landing is today. The Union armies continued to occupy the town until the end of the war."

She told us that only four homes survived the war. As we passed the Presbyterian Church on Main Street, she pointed to it and said, "That's the only public building still standing from that period of history."

After the war, Clifton emerged as a strong river port, welcoming large steamboats and barges carrying cotton and timber. She related how Clifton faced some hard times when the roads were built and river transportation became less important.

"Then came the Depression and the town fell into further decline. Most of the clothing mills in the area closed and people fled to the cities to find work. But it was during these difficult times that Clifton achieved special recognition. A local writer, T. S. Stribling, won the Pulitzer Prize for literature for his book

The Store, a novel that painted an unflattering picture of the town of Florence, Alabama. The people in Florence were very upset with the book and refused to let it be placed in the library. Store owners returned their copies to the publisher. The local newspaper pointed out that "Stribling belonged to Clifton, not Florence."

She told of another famous person who had visited Clifton. "I'm sure you've heard of General Erwin Rommel, known as Hitler's 'Desert Fox,' and considered one of the great military leaders in Germany today."

Wes nodded, but the name meant nothing to me.

"Well, anyway," she continued, "rumor has it that he spent a night in Clifton's Russ Hotel in the 1930s while studying the military tactics of General Nathan Bedford Forrest."

Wes said, "Gosh, you mean a famous German general actually stayed in that old hotel we just passed?"

"That's why reading is so important. You never know what you're going to learn from the pages of a book," she said as she steered the car toward the countryside outside Clifton.

The button factory was an unsightly old building made of hand-made bricks fired in the sun and laid in a strange, uneven pattern. It dated back to the Civil War when it was used by the Union Army for manufacturing gun powder. The powder was packed in small wooden kegs and loaded on boats destined for army posts along the river.

After being abandoned for many years, the building was restored and converted into the Woodward Button Factory. It was open five-and-a-half days a week and employed thirty full-time workers trained in making buttons out of mussel shells. The building had only a few small windows, which might have allowed some outside light if they hadn't been covered with a heavy film of dirt. The large room was dusty, noisy, and had an unpleasant odor of dead fish. The room was filled with men and women who were working at strange-looking machines attached to work benches. Overhanging fluorescent panels provided the only light for the workers.

Just inside the door, a glass bowl filled with buttons of different sizes sat on a large table. Granny Lee went straight to the bowl and began sifting through them and placing her selections into a brown paper bag. She filled one bag and gave it to a clerk who weighed it and wrote the price on the side of the bag. Granny Lee explained that she used the buttons for decorations on scarves and shawls, and made necklaces by stringing the buttons on colorful threads. She told us that the buttons in the bowl were rejects and could be purchased for five cents a pound.

"They have flaws in them," she said, as she held one up to the light to demonstrate, "but that doesn't make them less pretty."

A young man with lots of facial hair came over to greet us.

"This is Joseph Woodward," Granny Lee said, as she introduced us. "He's the grandson of the founder of this button factory and I've asked him to give you boys a tour of the place and explain the art of button-making."

It was obvious that Granny Lee had planned this before we arrived. We were pleased and thanked her for this special treat. As we followed Joseph, I noticed that Granny Lee was running her fingers through another bowl of rejects.

Joseph had worked in the factory since he was a small boy. He told us about the history of mother-of-pearl button-making and how his grandfather and father had kept the factory going through good times and bad.

"At one time, we had almost a hundred people working in this factory. During the thirties, factories up north started making plastic buttons and that put a lot of pearl button-makers out of business. When the war started, plastic was needed for wartime projects, and that put the pearl button industry back in business," he said as he walked briskly across the floor.

At the back of the building, a separate room, enclosed by a cinder block wall, contained several vats heated by electric coils. Two men were shoveling mussels into them. Joseph explained that the heat in the vats caused the mussels to open. They were then transferred to a rotating steel drum called a shaker. The shaking forced the opened shells to drop their meat into a metal container. The meat was transported to a grist mill where it was crushed and used for hog feed. Joseph pointed out that some factories bought empty shells from fishermen who had set up camps along the Tennessee River and had their own steam vats and shakers.

"I prefer buying fresh mussels and processing them here, where I can be sure the shells are cleaned properly."

"How do the fishermen catch so many mussels?" Wes asked, as he stared at the large piles in the storeroom.

"At one time, my grandfather and father used divers to go down to the bottom of the river and fill sacks with mussels. But that was slow and dangerous. Some divers drowned and others died of snake bites," Joseph explained.

"Today, most fishermen use the brailing method," he said, as he pointed to a large picture of a mussel fishing camp.

Wes and I studied the picture and asked Joseph to describe the method. Using a large pen and some brown wrapping paper, he drew a sketch of a brail. It had poles rigged with short chains to which hooks were attached. The hooks had four straight prongs and each one had been shaped to form a small bead. The fishermen built long, flat-bottomed boats large enough to accommodate several brails and hold a ton of mussels. The brails were dropped over the side of the boat and dragged along the bottom of the river.

"For some strange reason, the mussels clamp down on those beaded heads and hold on for dear life," Joseph said, laughing.

He told us that a good mussel fisherman can tell when a brail is full by testing the weight of the attached rope. The brail is then pulled up, spread out on the boat, and the shells are picked off the hooks. As soon as one brail is pulled from the bottom, another one is dropped.

"How many mussels can you catch on one of those brails?" I asked.

"About three hundred fifty pounds," Joseph answered.

"Now that you know how we get the mussels, I want to show you how we turn them into gleaming pearl buttons," Joseph said, as he moved over to one of the machines.

"The pearl capital of the world is located in a little town in Iowa. There was a time when there were hundreds of button-making factories along the Mississippi. Since mussels were pretty scarce in that area, they used clam shells for their buttons. Most of the machinery we have here was manufactured in Iowa," he explained.

He then asked the worker to demonstrate the process. The worker pointed to several machines on the table and began to explain what each did.

He used a saw to cut round pieces from a shell. "These are called blanks," he explained.

He took the blanks and put them under grindstones, where depressions were made in each one. The blanks were then put in revolving kegs where they were sanded with pumice stone and water to smooth the rough edges. Next, they were ground to a uniform thickness and the shell's brown outer surface was removed. Finally, holes were drilled for the thread and the finished button was polished to a pearly sheen. The worker put the finished buttons into a box, passed them down the line where they were sorted, and checked for flaws.

Before shipping to stores, the buttons were sewn onto cards. Joseph reappeared and explained that sewing buttons on cards was a small cottage industry for local women who preferred to work at home.

"If you boys lived around here, you could make some good pin money by delivering the buttons and cards back and forth from factory to home," he said.

We watched as the workman continued to cut, polish, and drill shell blanks into shiny buttons. "Bet you never gave a thought to where those buttons on your shirt came from," the workman said.

"You're right about that," Wes said, speaking for both of us.

Granny Lee met us as Joseph led the way to the front of the factory.

"I guess you boys are thoroughly schooled in button-making, since you've had the best teacher in the business," she said as she reached out to shake Joseph's hand.

"It's been my pleasure, Alma. It's easy when you have good students like these youngsters."

Wes said, "I can't wait to tell Mr. Webb, my history teacher, about our visit. He'll probably ask me to write an essay and read it to the whole class."

I was tired, hungry, and feeling sick from the smell of dead mussels. I managed a smile and thanked Mr. Woodward, and said, "It's been great. Every time I look at a button, I'll think about mussel shells."

And, probably smell them too, I thought.

Granny Lee, not one to miss an opportunity to make a point, said, "Let's remember that everything God has put on this earth has a purpose, even the lowly mussel. You see, beauty almost always comes with sacrifice. The mussel dies in order for us to have beautiful pearl buttons."

Joseph was nodding, but I don't think he knew what she was talking about, and neither did I. I fingered the button on my shirt and wondered if those mussels thought the sacrifice was worth it.

We left the factory with a bag filled with buttons of different shapes and sizes, and some of the shell casings with holes where the blanks had been cut out. Mr. Woodward thought the "holey" shells would be of interest to students in Wes' history class. I just hoped they didn't smell up the car.

Granny Lee drove over to one of the highest points on the bluff and pointed to a large rock where we would spread our picnic lunch. Wes and I carried the picnic hamper and a jug of lemonade. Granny Lee had brought along several quilts and some small towels. She spread the quilts at the base of the rock and opened the basket.

"I'm starving," I said, reaching for a plate and fork.

We feasted on chicken salad spread on homemade bread, sweet pickles, grapes, chunks of goat cheese, fried sweet potato chips, stuffed eggs, and pecan pie. We washed it down with lemonade cooled by ice cubes donated by Joseph.

As we ate, we watched a barge filled with logs move slowly down the river. Granny Lee continued her history lesson. "In 1918, that river froze over and some folks walked on it and others drove horse-drawn sleighs across it."

I was constantly amazed at how much she knew and wondered how she could keep all these things in her head. When I asked her about it, she smiled and said, "When you get to be my age, it's easier to remember what happened a long time ago than it is to remember what happened yesterday."

She told us stories about the Indian tribes that had settlements along the river.

"The Shawnee, Chickasaw, and Cherokee fought over the rights to certain areas. One settlement of Shawnees was wiped out by scarlet fever brought in by the white man. The fever was known to Indians as 'the death of robes' because the disease was contracted from germs in blankets and robes traded by the white man.

"There is a legend about an Indian that lived along the banks of the river here. Members of his tribe had been killed by white traders and he declared war on all river travelers. According to folklore, he lived in caves along the bluff and would keep an eye out for flat boats as they came down the river. He ambushed them, killed the settlers, burned their boats, and stole their goods. The river became so unsafe for the travelers that the governor sent a small band of soldiers to capture him. When they failed to force him out of the caves, about one hundred soldiers were sent to find him. Finally he was captured and sent to a prison in Florida."

After we finished our lunch, we put away what few leftovers there were and Wes and I stretched out on the quilts. Granny Lee pointed to the river and told us to watch the movement of the current.

In a soft and dreamy voice, as if talking to herself, she said, "The river flows trustingly without being sure of its source or its destination. It can also be shallow or deep and it's hard to tell just by looking at it. That's kinda like life, isn't it? About the only thing we can control is the flow. We're on a strange and wonderful journey and we have the power go with the current or redirect it." She paused and stared across the water for several minutes.

"There's a lady who lives over in Tuscumbia," she continued, "who was born blind and deaf. Her name is Helen Keller. After years of struggle, she overcame her handicap and now travels the world over lecturing and raising money for many social causes. She wrote that we should use our eyes as if tomorrow we would be stricken blind, and we should hear the music of voices, the songs of the bird, the mighty strains of an orchestra as if we would be stricken deaf tomorrow."

Finally, she said with fervor, "My dear, dear children, don't ever settle for less than the best that's in you. Create your own

170

vision and let it determine your destination. Don't accept shallowness. Open your lives to knowledge and curiosity so that there is depth to your existence. Dare to be risk-takers. Pick your heroes carefully. Ask the right questions and examine the answers thoughtfully. If you're willing to search for truth, you'll find it. A famous poet wrote about choosing the road less traveled. Like him, I think that can make a difference." She looked away from us and appeared to wipe tears from her cheeks.

Wes sat quietly, staring down at the river. As I thought about what she had said today and all the other times we had been with her, I realized that I had learned more about living from Granny Lee than from all the sermons I had heard my Daddy preach. I felt guilty even thinking such thoughts, but I knew something special happened that sunny afternoon sitting on the banks of the Tennessee River, listening to this remarkable woman. It was a moment I would treasure for the rest of my life.

She suddenly turned to us and said, "Enough of that. I'm beginning to sound like a babbling old lady. This is the day the Lord has made, let's rejoice in it."

She started singing a song she had taught us and motioned for us to sing with her.

This little light of mine, I'm gonna let it shine.
This little light of mine, I'm gonna let it shine, let it shine,
    let it shine.

Then we sang all the verses of *"Would you like to swing on a star, carry moonbeams home in a jar."* As we sang, we listened to the echo bounce off the granite wall across the river.

After we packed the car for the trip home, she walked over to the edge of the bluff and picked some wildflowers, and made a bouquet out of daffodils and bluebells. We didn't ask and she didn't say what she intended to do with them.

"You should've been a teacher, Granny Lee," Wes said as we drove onto the ferry.

"Or maybe a preacher," I said.

Wes retorted, "I've never heard of a woman preacher, have you?"

171

Granny Lee ignored the question about preachers, but said, "Well, I think of myself as a teacher. Although I don't have a classroom and chalkboard, I have many students."

When we crossed over the bridge from Savannah, Granny Lee turned the car onto the dirt road that led to the place where Junior had died. Without saying a word, we got out of the car and walked over to the edge of the water. Granny Lee tied the bouquet to a tree limb with a red ribbon. I wiped tears from my eyes. Wes turned away to hide his. Granny Lee did not speak. She hugged us and we walked arm in arm to the car and headed for home.

During dinner, Wes and I told Mother, Daddy, and Rue all about the things we had seen and heard that day. They asked lots of questions and shared our excitement about the day's adventures. There was also unspoken relief that we got home safely.

I was tired and looked forward to crawling into the covers and recalling the events of the day before going to sleep. Instead, I fell asleep almost immediately and entered into a sequence of unpleasant and frightening dreams. I dreamed I was a mussel scurrying around in the murky waters of a river, but I didn't look like the mussels we saw in Clifton. I had a tail and fins and was a swift swimmer. Whenever I heard the dragging of a brail along the bottom, I rushed ahead to warn the other mussels.

I yelled, "The brailers are coming. The brailers are coming. Don't be tempted to bite the hooks. Swim as fast as you can away from the barbs."

Most paid no attention as they innocently attached themselves to the moving brail. When I looked up through the murky water, I could see that one of the fishermen was Mr. Cowser.

A big catfish that looked a lot like Wes swam by and told me not to bother with those stupid mussels.

I cried, "But they don't understand, they just don't understand. They have a choice. They don't have to become buttons; they can live and die as mussels, not shells punched full of holes." Frustrated, I went looking for Granny Lee, but before I could find her, I woke up.

As I lay there, unable to sleep, many things passed through my mind. Whenever I closed my eyes, images seemed to dance in front of me—images of moving currents, Indians hiding in caves, mussels being steamed in a vat, a blind woman in Alabama, and a bouquet of daffodils and bluebells hanging from a tree. The last thought I had before falling asleep again was a prayer.

I said silently, "Please God, don't let me ever do anything to disappoint Granny Lee."

22

Because of extensive newspaper coverage of the tornado and the trial, Daddy had acquired a small amount of fame and was invited to speak to a number of civic and church groups in the region. He also had met with several county ministerial associations to discuss the church's role in meeting unexpected disasters. Today, he was speaking to the Rotary Club in Jackson and would miss the trial.

He called Uncle John and invited him to come over in the evening for dinner and fill him in on the day's testimony. What Uncle John reported was not what Daddy wanted to hear.

Judge Bascom called the court to order at 9:00 A.M. and Mitchell Hancock called his first witness, a federal bank examiner. The examiner testified that more than $25,000 in missing funds had been traced to Ben Cowser. The "paper trail" showed that false accounts had been set up using fictitious names. Mr. Cowser approved unsecured loans, transferred the money to a special account in a Nashville bank, and withdrew money with counter checks when he was in Nashville. Other times, money was wired from the Nashville account to his personal account in Adairsville.

J. Leonard Driscoll tried to elicit testimony from the examiner that would cast doubt on these allegations, but he did not succeed. The evidence for embezzlement was overwhelming and it appeared that Mr. Driscoll already knew it.

The prosecution then called three witnesses, officers in banks in Nashville, Atlanta, and Birmingham, who established the motive for Mr. Cowser's theft. They had become reluctant witnesses after subpoenas were issued. The banker from Nashville admitted to opening a special account for Mr. Cowser, and personally cashing counter checks and wiring funds. All three testified that playing poker was a favorite pastime of bankers at regional and national meetings.

They had become friends of Ben Cowser and played poker with him on many occasions. One recalled that Ben was a big loser over a period of several years.

"He was not very good at poker and didn't know when to walk away."

The three witnesses stated that they didn't know exactly how much Ben had lost but agreed it was in the thousands.

The banker from Georgia said, "Sometimes these games went on all night and the stakes were high. I know he was concerned about the amount of money he was losing, but he just couldn't quit. Ben was a habitual gambler and often talked about the excitement of trying to beat the odds. He bet on dog races, sports, elections, and anything else where there was a taker."

Another witness stated that Ben's friends were concerned about him because they knew "he had a psychological need to bet. He was seriously addicted to gambling."

Mr. Driscoll objected loudly, asking if the witness had a degree in psychiatry. The judge sustained the objection and asked the jury to disregard the remark.

The defense counsel pounded away at the three witnesses, challenging their credibility. He asked questions like: "If you were so concerned about Ben's welfare, why didn't you stop playing poker with him? Did Ben ever tell you he was stealing money from his bank to cover his losses? Was he the only big loser?" And the final question put to each witness: "Did you embezzle money in order to pay your gambling debts?"

Driscoll knew the answers to all of these questions, but wanted the jury to hear them from the witnesses. One of the bankers wept as he explained how his life would be ruined by his appearance as a witness.

"In spite of a good cross-examination," Uncle John said, "it was obvious to everyone in the room that Ben had a gambling problem and needed extra money to cover his debts."

The next witness was the coin collector from Nashville who testified that he had bought gold coins from Ben Cowser.

"That's what I paid Mr. Cowser for the coins," he said, pointing to a stub in his receipt book. The figure was $5,000.

"And what was the face value of those coins, sir?" Mr. Hancock asked.

"Four hundred and seventy dollars," the dealer answered.

There was a quiet, but obvious, stir among the spectators. One juror jotted down something on a piece of paper.

"And did you find among those coins this ten dollar Indian head gold piece?" Mr. Hancock asked, as he held up a plastic bag with the coin in it.

The dealer examined the coin and answered, "Yes, that looks like the one in the collection. I remember it because it's a rare coin and is in very good condition."

The prosecutor reminded the court and the jury that this coin was exactly like the one Lonnie Jackson gave to Junior Macgregor.

Driscoll did not spend much time with the witness. He asked if there was any doubt in the dealer's mind that Ben Cowser was the person who sold him the coins. The dealer, glancing at Mr. Cowser, answered that there was no doubt.

"Did Mr. Cowser tell you where he got the coins?" Driscoll asked.

"No sir, I didn't ask and he didn't tell me. But he didn't look like someone who came by them dishonestly."

"Your honor, please . . . ," Driscoll sighed.

"The jury will disregard the last statement. Just answer the questions, sir. We don't need opinions," the Judge admonished.

"How many coins do you handle in a period of say, six months?" Driscoll asked.

"I'm not exactly sure. Maybe fifty, maybe more," he said.

"And in your dealings, have you ever run across another ten dollar Indian head gold coin like this one?" Driscoll asked, pointing to the cellophane bag.

The dealer seemed unprepared for the question and hesitated before speaking. "Yeah, about two years ago a coin similar to that one came into my possession."

Mr. Driscoll probed further. "And if I showed you that coin today would you be able to distinguish it from the one in that bag?"

"Not if they were both in the same condition," he said, as he shifted in his chair and glanced over at Mr. Hancock.

"Thank you. I have no further questions of this witness," he said, looking at the jury as he walked away from the witness box.

The final witness was Lonnie Jackson. The spectators and the jury watched with curiosity as he walked slowly, dragging one foot, to the witness chair. For many in the room, this was their first look at the strange and mysterious man. It was apparent to them how he had acquired his nickname.

A tweed jacket covered an opened-collared, blue denim shirt. His tan trousers were cuffed just above the tops of his brogans. If he was nervous, he didn't show it. His dark eyes were piercing and his face stern as he placed his hand on the Bible and took the oath.

Lonnie's testimony was no different from what he had related to Daddy and the sheriff several months ago. He told of how he exchanged the coins for dollars so he could purchase food and other things from local merchants without arousing suspicion.

Mr. Hancock, trying to get Lonnie to impugn Ben Cowser's reputation, stated, "He sold your coins for more than ten times what he paid you, Mr. Jackson. Doesn't that make you angry?"

"No, it don't. As far as I'm concerned he was fair and square with me. Mr. Cowser has always been good to me and was a friend to my mother," he said, without any resentment.

When Mitchell Hancock realized that Lonnie wasn't going to say anything against Mr. Cowser, he ended his examination.

Leonard Driscoll surprised everyone with his first question. "Now Lonnie, I want you to look closely at this ten dollar coin and tell me if this is the one you gave Junior on the day he was killed."

Mitchell Hancock stood as if to ask a question, or make an objection, but did neither.

Lonnie took the coin from the bag, looked at it carefully, and said, "Well, it looks like the one I gave Junior but I can't say for sure."

Mr. Hancock jumped up and said, "Your honor, this is exactly like the coin Mr. Jackson described on two occasions to the sheriff and Brother Milton Turnage."

177

The judge fiddled with a paperclip and leaned forward in his chair to ask Hancock if there was an objection or question in his statement. Mr. Hancock, bewildered and speechless, sat down.

Leonard Driscoll smiled at Lonnie Jackson and asked, "Now, how do you suppose a coin that's so much like the one you gave Junior got into the hands of Mr. Cowser?"

Lonnie leaned forward, shifted his body to one side, and put his hands on the rail. Looking up at the late afternoon rays coming through the windows, he stared for a moment at Mr. Cowser and then the jury.

Finally he said, "I really don't know. I can only guess that I had two of those coins and I traded one to Mr. Cowser and gave the other to Junior."

Mitchell Hancock was on his feet, but the judge motioned him to sit down until Mr. Driscoll finished his inquiry.

"One final question, Mr. Jackson," Driscoll said as he stood in front of the jury box, "do you have any idea who shot you?"

Lonnie did not hesitate. "No sir, I don't, but I know it wasn't Mr. Cowser, if that's what you're asking."

Driscoll thanked him and said he had no other questions.

Mr. Hancock was on his feet asking for time for rebuttal questions. The judge nodded approval.

"Did you tell the sheriff and Brother Turnage back in November and again more recently that the 1907 ten dollar gold coin you gave Junior had an Indian head with stars on one side and an eagle on the other and underneath were the words 'E Pluribus Unum?' "

For the first time, Lonnie Jackson smiled as he answered, "Can't be sure I used all them big words, but if Brother Turnage says I did, then I did."

Taking the coin out of the bag again, he held it before Lonnie and asked, "Please describe this coin to the jury. Tell us everything you see on the coin."

Lonnie gave a detailed description of the coin, stumbling over the Latin words.

"That's a strange coincidence, isn't it Mr. Jackson? That's just the way you described the coin you gave to Junior," he said.

He paused and then said, "One more question. You testified today that Mr. Cowser didn't shoot you. Other times, you have stated that you didn't see the person who shot you. If you didn't see that person, then how are you so sure it wasn't Ben Cowser?"

Leonard Driscoll was on his feet, but before saying anything, Hancock said, "Withdrawn. No further questions."

Lonnie heaved a sigh of relief as he left the courtroom.

It was almost four o'clock and the judge announced that no other witnesses would be called today, and court would reconvene at 10:00 A.M. on Tuesday. After dismissing the jury, the judge requested a meeting in his chambers with the prosecuting and defense attorneys and Mr. Cowser. Court adjourned. Uncle John hung around the courthouse for a while, but was not able to find out why the judge requested the meeting.

After dinner, Uncle John, Daddy, and Mother went to the porch to continue their discussions of the events of the day. Sheriff Perkins drove up, got out of his car, and ambled up the side yard chewing on an unlit cigar.

"Looks like you folks didn't wait dinner for me," he said, laughing.

Mother said she might be able to find a piece of fried chicken or two.

"Just kidding," he said as he sat down on the steps, "but I sure could use a cup of coffee if you have any left over."

Mother went to the kitchen to get the coffee and added a fried apple pie.

"Speaking of coffee," the sheriff said, "I was sitting at the counter in the café the other morning having a cup when Pauley Caruthers came in and sat down next to me. Before he said anything, Ellie Mae came over and put something in front of him, and said, 'Here's your coffee—it's already been saucered and blowed.' Pauley picked up the saucer and started slurping his coffee. I had to move to the end of the counter to get away from him and what sounded like a cat lapping up milk."

Uncle John laughed and said, "Always wondered about Pauley. Never thought he had both oars in the water, especially after they found all those cats living with him in that shack of his."

179

As Mother returned with the coffee and pie, Sheriff Perkins said, "Well, he might be smarter than we think. Maybe he just wanted the taste of Ellie Mae's hot breath in that coffee."

Mother said, "Now Roy, watch your mouth. There's a lady and some children present."

I covered my face with a comic book and giggled. Wes punched me in the ribs with his elbow.

After some discussion of our trip to the button factory, Daddy asked the sheriff what he thought about today's testimony at the trial.

"Well, Milton, Ben looks like a fellow who fell out of a big tree and hit every branch on the way down," he said, sipping coffee and savoring the pie.

Uncle John agreed. "I'm not a lawyer, but I'm convinced that the money supported his gambling habits. And him a Sunday school superintendent and all," he said disgustingly.

Daddy frowned and slumped in his chair. "It's hard to believe. This just doesn't make any sense. And I thought I was a good judge of character. But I have to view this as some kind of sickness, something he can't control."

Ignoring Daddy's effort to find an excuse for Ben, Mother said, "How could he do this to his family?" It was more a statement than a question.

Several minutes of silence followed as there seemed to be a desire to change the subject.

Sheriff Perkins finally spoke up and said, "Well I'm proud to say, I cleaned up one mess in our community today."

"If it's good news, I sure would like to hear it," Uncle John said with a sigh.

The sheriff began telling about the pretty ladies who arrived unannounced in Adairsville a few months ago.

"Those ladies, dressed in fancy clothes and wearing broad-brimmed hats, just stepped off the train one day and sashayed over to a Chrysler station wagon that belonged to Billy Ray Plunkett. Word spread pretty fast and I got a call saying the ladies had moved into one of those shotgun houses out by the new clothing factory."

Mother seemed a little uneasy about where this conversation was going and suggested to Wes and me that we needed to

180

get started on our homework. I reminded Mother that we finished our homework before supper.

"I'm sure you have some chores to do before bedtime," she said firmly.

Wes and I moved from the porch to the living room where we sat by the open window and listened.

The sheriff continued. "I went over to the pool hall and had a man-to-man talk with Billy Ray. I told him what I had heard about the ladies and wanted him to understand that I had my suspicions about why they were here and I intended to keep an eye on them."

"And what did Billy Ray say about that?" Uncle John asked.

He said, "Roy, I'm surprised at you. These fine ladies came here from Memphis looking for good honest work in the mill. We're gonna see a lot of folks coming in from outside now that the factory is up and running."

"So I asked Billy Ray when he started working for the chamber of commerce. He just laughed and said he'd always been a civic-minded citizen," the sheriff said with a chuckle.

"I told Billy Ray that if I ever drove by that house and saw more than two cars parked there, I would be more than a little concerned about what was going on inside," the sheriff said.

With that, Mother left the porch and went to the kitchen to help Rue with the dishes.

"So the rumors were true," Uncle John said with a sly grin.

The sheriff went on to tell how he had gone out on Saturday night and found three cars parked in the drive and four out on the road.

"They had license plates from Alabama, Mississippi, Georgia, and one from Tennessee and they weren't looking for mill jobs," he said.

"I got one of my deputies out of bed and had him come to the house. Before we knocked on the door, we turned on our blue lights and wailed the siren a time or two. You should've seen the commotion. Men were scurrying out the front and scampering out the back, and, one of 'em, trying to climb out of a window, fell on the ground like a rock. It was a sight to see."

The sheriff said they found almost a hundred dollars in cash and some other items he'd rather not mention.

181

"The ladies were arrested and became guests of the county over the weekend. I escorted them to the train today, gave them some of their hard-earned money, and sent them back to Memphis," he said triumphantly.

"With the way my luck's running, I'm surprised they didn't claim to be Methodists," Daddy said with a smile.

Daddy and Uncle John complimented the sheriff on ridding the community of these "painted ladies," as Uncle John put it. They also suggested it might be a good excuse to rid our fair town of the notorious pool hall.

"Gosh," I said to Wes, "what in tarnation did those women do to deserve to be treated like that?"

Wes said I was too young to understand.

"Someday, I'll draw you a picture," he said impatiently.

I didn't want a picture; I just wanted to know what a "painted" lady was. And the more I thought about it, the more I was sure Wes didn't know either.

23

The court opened on Tuesday at 10:00 A.M. as announced, and no one, including Jacob Yancey of *The Clarion Standard*, was expecting what they heard. Judge Bascom called the court to order and stated that he had an important announcement to make. He adjusted his glasses and began reading from a piece of paper.

"After the court adjourned yesterday, all parties involved in this case met in my chambers to discuss a plea bargain. With the concurrence of the prosecutor's office and under the advisement of Attorney Leonard Driscoll, Mr. Cowser has agreed to plead guilty to bank fraud and embezzlement. These charges will be removed from the indictment and the accused cannot be questioned further about these matters. Appropriate sentencing will be made at a later date.

"The only thing before this court now is the charge of second degree murder against Ben Cowser. I realize this appears to be somewhat unconventional, but precedents support it. Both attorneys have agreed to abide by the ruling and not use it in any appeals that might be forthcoming. I have instructed the jury to accept this ruling without prejudice. In other words, they have been told that this separation of charges in no way reflects on the guilt or innocence of the accused with regard to the charges of the murder of Junior Macgregor. Counsel from both sides have requested a delay in the proceedings in order to review the case under these new exigencies and prepare accordingly. Therefore, I'm recessing the court until next Monday at 9:00 A.M., at which time Mr. Hancock will present his witnesses. Court is adjourned."

Jacob Yancey, his stenographer, and sketch artist were the first out the door. This would be the front-page story in tomorrow's *Standard*. Daddy and Uncle John made their way to the front of the room and spoke briefly to Mr. Cowser. Mrs. Cowser was in tears and unable to talk.

Uncle John reported that Robert Earl was confused and said tearfully, "Daddy, don't let them do this to you . . . to us . . . "

After Ben and his family left the courtroom, Leonard Driscoll approached Daddy and handed him an envelope.

"Milton, Ben wanted me to give you this letter."

Daddy put it in his pocket and, with sadness in his voice, asked, "Leonard, how does it look? Tell me honestly what you think about his chances now."

Mr. Driscoll was not a man to mince words or sugarcoat bad news. "He didn't do it, Milton, and it's my job to convince those twelve men that he didn't. This recess will give me a little more time to prepare a defense that will prove his innocence. It's not going to be easy but you know I'll give it my best."

At one time, Daddy hadn't felt comfortable around Mr. Driscoll but couldn't explain why. Today he trusted him and believed Ben was in good hands.

When Daddy was alone, he read Ben's letter. It was heartbreaking. Ben apologized for the shame he had brought on his family, the community, and the church. He wrote about his gambling addiction and the efforts that he had made over the past two years to overcome it.

"You've been a good friend and I've let you down, and that's one of the hardest things I have to live with," his letter stated.

He said he was resigning as Sunday school superintendent but hoped his family would still be welcome in church.

"And believe me when I tell you that, as God is my witness, I know nothing about the murder of Junior or the shooting of Lonnie Jackson. I've done some bad things, but I never could do anything like that.

"In closing, I've prayed for God's forgiveness and now I ask for yours. Please continue to be a pastor to my family. They need you and I need your friendship and counsel more than ever."

He signed it, "My regards to your wonderful family. Ben."

A watermark appeared on the letter. A tear that ran down Daddy's cheek and fell onto the paper formed it.

On Thursday, Mother and Daddy went over to visit with the Cowsers. Mother took them an angel food cake and some beef stew. Daddy told us when he returned that it was a good visit and they seemed to be holding up well. He said he told Ben how much he appreciated the letter and assured him that he would always be his friend and pastor. When Wes asked about Robert Earl, Daddy said he wasn't there.

Mother said, "I asked about him, but Mildred said he had gone out for a while. I had the impression that Robert Earl didn't want to see us."

I mentioned to Daddy that school would be closed Thursday and Friday next week for a teacher's conference and wondered if we could go to the trial with him. Daddy said he would give it some thought and let us know.

On our way home from school, Wes and I went by Jordan's Creek for a quick swim. We swung on the rope a few times before dropping into the chilly water. We shivered as we dried off with our shirt and put on our clothes. We decided to wait until warmer weather to do any more skinny-dipping.

When we got home, Rue told us that Parker was looking for us and wanted us to meet him in the orchard. Grabbing a couple of cold biscuits and a sugar cookie, we hurried across the road to find Parker. Seth and Moses were chasing butterflies with a fishing net.

Parker was in good spirits and called out to us as we approached. "What you boys been up to lately?" he said, laughing the way he used to.

Wes told about visiting the button factory with Granny Lee.

"Now, there's one smart lady," Parker said, as he picked up a bag of tools.

I told Seth and Moses about stopping by Jordan's Creek for a swim and almost freezing to death.

"It's too early for swimming. You get chilled like that and it can make you real sick," Parker said.

Parker then told us he needed our help to do some spring pruning. He put a ladder up against one of the apple trees and tied a tool belt around his waist. He explained that pruning was

necessary to keep the trees healthy so they would produce lots of apples. Parker began teaching just as he did at hog-killing.

"Before you start cutting on a tree, you've gotta think about what's helping the tree grow and produce and what's not. And you have to use sharp tools so you get clean cuts. Cause if you don't, you can do a lot of damage."

He took out his shears and began clipping small limbs and nipping at shoots. He told us our job was to pick up the branches and shoots and take them to the end of the orchard for burning later. "If you leave that stuff on the ground under the tree, the bugs and insects will use them for breeding and soon they'll be right back up in this tree."

We watched as he used his tools to cut out the broken limbs, suckers, and top branches.

As he threw down a large branch, he said, "You gotta make sure that all the branches of the tree get some sunlight, and that's why I cut out some of these limbs at the top. They're keeping the sun from getting to the other branches and that ain't good. You see, we're not growing shade trees; we growing apple trees," he said, laughing.

We followed along, gathered up the cuttings and hauled them to the edge of the orchard. We were looking forward to a big bonfire. After Parker had pruned about a dozen trees, we quit for the day. Parker asked if we could come back on Friday and help him finish the job.

"Mr. John will make it worth your time," he said, as he poured kerosene over the pile and lit it.

Even though it was spring, there was a chill in the air and the warm fire felt good to our bones.

Wes began sneezing and said he was still cold from the swim. I said I would fetch Moo Moo so he could go home and get warm. When I got home, Wes was stretched out on the couch with one of Granny Lee's afghans pulled up under his chin. Mother came in, inserted a thermometer under his tongue, and waited a few minutes before removing it.

"That's what I thought," she said, studying the instrument. "You've got a fever."

She felt his forehead and then had Wes open his mouth so she could look down his throat.

187

"Gosh," I said, "you think that cold water in Jordan's Creek did this to you?"

Wes didn't answer but gave me that Turnage stare. If Mother heard me, it didn't seem to be a matter of importance to her. I stood looking down at Wes and realized for the first time how much he looked like Daddy, especially when he was irritated.

Daddy was late getting home for supper and looked tired. He'd had a funeral in the early afternoon and had to go to Saltillo for the burial. He went into the living room and talked to Wes for a few minutes. Mother told him about the fever and suggested that Doc Townsend might want to take a look at him if he wasn't feeling better tomorrow.

After supper, we sat around the radio listening to the news, and then two of our favorite programs—*Jack Benny* and *Lum and Abner*. The news about the war made Daddy feel better.

"It's encouraging," was his reaction to Edward R. Murrow's commentary.

Rue came in from the kitchen and asked if she could listen to some music while she did her homework. I was sure it wouldn't be the kind of music I liked, so I went to the bedroom. Wes had already put on his pajamas and was propped up in bed reading a book. I slumped in a chair by the window and read the newest edition of *Captain Marvel*.

Wes was feeling worse the next morning and didn't go to school. His temperature was above 101 and he had no appetite. Mother sent Daddy to the drugstore for some cough medicine and aspirin and then called Doc Townsend.

"Just keep him warm and have him drink a lot of liquids," he said.

Liquids in our house meant milk, so Daddy had to go to the grocery store for some orange juice and soda pops. When I heard about this, I suggested kraut juice. Mother was puzzled by the idea and Wes was not amused.

After school, I worked with Parker and his boys picking up more branches and limbs for the bonfire. Parker told me that he had just the thing that would make Wes feel better, but he was sure "Brother Turnage wouldn't take too kindly to the idea."

Seth said, "When I have a cold or cough, I take Daddy's toddy and it sure makes me feel better. I just sleep and sleep."

Parker laughed and clapped his hands together. I thought about sneaking some of that toddy in and serving it to Wes in one of those communion glasses. On the other hand, maybe I should drink some of it to help me sleep now that Mother had moved me to the couch.

"You don't need to be sleeping in the same room with Wes. What he's got is contagious and I don't need both of you sick at the same time."

On Saturday, I rode the bicycle over to Granny Lee's house to help get her garden patch ready for seeding. I pulled up vines and stalks from last year's garden and raked the dirt smooth. Out behind the toolshed, Granny Lee always started building a compost pile in the fall with leaves, pine mulch, cow manure, and lime. During the winter, she put all the garbage that would disintegrate on top of the heap and turned it with a pitchfork about once a month. From time to time, she would add more manure and bags of phosphate. Although it put out an unpleasant odor, it was, in her opinion, the best natural fertilizer for a vegetable garden. She called it "organic fertilizer." It was the first time I'd ever heard that word.

With a pitchfork, I filled the wheelbarrow with compost, hauled it to the garden area, and dumped it in a pile. With shovels and rakes, we spread it until it covered the ground where her vegetables would be planted. She showed me a sketch where she had carefully laid out a plan for this year's garden. I smiled as I looked at it and wondered if Mother had ever thought of doing this.

Granny Lee's detailed plan revealed the location of every vine and stalk and stake for each vegetable. There were places for tomatoes, peas, cucumbers, radishes, pole beans, okra, Irish potatoes, and carrots. Over behind the old barn, she planted corn, cantaloupes, squash, and peanuts. In the potting shed, she had already filled stone jars with the seeds that would grow into fragrant plants for her herb garden.

"In Scotland, gardens were essential to survival. It took a lot of canning to get you through those long winters. Momma told me how families lived all winter off the food grown in the fields and gardens. I know I don't have to do that now, but I still like the independent feeling it gives me," she explained.

"Mother says she just likes to make things grow," I added.

"Your Mother has what they call a green thumb," she said, as she held up her hand. "You know what that is, Vance?"

"Yep," I said proudly, "It means you can grow just about anything you want to grow without much effort."

I knew I didn't have one and that was okay because I liked gardening about as much as I liked hoeing cotton.

We walked over to the strawberry patch and, as we pulled up some weeds, Granny Lee checked out the berries and snipped some suckers. There were large berries on every vine and they were beginning to show some color.

"Yep," she said, "they're going to be ripe and juicy for the festival next weekend. If you and Seth can come out on Friday and help me pick, I should have several crates ready for the bazaar on Saturday."

"Since there's no school on Friday, I'll be out early in the morning."

Granny Lee was concerned about Wes and said she would come for a visit on Sunday afternoon and bring her homemade fever remedy.

When I asked if it was like Parker's toddy, she laughed and said, "I think Parker might have some special ingredients in his that I don't use."

She said hers was a mixture of raw honey, lemon juice, vinegar, and a variety of dried herbs.

"Never fails," she said confidently.

"I have something else that will make him feel better," she said, as she took something from a piece of brown paper. "It's a sassafras root for tea. Your Mother will know what to do with it. Tell her to put in lots of honey after boiling the root."

Mother fixed the hot tea with honey and Wes drank it without complaining, although he said he'd rather have hot chocolate. I told him about my visit with Granny Lee and helping her spread that smelly compost pile. Wes smiled and said he remembered from last year. He was pleased when I told him that she was coming over tomorrow. I could tell he didn't feel like talking any more, so I left and went to the front yard to practice a new trick, called "Rock the Cradle," with my Duncan Yoyo.

Uncle John came across the road to ask how Wes was feeling.

"Tell him I've got a strong recipe that will get rid of that cold."

"That wouldn't be Parker's recipe, would it, Uncle John?"

He laughed and said, "Parker done gone and spoiled my fun. You tell your Daddy that I'm looking forward to our chess game tonight. I'll expect him about seven o'clock."

The Saturday night chess game had become a tradition. Daddy said it relaxed him and relieved some of the anxiety that he always had on the eve before Sunday.

We never asked and Daddy never told us who won those chess games.

24

I went to school on Monday without Wes, who was still running a fever. Nothing seemed to be helping, including Granny Lee's special potion. Mother bathed him with warm water mixed with rubbing alcohol and put Vicks Vapor Rub on his chest each night, but his temperature never fell below 102. She was concerned enough to call Doc Townsend to see if he could drop by sometime during the day and take a look at Wes. I was so worried that I thought about getting some of Parker's toddy and slipping Wes a cupful.

Uncle John and Daddy rode together to the courthouse for the trial. For some reason—maybe because it was late May and the warm weather kept farmers in the fields—the courtroom was not filled. Judge Bascom called the court into session at 9:10 A.M. and asked Mr. Hancock to call his first witness.

Throughout the day, Mr. Hancock questioned witnesses that would help make the case for second-degree murder against Ben Cowser. He led Special Agent Barry Timmons through the evidence related to the paint scrapings from Mr. Cowser's truck, the lug wrench with Junior's blood on it, the ten dollar gold coin, and the rat poison used to kill Lonnie's dog.

"Agent Timmons was a good witness. Very professional and believable," Daddy said later.

Leonard Driscoll tried to plant doubts in the minds of the jurors by raising the issue of circumstantial evidence. "Agent Timmons, the paint on the rock came from Ben Cowser's truck, you said. Do you have positive evidence that Mr. Cowser was driving that truck on that day?"

The answer was no.

"Were there any fingerprints on the lug wrench?"

"No," Agent Timmons mumbled.

"The rat poison found in Mr. Cowser's garage is a common product that can be found in almost every garage in this town, wouldn't you agree?"

Timmons paused a moment and then answered, "I wouldn't know, sir. All I know is the poison that killed the dog was the same kind found in *his* garage."

Driscoll studied the faces of the jury for a moment, and then asked his last question.

"Now, I want to talk about that $10 gold piece found in Ben Cowser's possession. You have testified that you believe this is the same one given to Junior Macgregor by Lonnie Jackson. Is that right?"

Agent Timmons nodded. The judge instructed him to speak up for the record.

"Yes, I do."

"But Mr. Jackson has testified that he's not sure if it's the same coin. Moreover, the Nashville coin dealer said he'd seen another just like this one over a year ago. My question is a simple one, Mr. Timmons. Is it possible that the coin Mr. Cowser sold to the dealer is a different one from the coin Junior had in his pocket the day he was killed? Is it possible? That's all I'm asking."

The Agent shifted in his chair and glanced over at Mitchell Hancock. Finally, he said, "Yes, it's possible." Driscoll thanked him and slumped down in his chair with a smile on his face.

Sheriff Perkins testified and went over some of the same evidence that the agent had just presented. He told of his meetings with Lonnie Jackson and the visit to his house when they found the dog dead and the house ransacked.

"Sheriff Perkins, you have stated it was a Monday when you found the poisoned dog and discovered the house had been broken into. I think you also stated that one of your deputies had gone to Mr. Jackson's house on that previous Thursday to check on things and feed the dog. Am I correct about that?" Mr. Hancock asked politely.

"Yes, that's correct. We had promised to watch after Mr. Jackson's house and dog while he was in jail."

Mr. Hancock glanced at a paper in his hand and then asked, "So the break-in could have occurred anytime from Thursday until Sunday night. Would that be an accurate statement?"

The sheriff agreed.

Mr. Hancock then asked about his meetings with Ben Cowser. The sheriff said they were friendly and informative meetings. "At any time during your investigation and your meetings with Ben Cowser, did you consider him a suspect?" Hancock asked.

The sheriff said he became convinced that Ben had embezzled money from the bank and that he had tried to steal the coins from Mr. Jackson's house.

Leonard Driscoll objected, reminding the judge that the embezzlement charge was not part of this trial. Judge Bascom overruled the objection, stating that in this context it was okay to mention it.

The prosecuting attorney thanked the judge and proceeded with his questions. "You've been a law enforcement officer in this county for many years, ten I think, and as you look at all this evidence, have you come to a conclusion about the guilt or innocence of this defendant?"

Sheriff Perkins had a pained look on his face and was obviously uncomfortable with the question, but he knew it was coming and he knew he had to answer it truthfully.

"Ben Cowser's my friend and I don't like saying this, but I'm convinced that the evidence is . . . well you know . . . it's conclusive."

Hancock pressed for a stronger statement. "You believe Ben Cowser, the defendant, killed Junior Macgregor?"

The sheriff looked at the jury and said quietly, "Yes, I do."

Hancock, pleased with his witness, turned him over to Defense Attorney Driscoll.

Mr. Driscoll didn't take much time with his cross-examination. His questions were similar to the ones he asked Agent Timmons. The purpose was to raise the circumstantial evidence issue again. His final series of questions, however, tested the patience of the sheriff.

"In your ten years as a law enforcement officer, have you ever investigated a case like this?"

The answer was no.

"In fact, Sheriff, most of your ten years have been spent picking up drunks on Saturday night, or settling domestic disputes, or dealing with a few stabbings. Isn't that right?"

The sheriff did not answer.

"I'm concerned that you come into this courtroom with no background in investigating capital crimes and with only a smattering of circumstantial evidence and can state categorically that you are convinced that this outstanding citizen, with no criminal record, is guilty of second-degree murder. I've been a lawyer longer than you've been a sheriff and I can tell you that kind of certitude with such flimsy evidence is mind-boggling."

Mr. Hancock was on his feet before Driscoll finished.

"Is Mr. Driscoll asking a question or making a speech?"

Judge Bascom asked if the defense counsel had any other questions.

"No, your honor, I have nothing further to say to or ask this witness." With that, he walked past the jury and let them see his disgust.

Daddy said later, and Uncle John agreed, that Mr. Driscoll's performance was demeaning and disgraceful. It reminded Daddy of why he had not liked Leonard Driscoll.

Jacob Yancey wrote in *The Clarion Standard* that the attack on the sheriff's credibility was a stroke of genius by the defense attorney.

"The defense team has every right to question the conclusions of the investigators. We don't think Mr. Driscoll was upbraiding the sheriff; we think he was challenging the validity of the evidence and raising appropriate questions about the credentials of the accusers. This is a murder trial and every effort should be made to ascertain the guilt or innocence of the accused," the article stated.

Doc Townsend was the next witness, but was on the stand only for a brief time. He testified that it was his conclusion that the lug wrench was used to kill Junior and someone standing behind him struck the blow.

Mitchell Hancock decided not to recall Lonnie Jackson. Instead, he made a motion that all the testimony previously given by Mr. Jackson that was relevant to the charge of the murder of Junior Macgregor become part of the record. The judge asked if the counsel for the defense had any objection. Mr. Driscoll did not object, but reminded the judge of his ruling that testimony related to the embezzlement charge could not be included. The judge agreed and accepted Mr. Hancock's motion.

Uncle John leaned over and whispered in Daddy's ear, "That's gonna be pretty hard to do, Milton. You know, keep those two things separate."

Daddy suggested that the jurors might need a Solomon in the deliberating room.

Mitchell Hancock rested his case.

The judge looked at his watch and said, "Due to the lateness of the hour, we'll adjourn until tomorrow morning at 9:00 A.M., at which time Mr. Driscoll will present the first witness for the defense."

There was a lot of speculation about whether Mr. Driscoll would let Ben Cowser take the stand in his own defense. *The Clarion Standard* presented the pros and cons of having a defendant testify in a murder trial.

"Although there is no direct evidence against Mr. Cowser and no eyewitnesses, the facts point to an inferential presumption of guilt. This may be the only way that Ben Cowser can convince the jury of his innocence. It would be his word against the controvertible testimony of his accusers and the inconclusive evidence based entirely on circumstances."

The consensus among the men in the back of Taylor's grocery store was that he should take the stand and tell his side of the story. Uncle John concurred with this opinion and wanted Daddy to try to persuade Ben to testify. Daddy refused, saying that Leonard Driscoll and Ben are the only ones who can make that decision.

"I just don't know," Daddy reflected, "how Ben would stand up under cross-examination by Mitchell Hancock. It could work against him."

When I got home from school, Mother was sitting by the bed reading Wes some poetry. The cough was worse and his temperature, which had gone down in the night, was now up to 104. Doc Townsend arrived about the same time that Daddy got home. Mother watched as Doc listened to Wes' chest and checked his pulse. He then put the stethoscope to his back and asked him to cough.

"Are you having any trouble with your bowels, son?" he asked.

Wes shook his head.

"Any trouble peeing?"

Wes again shook his head.

Doc Townsend patted him on the head and said, "We're gonna make you well soon. You just keep doing everything your folks tell you to do."

Wes forced a smile and thanked him.

Mother and Daddy talked to Doc Townsend in the living room and I overheard most of the conversation.

"I'm doing everything I know to do, and it concerns me that he is not responding to anything we've tried. I don't want to alarm you, but all the symptoms lead me to conclude that he's got a bacterial inflammation in one of his lungs, and that could mean pneumonia."

Mother gasped and walked to the kitchen. I could hear her crying.

Daddy said, "Doc we've lost one child to pneumonia. We don't want to lose another one. Don't you think we should take him to the hospital in Jackson or Memphis?"

Doc pondered the idea a moment and then said, "Not just yet. Traveling in a car that distance might drive the fever up and there's not much they can do at the hospital that we can't do here. Let's wait a couple of more days and see if we can get that fever down. I brought some medicine that's new on the market and I want you to give him a tablespoon every four or five hours. It has codeine in it and it'll make him very sleepy, but that's okay. Continue to give him alcohol baths and use plenty of Vicks around the upper part of his chest. Stop using the cough medicine; give him lozenges instead. I'll check on him to-morrow."

After Doc left, Daddy went to the kitchen and comforted Mother. He then went to the backyard and stood looking at the sky. I knew he was praying.

Wiping tears from my eyes, I went out the front of the house and ran as fast as I could to the pasture. I would fetch Moo Moo, but I needed time to be by myself and talk to God about Wes.

There was laughter in the courtroom. Mr. Hancock smiled and then continued. "After Friday night, you didn't see Mr. Cowser again until the dinner hour on Sunday. Is that correct?"

Stone nodded, and before the judge could instruct him said, "Yes, that's correct."

Hancock thanked the witness and sat down.

Curtis Shipley, owner of the car dealership and garage, testified about the dent in the pickup truck.

"When you talked to Ben about the damage, how did he explain it?" Driscoll asked.

Shipley testified that Ben had said he didn't know how the dent got there.

"He told me that somebody probably backed into him or he scraped one of those metal posts over by the lumberyard."

"Your witness," Driscoll said to Hancock.

"You don't know for sure how the dent got there or what scraped that paint off, do you?" Mr. Hancock asked.

The answer was no.

"You know, Mr. Shipley, that FBI Agent Timmons has testified that the paint from that truck matched the paint on the rock out at Lonnie Jackson's place," he stated.

Mr. Shipley said the sheriff had told him that. He added, "But I'm sure Ben has a good explanation."

"And we're all waiting eagerly to hear what that explanation might be," Hancock said sarcastically. As he walked back to his chair, he glared at Ben Cowser.

The judge announced that tomorrow's session would begin at 10:00 A.M. He then reminded everyone that it had been the custom of the court not to meet on Friday before the Strawberry Festival.

Looking down at Driscoll and Hancock, he said, "It's my wish that we complete testimony by Thursday afternoon so that we can hear the closing arguments Monday morning. This court, and I'm sure the jurors, would be most grateful if counsel would move expeditiously toward that objective. Court is adjourned."

On Wednesday, Leonard Driscoll called to the witness stand a professor of psychology from Memphis State College who testified that excessive gambling was an addiction, not a personality disorder.

"Our study of human behavior strongly supports the conclusion that gamblers are passive people and not prone toward violence," he said, as he wiped his glasses.

After Mr. Driscoll spent thirty minutes questioning him about his research, Matthew Hancock approached the witness.

In a tone of derision, he asked, "And how long have you been studying the idiosyncrasies of persons with a disposition for games of chance?"

Driscoll mumbled something to his associate but made no objection to the question.

The professor said he had been doing research in personality disorders for more than ten years.

With a smirk on his face, Hancock asked, "In those ten years of research, did you find that gamblers lie, cheat, steal, and enshroud themselves in a cloak of hypocrisy?"

Driscoll was on his feet protesting. "Your honor, I object to my opposing counsel's vitriolic attack on this man's credibility."

The judge overruled the objection, but admonished Hancock about courtroom courtesy.

Defensively, the witness agreed that some or all of these traits might be present in such a person. Then he added, "But not violence and certainly not murder."

"Your honor," Hancock bellowed, "if opposing counsel had given me timely notice of this witness, I could probably present dozens of qualified psychologists who would dispute these conclusions. I ask that you instruct the jury to disregard the testimony of this so-called expert."

It was obvious to the jury and the gallery that the judge was not pleased with Leonard Driscoll's ploy. The jurors were told that they could consider the testimony of the professor with the understanding that these conclusions are based on uncorroborated research.

"In other words, you are entitled to consider this evidence as fact, or you may consider it disputable. That's your prerogative."

Leonard Driscoll was on his feet objecting. "Your honor, you have no authority or expertise to question the results of scientific scholarship."

The judge was not amused. "You're right, but I do have the authority to instruct the jury as to the merits of testimony based on what is not widely accepted by leading sociologists and psychologists. You see, Mr. Driscoll, I have also done my homework. Call your next witness."

During a brief recess, Daddy talked to Uncle John and Granny Lee.

"The judge is right about that. I've studied a little psychology myself and those conclusions are still being debated. However, something else is going on here. I think Leonard's stalling for time."

The rest of the day was taken up with other "expert" witnesses who talked about forensic science as being imperfect and prone to different interpretations and conclusions.

Driscoll picked up the wrench on the evidence table and addressed the witness, "In other words, you are saying that there might be a variance among technicians about the blood on the lug wrench?"

The witness stated that faulty forensic analysis could send an innocent man to prison.

Mitchell Hancock did not approach the witness. He stood beside his chair, and in a caustic tone, asked, "You are employed by Synergy Labs in Atlanta and you conduct tests for private clients at a substantial fee. Isn't that right?"

The witness said, "Yes, we are a private business and we do get paid for our work. Whether it's substantial is for the client to judge, not you."

"Do you also get paid for testifying at trials like these?"

The answer was yes.

"One final question, are you suggesting that the F.B.I. laboratory in Washington D.C., which, by the way, is financed by taxpayers, not private companies, is guilty of conducting faulty tests on blood samples?"

Before he got an answer, Hancock said, "No further questions," and sat down.

By mid-afternoon, the judge was perspiring and showing signs of impatience. The windows were open but there was no breeze. The ceiling fans hummed annoyingly, agitating the hot air. Men took off their jackets and loosened their ties. Ladies tried valiantly to cool their flushed faces with fans furnished by the local funeral home.

During the recess, Mr. Driscoll conferred privately with Ben and his family. There seemed to be some disagreement among them, but even Jacob Yancey couldn't get close enough to hear their discussions.

The judge called the court back into session and asked if Mr. Driscoll was ready to proceed. Leonard Driscoll rose, buttoned his coat, and addressed the judge.

"Your honor, I have no other witnesses to call today."

There was a sigh of relief from the bench and the jury.

"I do, however, wish to notify my opposing counsel and the court that I will be calling a final witness tomorrow and I anticipate that he will require the court's attention for most of the day."

"And might the court be privy to the name of your final witness?" he asked with a smile.

"My final witness will be the defendant, Mr. Ben Cowser."

Driscoll then sat down, studied the faces of the jurors, and listened to the murmurs among the spectators.

Jacob Yancey was on his feet and out of the room before the judge could respond. "We look forward to hearing from Mr. Cowser tomorrow. Court is adjourned," he said, as he pounded the gavel.

I was sitting in the room with Wes when Daddy arrived home. Mother had been putting cold cloths on his forehead and wiping away remnants of green mucus he coughed up. Daddy sat down on the other side of the bed and said, "Are you up to hearing about what happened in court today?"

Wes nodded.

Daddy related everything he could remember about the day and then told us that Ben Cowser was going to testify tomorrow. I reminded Daddy that I didn't have to go to school, and pleaded with him to let me go with him to the trial. Mother was hesitant, but Daddy said he thought it would be a good learning experience.

"I'm sorry you can't be there too, Wesley, but I'm sure you'll get all the details tomorrow night," he said, as he patted him on the head before leaving the room.

When I went to the kitchen for a glass of milk, I heard Mother tell Daddy that the fever had reached 104 during the day and the coughing was much worse than before. Rue came in to help with supper and asked me to set the table. Daddy went out to milk the cow and feed the chickens. Mother called Doc Townsend.

During supper, we talked about the Strawberry Festival and the weekend activities. Rue invited me to go with her and Johnny Fesmire to the park on Friday night for the annual jamboree. Johnny wanted Rue to enter the festival pageant that selects the queen, but Daddy and Mother objected, believing that beauty contests were vulgar and demeaning. Rue didn't seem to mind but she told me later that Johnny was disappointed.

"He said he was sure I'd win and then he'd get to ride in that convertible with me on Saturday."

In spite of her smile, there was regret in her voice.

26

The courtroom was packed. People who could not get seats stood along the back wall. We got there early enough to get seats in the fourth row near a window. I had been in the room once when Mr. Webb took our class on a tour of the courthouse and the jail, but I had never been there during a trial.

Uncle John and Granny Lee sat behind us. The sheriff stood at the back near the door and was wearing his gun. Lonnie Jackson sat in the last row near the side wall. I noticed that Mrs. Cowser, Betty Lou and Robert Earl were sitting in the front row, just behind the table where Mr. Driscoll, his assistant, and Mr. Cowser were seated.

The jury came through a door at the front of the room and took their places on elevated benches, separated from the courtroom by a wooden rail. It looked like a choir loft in a church. I now knew why they called it a "box."

Some of the jurors looked around the courtroom and smiled as they spotted a friend or relative. I recognized a few of them. I don't know why, but it startled me when I realized that the person just in front of us was Mr. Macgregor. Daddy leaned over and whispered something to him, and Mr. Macgregor nodded, but said nothing.

Suddenly a door on the opposite side from the jury swung open. A man in a black robe entered and sat down behind the desk. He hit a wooden hammer on the desk and turned to Mr. Driscoll. "Are you ready to call your witness?"

Mr. Ben Cowser walked to the front, raised his hand, and took an oath to tell the truth.

It's hard to describe the excitement I felt as I watched Mr. Cowser take a seat in what Daddy had explained was the witness box. It was the way I imagined they made movies. "Wes would love this," I whispered to Daddy.

Granny Lee overheard the comment and smiled in agreement, as she patted my shoulder.

Daddy tapped me on the arm and pointed to Mr. Yancey's secretary, who had a large pad in her lap and a pencil in hand.

"Watch her today, son, and you'll see why *The Standard* is able to report almost everything said in the courtroom."

I thought of Wes as I watched a sketch artist drawing a face on a sheet of paper. It looked like he was using a piece of charcoal.

Mr. Driscoll approached the witness and greeted him warmly.

"Mr. Cowser, it's important that this court and the jury hear your side of the story. You understand what it means to testify under oath and you know the penalty for perjury?"

With a strong voice, Mr. Cowser answered "Yes."

Ben Cowser admitted to taking coins as "collateral" for money he had advanced to Lonnie Jackson and stated that he had sold the coins at a sizeable profit to the dealer in Nashville. Without any apology, he described how his gambling habits had led him to embezzle money from the bank, mortgage some farm land he had inherited, and sell the coins, even though he had promised to keep them in a safe-deposit box.

When asked about the weekend of the break-in at Lonnie's house, Mr. Cowser told the same story that Mr. Stone had related the day before.

"My family was taking the sedan to Florence for the weekend, so I had Mildred drive me to the station, and I rode the train to Memphis and didn't return until Monday."

"So, if you were in Memphis those three days, you couldn't have driven your pickup out to the ridge, ransacked Mr. Jackson's house, and scraped the fender on a rock, could you?"

Mr. Cowser glanced over to the jury box before he answered.

"No, I couldn't have and I wouldn't have."

"Do you have any idea how the pickup got that dent in it?"

Mr. Cowser said, "I really couldn't say. I don't drive the truck much, and when I noticed it had a bad scrape on the fender, I took it to the garage to get it repaired. Sometimes my yardman drives it to pick up mulch and compost, and I assumed he might have hit something or I might have scraped one of the posts at the lumberyard. It was no big deal and I didn't make inquiries about it."

When asked about the lug wrench with the blood on it, Mr. Cowser said he had no idea how the blood got on it, or why it was stuffed under the seat in the truck. He testified that he had not used the wrench for more than a year and had even forgotten where he kept it.

Mr. Driscoll quickly disposed of the rat poison evidence by having Mr. Cowser state that he used it to kill rats and mice that nested in a storehouse behind the garage.

"Since the prosecutor has brought this up, let me ask you about the shooting of Lonnie Jackson," Mr. Driscoll said.

Mr. Cowser testified that on the day Lonnie was shot, he had gone out to his house to talk to him about the coins but didn't shoot him.

"I was as shocked as everyone else when I heard the news. I have no reason to cause any harm to Lonnie Jackson," he said with conviction.

"I have just a few more questions, Mr. Cowser, and the jury will be very interested in your responses, so take your time and answer carefully. Did you know Junior Macgregor well and did you have any personal contact with him?"

Mr. Cowser looked directly at Mr. Macgregor and answered, "I know J. C. Macgregor well. He's my friend, but I didn't know his son except for informal situations, like at church or at school meetings. He seemed like a fine young man and was a friend of Robert Earl's, my son."

I cringed when I heard that and started to say something to Daddy, but he put his finger to his lips to shush me. I looked over at Robert Earl and his head was lowered so much that his chin touched his chest.

"Do you remember where you were on the day Junior Macgregor was killed?" Mr. Driscoll asked, as he moved to the edge of the jury box.

"I was working at our farm most of the day. We were mending some fences and hauling hay to the barn."

Driscoll asked, "When you say we, to whom are you referring?"

Mr. Cowser said he had hired some of Mr. Parson's sharecroppers to help him and, except for an hour or so at lunchtime, he was with them all day. He said Sheriff Perkins had talked to some of the workers and they told the same story.

"And during that hour or so when you were not at the farm, where were you, and did anyone see you?" Mr. Driscoll asked quietly.

"I came to town to wash up and get a bite of lunch. Mildred was at a circle meeting. Robert Earl was at the park and Betty Lou was with some friends at the drugstore. I didn't see anyone while I was in town."

"I have just two final questions, Mr. Cowser. Did you have any reason to cause harm or injury to Junior Macgregor?"

"No, I did not."

"Did you kill Junior Macgregor?"

There was a hush in the room as Mr. Cowser looked over at the jury and said, "No, I didn't kill that boy."

Mr. Driscoll indicated to the judge that he had no other questions.

The judge said, "The court is now in recess and will reconvene at 1:00 P.M. this afternoon."

Uncle John, Granny Lee, Daddy, and I headed for Fesmire's Drug Store to get some lunch. I got an earful listening to the three of them talk about Mr. Cowser's testimony while I ate a grilled cheese sandwich stuffed with sliced pickles and covered with a generous amount of catsup. Granny Lee looked at my sandwich with curiosity, but said nothing. I washed it down with a strawberry milkshake.

Granny Lee said she didn't see how a jury could convict him after hearing his testimony this morning. Uncle John agreed and offered his opinions about the questions and answers. Daddy was not so sure and said he was worried about Mitchell Hancock.

"The prosecutor is tough and smart. Ben had better be ready for anything Hancock throws at him this afternoon."

I wasn't sure my opinion was worth anything, but I decided to say what I was thinking.

"I don't know why, but when I listened to Mr. Cowser, I thought he was telling the truth . . . you know what I mean. I just can't believe a man like that would do something so awful to a kid."

Daddy said, "Let's hope you're right, son."

On our way out, Mr. Fesmire asked about Wes and gave Daddy a sack of candy. "That'll cheer him up. And you make him share some of it with you, Vance."

Mr. Cowser took the stand a few minutes after 1:00 o'clock. The judge reminded him that he was still under oath. Mitchell Hancock approached the witness and began his cross-examination.

The Clarion Standard described Mr. Hancock's opening question as being "acrimonious and spoken with contempt."

"Mr. Cowser, you have already confessed to embezzlement, the theft of gold coins, and leading a deceptive and sordid life that is not consistent with your role as a Sunday school superintendent, Mason, Rotarian, and family man. You lied to Lonnie Jackson, the bank auditors, the F.B.I., Sheriff Perkins, your wife, and your preacher. Now, I ask you sir, tell me and this court why we should believe you when you say you didn't shoot Mr. Jackson and you didn't kill Junior Macgregor?"

Leonard Driscoll stood for a moment but said nothing.

Mr. Cowser said he told lies about his gambling because he was distressed and ashamed.

"I know what I did was wrong. How many more times do you want to hear it? I did lie and I've brought dishonor to the Cowser name, disgraced myself, and caused untold suffering to my family, but I have never physically harmed anyone."

"Okay, Mr. Cowser, let's proceed. You testified this morning that you didn't know how the pickup got dented. Tell the court where the pickup was during the weekend you were in Memphis."

"I assume it was parked in my driveway at home. That's where it was when I got back on Monday," he said wearily.

"Who else besides the yardman is allowed to drive that truck?" Hancock asked.

Mr. Cowser said his wife drove it only in case of an emergency. He paused a moment as Mr. Hancock waited, and then he said, "I taught Robert Earl to drive but he doesn't have a permit yet, and isn't allowed to go out by himself."

"And you have testified that you don't know how blood got on your lug wrench or who wrapped it in a towel and hid it under the seat. Forgive me, Mr. Cowser, but I'm a little confused. It is your pickup and you drove it more than anyone else, didn't you?"

Ben seemed a little rattled, and hesitated before answering. "I drove it when my wife was using the sedan, but I didn't drive it every day. That's what I said."

"I know that's what you said, but it seems odd to me that you don't know much about a vehicle that you own and drive most of the time. You weren't immediately aware of the dent in the fender and you didn't notice that you were missing a lug wrench. Most of us wouldn't start out anywhere without a lug wrench, Mr. Cowser."

Ben said nothing.

Mr. Hancock hesitated a moment before continuing.

"Did you know that Lonnie Jackson and Junior Macgregor were friends and that they spent a lot of time together?"

Mr. Cowser said Lonnie had once told him that Junior was the best friend he had.

"He told me that they fished down at the river and Junior helped him buy supplies over in Savannah."

"So would it be fair to say that Mr. Jackson and Junior shared a lot of things with one another, even secrets?" Mr. Hancock asked.

Mr. Cowser said he wouldn't know what they talked about or what secrets they shared.

Mr. Hancock positioned himself between Leonard Driscoll and the witness.

"Now, let's talk about where you were when Mr. Jackson was shot and Junior Macgregor was murdered. You can account for part of the time in question, but you have produced no witnesses to verify your whereabouts during other periods of time. In other words, Mr. Cowser, there are gaps in your alibi. Can you explain that?"

Mr. Cowser glared at the prosecutor, and it was apparent that he was irritated and running out of patience.

"I might be able to answer your questions if they were more precise and your manner less offensive."

Mr. Hancock looked straight at Ben Cowser and pondered the obvious reproach for a few seconds. He glanced at the judge but realized he would get no support from the bench.

"Alright, Mr. Cowser," he continued, "let me be very precise. Within a time-frame of four days, someone ransacked Mr. Jackson's house looking for gold coins and poisoned his dog. At some point, your truck hit the rock at the entrance to the house and left red paint on it. Now, you have said you took the train to Memphis on Friday, leaving the truck in your driveway. Witnesses have testified that they were with you on Friday but did not see you again until Sunday evening. That's one of the time gaps I'm talking about. Is that explicit enough for you?"

"I worked at the bank all day on Thursday and was seen by clerks and tellers. I took the train early on Friday and was in Memphis until Monday. I attended the general meeting of the Tennessee Bankers Association on Saturday and Sunday. There were more than 200 people at the conference and I don't know if anyone would remember seeing me. I did not spend any time with friends on those two days. You have the letter from The Peabody that I paid for a room for three nights. If you're suggesting that I came back to Adairsville on Saturday and returned on Sunday, then you don't know much about train schedules."

"Oh, but I do, Mr. Cowser. I know there's a train that leaves Memphis on Saturday at 6:00 A.M. and arrives in Adairsville at 9:30 A.M. There is another train that leaves on Sunday morning at 11:00 A.M. and arrives in Memphis at 1:45 P.M. So it would have been possible for you to return, pick up your truck, go out to the Ridges, and break into Mr. Jackson's house." Mitchell Hancock appeared to be pleased with his performance.

"All I can do is repeat my testimony and tell this court that I was in Memphis during the entire weekend, and I didn't have anything to do with the incident you have described," Mr. Cowser said with a heavy sigh.

I leaned forward in an effort to catch sight of Mrs. Cowser and Robert Earl. Mrs. Cowser looked older than I remembered and Robert Earl was nervously chewing on a toothpick. I wondered what it would be like to sit in a courtroom and watch your father being mocked and ridiculed by a lawyer who was trying to convict him of murder. I wanted to feel sorry for Robert Earl—I even wanted to like him—but I couldn't.

Mitchell Hancock shuffled through some papers on the table and then continued his inquiry.

"Before we get to the day Junior Macgregor was killed, let's talk about the day Mr. Lonnie Jackson was shot. Didn't you go out to his house that day to force him to get those other coins from the sheriff and give them to you? Isn't that what happened, Mr. Cowser?"

Mr. Cowser sat up straight in the chair and for the first time raised his voice.

"No, that's not true. I went out to tell him that the coins he had given me for safekeeping were missing."

"Missing? Is that what you told him? Is that what you call an act of deception and thievery? Is that how you describe the betrayal of a trust? Using 'missing' to describe this situation appears to me to be a denigration of the English language. Is that how you explain the theft of twenty-five thousand dollars from your bank?"

Mr. Driscoll stood up so forcefully that he knocked over his chair. "I object . . . object strenuously . . . to this kind of characterization cloaked in the form of a question, and I object to the devious way my opposing counsel has slipped in the embezzlement issue. Mr. Hancock is being argumentative and disrespectful of my client, and I do not think this court should permit sarcasm as a method of examination."

The judge watched as Mr. Driscoll's associate picked up the chair, then said, "Objection is sustained. Mr. Hancock, I implore you to refrain from unseemly conduct that is not in accordance with accepted rules of this court."

"My apologies, your honor," Mr. Hancock said, and then turned his attention back to Mr. Cowser. "So how did Mr. Jackson react when you told him that his coins were missing?"

Mr. Cowser seemed to be looking over the heads of the spectators to catch a glimpse of Lonnie Jackson.

"He said it was okay because he didn't feel they were his coins anyway. He was very understanding."

Mr. Hancock paced in front of the jury box as he continued his questioning. "Good old Lonnie. He didn't ask you how those coins just disappeared in thin air. He didn't get mad or threaten to go to the sheriff or to Mr. Yancey at *The Clarion Standard*? He was very understanding. He just said it didn't matter."

Mr. Cowser loosened his tie and wiped sweat from his brow. "That's what he said."

Abruptly, Mr. Hancock said, "Sounds like you had some fairy dust sprinkled on your oatmeal this morning to come up with a story like that."

Before he finished his sentence, Mr. Driscoll was on his feet objecting loudly. "Your honor, please remind Mr. Hancock that this is not a Chautauqua. We don't need these kinds of theatrics in a courtroom."

Judge Bascom was red in the face. "I agree."

Turning to Mr. Hancock, he said sternly, "I am giving you one last warning, Mr. Hancock. I will not tolerate this kind of indecorous conduct in my courtroom. Another admonition will carry with it a contempt citation and a sizeable fine."

Mr. Hancock had a smirk on his face as he spoke.

"My apologies, your honor. I don't mean to be contentious, but you must admit that this witness has challenged credibility with his disingenuous testimony. From the moment he began testifying, a heavy cloud of mendacity has been cast over this courtroom."

Granny Lee leaned forward and whispered. "He ought to be in Hollywood making movies. What a great actor!"

Daddy frowned and said, "Yep, and the jury is eating it up."

The judge peered down over his glasses and responded.

"And I have been overwhelmed by the egregious tactics of the prosecution. And as for the veracity of the testimony, that's for this court and jury to decide, not you. Now, if you can conduct yourself with more civility and correctitude, you may proceed."

For the first time, Mr. Hancock seemed uncertain about his next question. He paused before moving close to the witness box.

"Mr. Cowser, it's the belief of the prosecution that you were about to be exposed as a thief and fraud, and that's why you killed Junior Macgregor. And when Lonnie Jackson refused to give you the other coins, you slipped out there, took his rifle from the house, and waited until he returned from the lumberyard. You then sneaked up behind him and shot him, hoping to kill him. Isn't that right?"

Before Mr. Hancock could finish the statement, the associate at the defense table rose to object. Before he said anything, Mr. Driscoll pulled on his sleeve and shook his head. The judge watched with interest and seemed surprised that no objection was offered.

"Isn't that right, Mr. Cowser?" Hancock repeated more loudly.

Mr. Cowser leaned forward and gripped the rail. With tears in his eyes, he said, "No, no, that's not true. You don't understand. I could never do anything like that."

"You could never do anything like what, Mr. Cowser?" Hancock bellowed.

Mr. Cowser paused for a moment, wiped the tears from his cheeks, and sat erect in his chair.

"Lonnie Jackson is my brother, and I would never harm him."

There was a collective gasp in the courtroom. Robert Earl was on his feet and yelling before his father finished his statement.

"No, Daddy, it's not true . . . it's not true! You don't have to say that. They can't make you. Please . . . don't do this to me."

Mr. Cowser reached out his hand like he was trying to touch Robert Earl across the room, and said, almost in a whisper, "It's true, son, and there's no reason to be ashamed or hide it any longer."

Sobbing loudly, Robert Earl ran up the aisle and bolted through the door.

"Oh my God," Mr. Hancock was overheard to say as he folded his hands across his chest.

The sheriff stood motionless and had a stunned expression on his face. Lonnie Jackson sat quietly looking up at the ceiling and shaking his head. Mrs. Cowser stared straight ahead. The gasps from spectators had now turned into murmuring and restless movement.

Daddy looked up at Mr. Cowser and nodded. He then turned to me and said, "Son, you stay here, and if I'm not back by the time court ends, John will take you home. I'm going to find Robert Earl."

After the judge finally restored order in the courtroom, Mr. Cowser calmly explained that Melvin, his father, had an affair with Maribelle Bove one summer when she was home from college. As a result of the affair, Maribelle gave birth to a child. That child was Lonnie Jackson. Mr. Cowser told how the family, to avoid shame and embarrassment, concocted a story about Maribelle's marriage to an army officer named Jackson. He told how his father provided for Maribelle and Lonnie as long as he lived.

"On his deathbed, my father made me swear to watch after Lonnie and Maribelle. I did all I could for them without stirring up gossip and hurting my family. I tried to protect Maribelle while she was living and I didn't want to do anything to cause embarrassment for Lonnie. He knew he was my half brother, but he never tried to use it to his advantage." Mr. Cowser slumped in his chair and appeared to be exhausted.

Mr. Hancock, who was still in a state of shock, requested that, in light of the defendant's unexpected testimony, the court adjourn until Monday. The judge seemed eager to grant the motion. As he rapped his gavel, the reporters rushed toward the door and spectators moved quietly out of the room.

Granny Lee went over to talk to Mrs. Cowser. As Uncle John and I left, Lonnie was sitting in the back row with his head against the wall. I gave him a slight wave of the hand. He smiled and waved back.

215

27

Mother moved the radio into Wes' room so he could hear the Cardinals' ball game. The first thing he said to me when I got home was, "Musial hit two home runs and the Cardinals beat the Giants six to nothing."

In the kitchen, Mother told me that Doc Townsend was coming tomorrow and, if the fever wasn't down, they were going to take Wes to the hospital on Saturday.

For the rest of the afternoon, I tried to tell Mother and Wes what had happened in the courtroom. Daddy filled in the gaps when he got home. Wes said he hadn't seen me so excited for a long time.

They were shocked to hear that Slowfoot was Mr. Cowser's half brother.

"Does that mean he's Robert Earl's uncle?" Wes asked.

Daddy nodded.

Daddy had not been able to find Robert Earl and assumed that the reason he ran from the courtroom in tears was because of the shame he felt about being related to Lonnie Jackson.

"I wish you could've heard the judge yell at Mr. Hancock," I said. "And boy, did they use big words! If I ever go to another trial, I'm taking a dictionary with me."

I realized Wes had heard enough, so I told him he could read the rest in tomorrow's *Clarion Standard*. I went out to do my chores.

On Friday Seth and I picked buckets of strawberries for Granny Lee. We put them in quart boxes, crated them, and loaded several containers into the trunk of her car. I got home in time to round up Moo Moo and clean up for the strawberry festivities. I went in to say good-bye to Wes but he was sleeping.

The Jefferson Davis Park was lit up with hanging lanterns and strings of Christmas lights. Rue and Johnny held hands as we walked toward the large pavilion, which was also called a bandstand, because that's where people came with picnic baskets and blankets to enjoy summer concerts.

Every year local talent from the surrounding area, as well as professional musicians from Memphis and Nashville, performed at the Strawberry Festival. Last year, Roy Acuff and the Smoky Mountain Boys from the Grand Ole Opry were the main attraction.

Granny Lee had arranged for a bagpiper to open the ceremonies. He wore a bright garment of pleated tartan cloth that barely reached his knees. Granny Lee called it a "kilt." I thought it looked like a girl's dress and knew I would never be caught dead wearing one.

He marched through the crowd playing Scottish and Irish songs. To the tune of "O Danny Boy," he led the Strawberry Festival Queen up the steps of the pavilion. The queen took a bow and everyone applauded. He then stood at the top of the pavilion steps and played "Amazing Grace," and, from that moment on, I loved the music of bagpipes. After the Presbyterian minister said a prayer, everyone stood with hands over their hearts as the high school band played the National Anthem.

It seemed like almost everyone in Adairsville was at the park that night. As the gospel quartet began singing, I left Rue and Johnny and went looking for food. There were vendors selling hot dogs with mustard and relish; hamburgers stacked with pickles, lettuce, tomatoes, and onions. Barbecued ribs came with potato salad and baked beans. Funnel cakes, fried pies, and ice cream covered with strawberries were big hits. The concession stand, where a man was serving paper cones filled with shaved ice and covered with sweet, flavored syrup, was always busy.

Away from the bandstand young children watched a puppet show and older kids tried to figure out the magic of an illusionist. Daddy and Uncle John were enjoying a barbecue sandwich as they watched a jump rope contest. We strolled over to the bandstand to listen to the Tennessee Troubadours singing mountain folk songs, accompanied by fiddles, guitars, and a harmonica.

217

Daddy and Uncle John waved good-bye as they left the park. If Wes had been there, it would have been a perfect evening.

I caught up with Johnny and Rue just in time for the jitterbug contest. A large dance floor had been constructed over by the pond and contestants were lining up for the event. Some of the girls sported beehive hairdos and polka-dotted flared skirts. The boys wore tight shirts and colorful pants, and a few of them had on white bucks.

Granny Lee spread a large quilt for us to sit on. Daddy didn't approve of dancing, but he said it was alright for us to watch jitterbugging since the dancers never got that close to one another. I never questioned Daddy, but I often wondered why Methodists considered dancing a sin.

While we were watching the couples pin hand-numbered cards on their backs, I said, "Granny Lee, can Presbyterians dance?"

"Well," she said as she tilted her head to one side and smiled, "some can and some can't."

There was a moment of silence and then we all burst out laughing. Johnny thought it was one of the funniest things he'd ever heard.

Near the dance floor, there was a printed sign which read: AN OLD-FASHIONED, JUMPING AND JIVING, SWINGING AND SWAYING, FUN AND FROLICKING JITTERBUG CONTEST.

The master of ceremonies went to the microphone and, after welcoming everyone, read the rules. He warned against "side-by-side" routines or "colliding with other dancers." He said that judges would be watching for originality, timing, variety, and interpretation. In addition to trophies, the first, second, and third place winners would receive cash and tickets to the Dixie Theater.

He then yelled into the microphone, "Let the contest began."

The Dixie Rebels, a small band from Jackson, began playing, and the dancers, four couples at a time, moved, as Granny Lee described it, "with different degrees of grace and supple fluidity."

I was having a good time, but I missed Wes and felt bad that he was not there enjoying the music and food and other festivities. It was beginning to get dark and I knew Rue and

Johnny would stay until the last note was played, so I decided to walk home. I thanked Johnny and Rue for bringing me and said good-bye to Granny Lee.

A few blocks from the house, I sat down on a tree stump by the side of the road. The moon had slipped behind the clouds and darkness was beginning to settle in. I stared at the sky, watching the clouds as they moved with the force of warm winds. Suddenly I saw a bright star in the western sky. I stood up and said:

Star light, star bright, first star I see tonight.
I wish I may, I wish I might,
Have the wish, I wish tonight.

I closed my eyes real tight and made a silent wish. When I opened them, I saw a tiny blinking light a few feet away.

"It's a lightning bug," I said out loud.

I knew that lightning bugs don't usually appear until mid-June or later, after it got hotter.

All of a sudden, it came to me and I knew what I had to do. I ran home and found an empty fruit jar. Fumbling in the kitchen drawer, I retrieved an ice pick and used it to punch holes in the lid of the jar. Mother and Daddy were sitting in the living room listening to the radio and asked why I was home so early. I don't remember what reason I gave, but I told them I was going to the backyard to get something that would make Wes feel better.

Daddy looked up from his book, furrowed his brow, but said nothing. Mother smiled and continued knitting.

It took about thirty minutes to catch a dozen or so fireflies. I held the jar up to the darkness and watched with delight as the rear ends of these strange insects lit up like tiny lightbulbs.

I said to myself, *Now, what did God have in mind when he made bugs that glow in the dark?*

The answer came to me as I realized a smile had replaced the frown that had been on my face ever since Wes got sick.

I ran into the house and hurried to Wes' room. He was awake but lying very still. The fever and loss of appetite had weakened him to the point that he could hardly talk.

Holding the jar behind my back, I said, "Wes, I've got something that's gonna make you feel better."

I turned off the lamp by the bed, and held the jar in front of him, and exclaimed, "Look, I've brought something that'll cheer you up. Just like that silly song says . . . moonbeams in a jar."

Mother came into the room and asked why we were sitting in the dark. I smiled at her, then said to Wes, "Did you ever wonder why God made these little creatures and gave them tails that twinkle?"

I answered my own question. "He put them here for us to enjoy. They bring happiness. They cause us to laugh when we chase after them or watch them flashing on and off in the darkness of night."

Mother, who had written a poem about fireflies, said, "You're right, son. Fireflies are like moonbeams delighting us with their bright flickering and strange gifts. But they need space and air to live so that everyone can enjoy them. That kind of mystery shouldn't be contained in a jar."

I knew she had given the answer to a question before I asked it. She and Granny Lee shared this uncanny ability to anticipate and respond with insight. She rose and went to the kitchen to get a wet cloth to put on Wes' forehead. I stared at the jar and then at Wes.

He smiled and, in a weak voice, said, "Thanks, Vance. You and those funny-looking bugs have made me feel a lot better. But Mother's right."

I picked up the jar, walked to the front yard, opened the lid and watched as they flew out into the darkness with their tails flashing brightly.

"Moonbeams don't belong in a jar," I said quietly to myself.

In the middle of the night, I was jolted out of a sound sleep. I raised my head from the pillow on the couch and realized there was a bright beam streaming across the living room. I turned to see where it was coming from. Through the window, I saw a full moon that lit up the sky like fireworks on the Fourth of July.

I lay very still, watching the tiny specks dancing in that mysterious shaft of light that brightened the room. All of a sudden, I became aware of movement in the room. Startled, I

221

abruptly raised up, and before I could say anything, the light beam revealed Mother's form.

She whispered, "I'm sorry to wake you but I thought you'd want to know that the fever has broken. His forehead's cool and the cough's gone."

I jumped off the couch and followed her into the bedroom. Daddy came in behind us and turned on the light. Wes was sitting on the side of the bed sipping water from a glass. He smiled and said, "I'm feeling a lot better."

Mother took his temperature and it was below a hundred. Rue heard the talking and came in to share the good news. We were puzzled, amazed, and thankful. We all stood by the bed and held hands, and Daddy said a prayer.

"I think I can eat some eggs and biscuits," Wes said.

"You don't want to rush things, Wesley," Mother said softly. "How about some hot oatmeal and toast for breakfast in the morning?"

I was awake for a while trying to sort things out. Everything that had happened—the wish, the fireflies, the light—was swirling around in my head. For a moment, I thought it might have been a dream—not a nightmare—just a good dream. But I knew it was real and I knew Wes was going to be okay. Just before I fell asleep, I realized the room was once again dark. The clouds had covered the moon and turned off the beam.

28

I slept soundly in one position for about five hours and woke up on Saturday with a stiff neck. I went to the bedroom and Wes was sitting up in bed reading a magazine and drinking a hot cup of coffee. He hadn't wanted coffee since he got sick. His temperature was back to normal and there was no sign of any congestion in his chest. Mother and Daddy were so excited they woke up Doc Townsend to tell him the news.

I hurried through breakfast and did my chores so I could get downtown before the parade began. I promised to help Granny Lee at the Presbyterian bazaar and then take my turn cranking the ice cream freezers at the Methodist Church. Mother and Rue would be working there most of the day. Daddy said he would take Wes in the car and park where he could see the floats and hear the bands. I didn't know until later that Daddy would get an urgent call that changed his plans.

This was one of the biggest events of the year for Adairsville and almost everybody in town turned out. Main Street was lined from one end to the other with people eagerly waiting for the Strawberry Festival parade to begin. Green banners with red berries painted on them hung from light posts and storefronts. All the merchants along the street closed for two hours so their workers and families could watch the parade. City and county officials and Congressman Murphy sat on folding chairs in the grandstand, which was positioned midpoint in the parade route. That's also where the men and women who judged the floats and the marching bands sat.

I was trying to find the best spot when Uncle John called me to come over to where he was standing with Mr. Fesmire and Mr. Macgregor. Uncle John told me that Johnny had gone to pick up Rue and Wes and they were going to park in J. C.'s driveway, where they would have a good view of the parade. I was so excited, it didn't occur to me to ask why Wes wasn't coming with Daddy.

The sound of music coming from one of the bands let us know that the parade had left the courthouse square and was turning down Main Street. Boy Scout Troops led the way, carrying signs indicating their names and sponsors. Two flags, American and Tennessee, waved proudly in the breeze. After they passed, I caught sight of Parker and his family standing over by the Esso station. I waved and they waved back.

*   *   *

Thirty minutes before the parade started, Sheriff Perkins cautiously approached a red pickup truck parked in a grove of trees out by the Ridges.

"I didn't mean to kill him, I swear. I just wanted to scare him . . . to get even with him for the things he said," Robert Earl blurted out when the sheriff found him sitting in the truck.

A Winchester rifle was cradled in his arms and several cartridges lay on the seat beside him. After carefully removing the rifle, the sheriff cuffed him and took him to the jail where Ben Cowser was waiting.

Daddy was called and went immediately to the jail. In a cramped, sparsely furnished room, the sheriff sat across the table from Robert Earl and an unpleasant Leonard Driscoll. Daddy took a chair in the corner. Molly, the sheriff's assistant, sat down at a small desk and placed a notebook and pencil on it. Ben Cowser waited in the sheriff's office.

*   *   *

The Adairsville High School Marching Band, dressed in bright orange uniforms, and led by pretty majorettes twirling batons, followed the scout troops. Mary Beth Shipley was one of the junior majorettes, and when I saw her, I said to myself, *Wow, I hope Wes gets a good look at her in that outfit.*

224

Vigorous applause could be heard rippling down the street as they passed. It was one of the finest bands in West Tennessee and often won top honors in band competitions.

Cheers and whistles went up as the yellow Chevrolet convertible carrying the queen passed the grandstand. The marching band from Jackson Central High School, which was once invited to perform at the Rose Bowl, gave a rousing rendition of one of Sousa's marches. A maroon convertible carrying the mayor and the President of the Chamber of Commerce followed it. The car had a printed sign stuck on the side that advertised Shipley's automobile dealership.

*   *   *

"Start from the beginning, son, and tell us everything that happened," the sheriff said calmly.

Mr. Driscoll, after several failed attempts to keep Robert Earl from talking, agreed to the confession with the stipulation that his cooperation would be given consideration at the time of sentencing. It was apparent to everyone in the room that Robert Earl wanted to get it out of his system.

"You gotta believe me, Sheriff. I didn't mean for it to happen. But Junior made fun of me and teased me constantly. He did everything he could to make me mad and . . . you know . . . get my dander up. That day—you know the day he, ah, died, I saw him at the park and he started mocking me and bragging about this gold coin he had. When I double-dog dared him to show it to me . . . he pulled it out and held it up to the sun. I told him I didn't believe it was real. He laughed and said it was worth ten dollars and that there were lots more of them and he knew where they were." Robert Earl started coughing and asked for something to drink. Molly got him a bottle of Orange Crush.

"I tried to get him to let me hold it and he just laughed at me and stuffed it in his pocket. We got into a fight and he hit me hard in the stomach and knocked me down. As he got on his bike, he was calling me names . . . names I wouldn't repeat . . . and said he was gonna tell everybody what he knew about me and my family. I got real mad and threw rocks at him as he rode away."

The floats were better than last year. One, built to look like a Roman chariot, was pulled by a white horse. Another told the story of the American flag. A woman posing as Betsy Ross sat on a stool sewing stars on a piece of cloth. The Future Farmers of America float, pulled by a John Deere Tractor, was decorated with cornstalks and sheaves of wheat. Boys, dressed in overalls and holding pitchforks, sat on a bale of cotton.

The Liberty Mutual Insurance Company of America sponsored one of my favorites. A beautiful girl posed as the Statue of Liberty, holding a torch high above her head. The inscription read: LAND OF THE FREE AND HOME OF THE BRAVE. Most people in Adairsville had only seen pictures of the Statue but they understood what it stands for and they greeted the float with loud applause.

Uncle John leaned over and said, "Bet this will be one of the winners."

*   *   *

Robert Earl was calmer as he continued his story. "I went home and got the lug wrench out of the back of the truck and rode my bike down to the river. I never intended to hurt him. All I was gonna do was try and scare him and make him fess up about what he knew. I got down there and he was sitting by the bank staring at that stupid coin. He saw me coming and yelled for me to leave him alone or I'd be sorry. He stood up and started coming at me. I took the lug wrench from the basket on my bike and waved it in the air . . . you know, just, ah, trying to scare him. He grabbed my arm and tried to take the wrench away from me, but I fought him and finally wrestled him to the ground. I pinned him down and threatened him. I said if he didn't tell me where the coins were, I'd make him wish he had."

Daddy said later that when Robert Earl described that threat, he had a "menacing" look on his face.

"I got chills just looking at him," Daddy reported.

"I could tell by the look in his eyes," Robert Earl continued with a gleeful smile, "that he was really scared. I never saw

Junior afraid of anything before that day. He told me that Slow-foot had given him the coin and that he . . . Slowfoot . . . had a metal box full of other coins just like that one. He told me that him and Slowfoot were real good friends and that he knew where the coins were hid and that he'd share them with me. He cried and begged me to let him up."

*   *   *

The last float passed by and, as I started to leave, I noticed a man dressed in a long black coat and a broad-brimmed hat coming down the middle of Main Street. He was carrying a Bible and a sound as clear as a songbird was coming from his mouth. I had never heard anyone whistle like that. As he came closer, I recognized him. It was Clovis Blanchard, the loser in the fight with Randy Woods at the basketball game.

Uncle John said that he was now known all over West Tennessee, not so much for his preaching, but for his amazing ability to whistle gospel hymns. He was called the "Whistling Preacher." I mentioned that I remembered that Clovis had something wrong with his lip and couldn't talk plain.

Uncle John chuckled and said, "It seems that when Doc Townsend sewed up the gashes around his mouth, he corrected Clovis' harelip problem, and by some strange miracle, created a unique whistling talent."

"I guess Daddy's right, God does work in strange ways," I said.

I headed over to the Presbyterian Church to find Granny Lee. The large lawn in front of the church looked like one of those flea markets at the county fair. Tables were filled with an assortment of stuff that had been donated for the sale. The money raised would go to a fund to buy new hymnals and replace worn choir robes. Many of the items had been handcrafted by local artisans. There were carved teak bowls, straw baskets, pottery pieces, sculptures, and paintings.

"Someday, Wes will have paintings to donate to your sale," I said to Granny Lee. She smiled and nodded.

On one table, there was an assortment of hand-made bird houses and feeders. Granny Lee told me to pick one that I liked and it would be a present for helping with the bazaar.

I was fascinated with the table that displayed jewelry. There were all sorts of rings and beads and necklaces. Granny Lee showed me several of her jewelry pieces made with buttons and quartz. In between two tables, she had stretched a clothesline and hung two of her most prized quilts. When I had seen these quilts in her studio, she told me and Wes that those were her favorites, so I asked her why she was selling them.

She shrugged and replied, "It's for a good cause and I can always make more quilts."

*   *   *

"I believed him and thought he would keep his word. But soon as I let go of him, he ran to the edge of the river and picked up a large stick—something that looked like a walking cane. He held it with both hands and started toward me. I backed away and thought about running, but he started laughing at me . . . in that weird way . . . he just kept laughing, and that's when he told me that Slowfoot . . . er . . . Lonnie Jackson . . . was my uncle. I called him a liar and lunged at him. He just kept mocking me and saying that my father and Slowfoot were brothers; that my grandfather had . . . ah . . . , well, you know, had got Miss Maribelle in trouble. I screamed at him and kept calling him a liar. He just grinned and said he was gonna tell it all over town about Slowfoot and my daddy."

Looking pleadingly at Daddy and the sheriff, he said defiantly, "You know, I couldn't let him do that . . . I just couldn't."

*   *   *

For an hour or so, I unpacked boxes and wrapped purchases for Granny Lee at her booth. We stopped long enough to eat lunch from her picnic basket. I told her how the beam came into the living room on the night Wes' fever broke.

"It was strange, you know . . . like a ghost or something."

"Vance, the body is full of mystery, and there's a lot we don't know about sickness and healing. Doc Townsend used all his knowledge and skill to find a cure for Wes. You and your parents provided love and caring, and many people offered prayers."

228

She wiped her glasses on her apron, and then continued. "I believe that God uses people, medicines, faith, and prayer in ways that we may never understand. That's why we must listen, learn, and dedicate our minds and hearts to helping others. St. Paul said, 'We see through a glass darkly, but someday we shall see face-to-face.' People who use platitudes and give easy answers do not understand what the real problem of suffering is. The most important thing is that Wes got well and, perhaps, the how and why is not for us to fathom."

I remembered Daddy's sermon on suffering after the tornado, and I was sure that I would never fully understand this mystery.

I wandered off a couple of times to see the merchandise being sold at other booths. Jams, jellies, preserves, and an array of canned vegetables filled one table. At the candy booth, a lady was pulling long strings of cream-colored taffy; another was dipping juicy strawberries into a pan of dark-brown chocolate. The aromas coming from the taffy vat and the chocolate pot were almost too much to resist, but the thought of strawberries and cream helped me overcome the temptation.

*　　*　　*

"I lunged toward him . . . he backed up . . . slipped and fell." Robert Earl said.

"I knocked the cane out of his hand and screamed at him. I don't remember much about what happened next. It was all just like, you know . . . like I went a little crazy. I just know that when he turned around to pick up the stick, I hit him on the back of the head with the wrench. He made a strange . . . ah . . . kind of gurgling sound, and then just fell to the ground. It was awful . . . just awful. Blood was coming out the back of his head and he wouldn't move. I yelled for him to get up and even kicked him, but he just laid there. He wouldn't move. I went over by a tree and threw up, and then started crying . . . crying like a baby."

He put his head down on the table and waited a few moments before continuing. "After a while, I knew he was dead. Anyway, he looked dead. I sat down and tried to figure out what

One of the pleasures of being a "cranker" was getting to lick the paddle after it was removed from the container.

When Johnny and I finished with one freezer, we moved on to another. By the end of the day, my arm was so sore I could hardly lift it.

*   *   *

"Why did you try to steal Lonnie's coins?" the sheriff asked.

Before answering, Robert Earl drank some cola.

"I found out my daddy was in some kind of trouble. I heard him and Momma talking one night and I knew he needed money. I just thought I might be able to help him. I guess I never done anything really good to make my daddy proud of me. Most of the time . . . you know, I felt like he didn't even like me. I just wanted to prove something to him. Prove that I wasn't as dumb as everyone thought."

Daddy started to say something, but changed his mind.

"Go on, son," the sheriff said.

In a calm, deliberate voice, he continued. "While Slowfoot was in jail, I went out to look for the coins. Momma wanted me to go with her and Betty Lou to Florence, but I told her I was going camping with some friends that weekend. We never told Daddy because we knew he wouldn't like it if Momma left me alone for a weekend. Didn't think I could take care of myself, I guess.

"On Saturday I drove the pickup out to Slowfoot's house. The dog looked real mean and I couldn't even get out of the car. I went back to the house, got some hamburger meat from the refrigerator, and put rat poison in it."

He laughed as he told how the dog ate most of it and fell over dead. "I tore up the place but couldn't find anything. I was angry because I thought Junior had played another trick on me. I was in a hurry to get outta there and that's when I hit that rock and scraped the fender."

*   *   *

There was a long line of people waiting for dessert. Bowls with heaping scoops of ice cream covering shortcake were

232

handed to each person. As they moved down the line, they helped themselves to sliced strawberries and fresh whipped cream. Second helpings were free.

Other tables displayed jars of all kinds of jellies and jams made from strawberries. The Bykota Guild, which Mother had explained meant "Be Ye Kind One to Another," had collected every strawberry recipe imaginable, and Mr. Crowe had donated time and material for a special printing of the cookbook. By the end of the day, they would all be sold.

*   *   *

Daddy asked Robert Earl why he tried to kill Lonnie.

"I never meant to hurt him . . . you know. I just wanted him to give me the coins. He told me he didn't have them . . . and even if he did, he wouldn't give them to me. What really made me mad was when he said my father was a good man and it was too bad he had a rotten kid like me. I wanted to hit him, but he just turned his back and told me to get off his property. After he left, I went into the house to look for the coins. That's when I saw the rifle. I thought if I killed him, no one would ever know about him and Daddy. 'Course, I didn't know then that . . . that my daddy would blab it to the whole town."

*   *   *

After most of the ice cream was gone, Johnny and I started cleaning up. We poured out the brine and rinsed out each freezer. When we had finished our chores, we went over where Rue and Mother were having their first taste of strawberries and cream. Johnny and Rue talked about what they would do after graduation. Johnny was excited about going to college on a basketball scholarship, but said the war might change his plans.

Mattie Malone came by to complain about Daddy's absence. "I haven't seen Brother Turnage all day, and I know the ladies are disappointed that our preacher didn't show up to give his support to one of the most important fund-raising activities of the year."

Mother clenched her fist, and when she spoke, it sounded like she was grinding her teeth. "My husband has never missed

233

the annual bazaar since he's been pastor here, and he wouldn't have missed this one if he hadn't been called to take care of an urgent matter."

Rue stood up and, for a moment, I was afraid she was gonna punch the busy-body in the nose.

As she walked away, Mattie tilted her head to one side and said, "Well, I certainly hope it's more important than the Strawberry Festival bazaar we ladies have worked so hard on."

We looked at each other for a moment and then, realizing how silly the whole thing was, began laughing. It was apparent that our laughter reached the ears of Mattie Malone.

*   *   *

The final question was about how the ten dollar gold piece got into Mr. Cowser's possession. Robert Earl said that one day when he stopped by the bank, his daddy opened the lockbox and showed him the coins.

"He said he had bought them from a customer, and if anything happened to him, they would belong to me. I kept Junior's coin in a pouch . . . you know . . . a Bull Durham tobacco sack . . . and when Daddy left the room to answer the phone, I threw the coin in the box 'cause I didn't wanna get caught with it and . . . it was like, you know . . . giving something to Daddy."

Robert Earl suddenly started crying and rambling on about his feelings and how angry he was when he was sent away to military school. He spoke in broken sentences and seemed irrational at times. He finally broke down and sobbed.

"I've done some awful things, and my Daddy will never forgive me. He won't ever love me again . . . if he ever did. What's gonna happen to me?"

Daddy put his hand on Robert Earl's shoulder and said, "Your daddy and mother will always love you and we'll do everything we can to help you and your family."

Leonard Driscoll went to the hallway and phoned Judge Bascom. The sheriff talked to Matthew Hancock and then dialed Jacob Yancey's number. Parts of the confession would eventually appear on the front page of *The Clarion Standard*. As Daddy was leaving, he saw Ben Cowser put his arm around Robert Earl and whisper something in his ear.

Wes and I sat on the porch that evening thinking about Robert Earl's confession. Daddy wearily related everything he could remember, but soon grew impatient with our questioning. We took our signal from one of Mother's raised—eyebrow looks and left the room. Uncle John came by to remind Daddy about their chess game, but he said he would be busy writing a sermon.

"Now, Milton, I know you've never waited 'til Saturday night to write a sermon," Uncle John protested.

"You're right, but the sermon I prepared for tomorrow will have to wait. I'm trying to make some sense out of all this wretchedness and, with God's help, something hopeful and redemptive might be revealed."

As Wes and I passed through the living room on our way to bed, Daddy hardly looked up when he said good night. Sitting at the kitchen table, he was hastily scribbling notes on a lined tablet.

29

When the congregation and choir stood to sing the opening hymn on Sunday morning, a man on the back pew rose and opened the Cokesbury Hymnal, but did not sing. It was the first time Lonnie Jackson had been inside a church.

Daddy opened his sermon by reading from the seventh chapter of the Gospel According to Matthew. "Judge not, that ye be not judged. For with what judgment ye judge, ye shall be judged; and with what measure ye mete, it shall be measured to you again."

The tone and tenor of the sermon was one of forgiveness, acceptance, love and personal compassion.

"In order for our community to be restored to wholeness, we must begin by curbing a base desire to be judgmental. We must find it in our hearts to forgive those who have committed egregious acts against God and man. I know this isn't easy. It's natural to see only the mote in our brother's eye and not consider the beam, our own shortcomings, in our eye."

I could sense a slight stirring among the listeners. Mother began to twist her handkerchief.

"We are called upon to bear one another's burdens and lift up the fallen. The old hymn instructs us to throw out a lifeline when someone is sinking. There are people sinking in the tumultuous wakes of a stormy sea. And we can be keepers of the lighthouse, casting lifelines and sending forth beams into the darkness. Some may say, 'Let them drown,' they deserve it. But

God says, 'Rescue the the perishing, weep over the erring ones, and lift up the fallen.' To love the sinner is not to condone the sin. To love the evildoer does not mean that we take evil less seriously. But the consequence of deeds of greed and avarice should not be excommunication. Ben Cowser is our brother and we must be our brother's keeper."

A quiet "Amen" was heard, but I could not tell where it came from or who said it. Wes leaned over and whispered, "If I hear 'praise the Lord,' I'll know Daddy is really preaching."

"Yes, we must hate the crime, but not the criminal. One who commits a heinous act of murder and attempted murder must be punished, but he must also be forgiven. Robert Earl Cowser is not only Ben and Mildred's son, he is our son and he is still part of this Christian family and this community. The Scripture says, 'Blessed are the merciful, for they shall obtain mercy'!"

There was another "Amen" and it came from the pew just in front of us. Several heads turned cautiously toward the man who had uttered the affirmation. It was J. C. Macgregor.

"So, instead of casting stones, let's use the stones to build a foundation of new beginnings; a foundation of renewal for this community that we all love so much. We don't understand all the reasons why these things happen. Only God is omniscient. Like St. Paul, we are puzzled by 'the mystery of iniquity,' but can any attempt to interpret this dark enigma be anything but inadequate?"

He closed with a quotation from I Corinthians 13: *"And now abideth faith, hope, charity, these three; but the greatest of them is charity."*

The closing hymn was one I had heard many times, but it had a different meaning today. The congregation stood and sang it joyfully.

Look all around you, find someone in need, Help some-
    body today!
Tho' it be little—a neighborly deed—Help somebody today!
Many are waiting a kind, loving word, Help somebody
    today!
Thou hast a message, O let it be heard, Help somebody
    today!
Many have burdens too heavy to bear, Help somebody today!
Grief is the portion of some everywhere, Help somebody
    today!
Some are discouraged and weary in heart, Help somebody
    today!

After each verse, the congregation sang the chorus with en-
thusiasm.

Help somebody today, somebody along life's way;
Let sorrow be ended, the friendless befriended,
Oh, help somebody today!

Lonnie Jackson shook Daddy's hand and said, "Thank you,
Brother Turnage. You know I'm not a religious person, but I
liked what I heard this morning. You keep talking that way and
it just might make a difference in this town."

As he walked by us, he winked and said, "You boys haven't
been teasing any snakes lately, have you?"

Almost in unison, we said, "No sir, Mr. Jackson."

"That's good, cause you ain't no match for a copperhead."
He tilted his hat to one side and walked toward the cemetery.

When the treasurer emptied the offering plates, a twenty-
dollar gold coin was found.

Almost everyone agreed that this was one of Daddy's finest
sermons and would help create an atmosphere of healing and
hope for the community.

After a lunch of pot roast, potatoes, carrots, and string
beans, we all went over to Uncle John's for hot apple pie topped
with ice cream.

Granny Lee brought over a crate of strawberries that we
would share with the Menloes. "Sorry I missed that sermon,

Milton. Maggie told me it was one of your best. If I didn't have so much Scottish blood in me, I'd probably become a Methodist."

"You'd be in good company, Alma. John Fletcher, John Wesley's heir apparent, was born and raised in Scotland," Daddy said with a smile.

Wes and I stretched out on a quilt in the soft grass and listened to the adults talk about what would happen to Robert Earl. Sitting in a swing under the grape arbor, Rue and Johnny held hands and talked quietly.

Daddy told us what Lonnie Jackson had said to him after church. "I have no doubt about where that gold coin came from," he added.

On their way home from church, Parker and his family, dressed in their Sunday best, stopped by to say hello and check up on Wes.

Seth, grinning like a treed possum, said to Wes, "I'm sure glad you got well 'cause I'm gonna pick more cotton than you come fall."

Wes smiled broadly and said, "I'll be ready for you, Seth."

As we were putting away the dishes and folding the quilt, Sheriff Perkins drove up and slowly made his way from the drive to the backyard. He was not in a pleasant mood and declined an offer of pie and ice cream. He reported that he had met with the judge and the lawyers, and they agreed to have a hearing on Monday to consider the guilty plea and discuss sentencing.

"How do you think that'll go, Roy?" Uncle John asked.

"I really don't know, but what I do know is that this is the worst thing that's ever happened in this town, and somebody's gotta pay for it. Maybe they ought to put both of them in the same cell and lock 'em up for life."

Uncle John's wife surprised everyone with the tone of her response to the sheriff.

"If you had been in church this morning and heard Brother Turnage's sermon, maybe you could find it in your heart to be a little more charitable and forgiving."

The sheriff, surprised by the rebuke, stammered a bit when he replied. "I wish I could, Loretta, but I just don't feel that way.

Maybe it's my job or maybe it's just that I'm not as good a person as the rest of you."

Daddy came to his defense.

"You don't have to apologize to us, Roy. We know you're a good and decent person and we sure know you're the best sheriff this county will ever have."

The sheriff's frown turned into to a slight smile and, as he walked away, he said, "Save a piece of that pie. I might be in a mood to eat it later."

As Wes and I were leaving, I overheard Uncle John say to Daddy, "Now, Milton, how about that chess game?"

Daddy said, "You're on."

The ladies went to the kitchen. Rue and Johnny drove off toward the park.

When Wes and I got home, I turned on the radio and closed the curtains. Wes fluffed up two pillows and plopped down on the couch. I put some cushions on the floor and stretched out for our favorite Sunday afternoon pastime—Cardinals baseball and a nap.

Wes quietly said, "You know, Vance, Robert Earl could've come after one of *us*. While I was lying in bed this past week, I had plenty of time to think about him, and couldn't help but wonder what made him so mean and spiteful."

I thought about that for a while and said, "You're right. I guess that's why I stayed away from him as much as I could. There were times when he scared the bejeebers out of me. Daddy said Robert Earl felt nobody loved him, and that's what brought on a lot of his anger and hate."

"Guess we'll never know, will we?"

The Cardinals were leading four to one in the fifth inning, but we were not paying much attention to the game.

"So, Vance, what're you gonna be when you grow up?" Wes suddenly asked.

The question surprised me because we hadn't talked much about this.

"Well, you know I'm not gonna be a farmer," I said laughing.

"I'd guess you just might be a preacher, like Daddy."

"No way," I protested. "I'm not that smart and I sure don't wanna have to be that good."

Reflectively, I said, "I guess I'd like to travel the world and write stories about all my adventures. Yeah, that's what I'd really like to do."

Wes studied that thought for a moment, and then said, "You'd be good at that, Vance. However, you don't have to travel all over the world to find stories to tell. There's lots of good stories close to home."

"And what do you wanna do, Wes?" I asked.

Without hesitating, he said, "I want to be a really good artist. I would like to do with paint and brush what writers do with words. I want to put stories on canvasses and hang them in museums and art galleries so people could come and look at them and maybe hang them on their walls. That's what would make me happy."

"Okay," I said teasingly, "you paint and I'll write, but how're we gonna make a living?"

We both dozed off and missed the last two innings of the ball game.

Epilogue

Rue graduated from high school with honors and announced her intention to attend Lambuth College in Jackson in the fall. Johnny Fesmire made the All-State Team and was awarded an athletic scholarship to the University of Tennessee. The scholarship would have to wait. Knowing that he would be drafted, he joined the navy and left for boot camp. Rue and Johnny promised to write every day. Six months later, Johnny was killed when a Japanese submarine torpedoed the PT boat to which he was assigned.

Ben Cowser was sentenced to eleven months in a federal penitentiary and ordered to repay the money he had embezzled. Robert Earl was sent to a juvenile detention center, where he would serve until he reached the age of eighteen. He would then be transferred to a state prison to serve out the rest of a twenty-five year-to-life sentence.

Mildred Cowser and her daughter, Betty Lou, moved to Florence, Alabama, to live near Mildred's sister. Ben and Mildred divorced and neither one ever returned to Adairsville.

Lonnie Jackson donated the Bove property on Chapel Hill Road to the county and gave $2,000 to start a fund to build a home for orphans. He moved to New Orleans to live with "Aunt Ruby," the illegitimate daughter of Justin Bove and the half sister of Maribelle Jackson.

Granny Lee booked passage on the *Queen Mary* and spent three months touring Scotland and visiting ancestral sites.

Governor Prentice Cooper, at the state capitol in Nashville, presented Parker and his family with Euclid's Medal of Honor. Uncle John and Loretta provided transportation for the family.

243

The county school board authorized the use of a bus to carry twenty-five Negro students to the ceremony.

J. C. Macgregor bought the pool hall and converted it into a bicycle sales and repair shop. The sign over the door read: JUNIOR'S BIKE EMPORIUM.

After resigning as principal and teacher, Mr. Butterfield became the full-time pastor of the Baptist Church at Pickwick.

In early September, the Bishop appointed Daddy to a church in Memphis. The news upset Mother. She had come to love Adairsville and did not want to leave her friends. She cried all the way back to Memphis.

John Wesley Turnage enrolled in the freshman class at Humes High School and, on Saturdays, took special art courses at the Memphis Academy of Art.

Luther Vincent Turnage traded his cotton sack for a smaller shoulder bag and became a paperboy, delivering the *Memphis Press Scimitar*. Each evening before going to bed, he wrote in a leather-bound journal, a present from Granny Lee.

For the next few years, Wes and Vance would spend two weeks each summer visiting Uncle John and Granny Lee in Adairsville.